Bluestone Shadows

Chronicle of Ceres, Book 4

CL LaVigne

Cover Designed by MiblArt

Bluestone Shadows

(Chronicle of Ceres, Book Four) - 1st Edition

www.cllavigne.com

www.facebook.com/CLLaVigneAuthor

ISBN (paperback): 979-8-9884845-3-0

ISBN (eBook): 979-8-9884845-4-7

The ancients reach out to us with the wisdom of the universe. Only those who see clearly with their heart will understand how to use that knowledge.

Contents

Chapter 1

The Family Records

Keeper of the Records, a warrior stands.
From Amesbury the bugles blow
And, the light casts its shadow on bluestone.
The time is nigh. The battle approaches.
Gather the troops and reclaim the forgotten throne.

CHANCE SOARED OVER THE Welsh countryside on outstretched arms. Mount Snowdon, born of ancient volcanoes and home to mythical creatures, loomed in the distance and thrummed energetic pulses to its lost son. Patches of greens, browns, and yellows hurried below. Sheep bleated as he zipped over their pasture. And, like a migrating bird, Chance followed the invisible magnetic threads that pulled him home.

Although he had never visited Wales, Chance knew exactly where he was heading. His intuition led him over rocky crags and past tumbling waterfalls. He rolled easily on the wind currents as he circled toward the mountain's peak, which stabbed into the clear blue sky.

Pangs of excitement played in Chance's belly and joy filled his heart. Forgotten words to an ancient melody trickled through his brain, and he absently whistled the tune into the wind.

As he approached the snowy peak, a thunderstorm rolled in from the east enshrouding the summit with black, boiling clouds. Lightning bolts stabbed the mountain continuously and thunderous explosions followed each strike.

This looks familiar, he thought as he landed on the slope. *Reminds me of the nor'easter at The Nine Muses. And Stygian.*

Screech!

An immense black dragon dropped out of the superstorm and slammed Chance to the ground pinning him with a clawed foot. Chance reached for his weapon, but the sword was no longer fastened to his back. Enraged, he grabbed one of the dragon's scaly toes and bent it backwards as he screamed into the fury of the storm.

Within seconds, the beast morphed into three dark figures who tumbled to the ground and jumped on Chance kicking, punching, and subduing him with incantations. Their assault was so swift he had no time to react to the spells that drained his powers and rendered him too weak to fight.

A tall man wearing all black ordered his comrades to neutralize Chance's powers with high magic and suspend his body in front of a boulder. Chance was quickly spread eagle and held in place by unseen forces. The leader stepped forward, grabbed a fistful of Chance's hair, and yanked his head backward exposing his throat.

"You'll pay dearly for what you've done, Hilly," the dark man hissed.

Hilly? Chance thought.

A distant voice hailed Chance. The spells had muddled his mind, and he struggled to see who might be calling his name.

"Chance! Wake up!" a female voice cried out.

He fought against his invisible restraints, but his energy had been sapped. Lethargic and weak, he scanned the sky for the person trying to get his attention, but his eyes slowly closed as he fell into a forced slumber.

"CHANCE!" the voice screamed. "WAKE UP!"

Chance bolted into a sitting position. His heart hammered and he gasped while clenching his fists in front of his chest, prepared to fight. He looked around the dark room trying to make sense of where he was and what had happened.

I was flying to a mountain...but I don't have the ability to fly.

A man called me Hilly.

A woman called me Chance.

The nightmare's tentacles slowly released their grip when he realized he was safe in his bedroom. He glanced to the other side of the bed where his wife, Janet, slept peacefully curled up on one side. She softly murmured.

Chance relaxed. His fists unclenched and his breathing calmed. He closed his eyes and drew in a long, cleansing breath, held it for a few seconds, and then exhaled through his mouth slowly.

Sybil.

The name popped into his mind.

Sybil had done this before. She had penetrated Chance's dreams, dropped glimpses of the future and then yanked him back into the land of the waking. Sybil was an ancient book that contained hand-written accounts from members of the world's magical families. She could lead Chance through the veil that separated the physical and spiritual realms to reveal future events she deemed important.

Chance affectionately named her Sybil after the Greek prophetess.

The massive book filled with parchment pages recounting the history of all the mystical beings on earth was given to Chance during his Revelation six months earlier. When Darrius placed the book into his hands, Sybil psychically joined with Chance's energy and established a symbiotic partnership. This close relationship continued to grow as Chance's memories returned and his supernatural powers strengthened.

"Okay, Sybil," he whispered into the darkness. "I'll be right down."

Although Chance read the tome almost daily, that didn't stop Sybil from poking him at unusual hours and insisting he visit her in the wine cellar where she was hidden. He dared not ignore her intrusions for fear of missing an important event that would impact the future of his family or the world.

Although her voice had pulled him from his dream, she didn't speak to him now. Instead, she reached out to him with a sense of urgency that raced through his mind as if the world would abruptly end if he didn't jump out of bed and consult her pages.

He glanced at Janet who had flipped to her other side and now faced him. Her palms were pressed together under her head. A slight smile gave her the appearance of an angelic child. Although she was fifty-one, she had retained her youthful appearance. He grinned at her as she mumbled something unintelligible, shifted her legs, then settled down again.

He touched his fingers to his lips before lightly brushing them against Janet's mouth. "Love you, baby girl," he whispered before quietly sliding out from under the sheets and tiptoeing into their walk-in closet. He threw a blue T-shirt over his boxers and headed downstairs.

It was three in the morning. The house was quiet. Barefoot, Chance headed down the staircase, careful not to wake his teenage son and twin daughters. When he reached the kitchen, he flipped on a light and added fresh dark roast to the coffee pot.

While the eight-cup coffee maker burped and sizzled, he visited the library, a room across the hall from the kitchen where three walls were lined with dark mahogany bookcases that nearly reached the twelve-foot ceilings. Each shelf was full of books of all sizes and genres. Chance had meticulously arranged each collection by genre and then alpha by the author's last name.

He grabbed the rolling wooden ladder, moved it to the center of one bookcase, and climbed up until he reached the shelf containing novels by H. G. Wells. Lightly running his finger along the book spines, left to right, he located *The War of the Worlds*. He removed it and flipped to the back cover where he had hidden a skeleton key in a specially designed compartment. He extracted the key and held it aloft as he momentarily considered where he could place it as he climbed down.

Without a pocket in his boxers or shirt, he clenched the key between his teeth. Then he replaced the book on the shelf taking the time to align the spine flush with its companions, descended the ladder, moved it back to a neutral starting position, and exited the library.

He filled a large mug with black coffee, then headed down the hallway toward the door to the wine cellar. An unusual metal lock hung on the door. It required two keys: the skeleton key in his hand and a much smaller key that was fastened to a chain around his neck. He took a long sip of the coffee and placed the mug on the floor before he lifted the chain over his head. Holding a key in each hand, he inserted them simultaneously into the lock and turned them clockwise.

Clunk.

The familiar noise made him smile. He had worked especially hard on the manual double lock system, one of many security layers, traditional and magical, that protected Sybil as she lay hidden in the wine room.

Chance extracted the keys and entered the next room pulling the door shut behind him. Then he repeated the process in reverse by placing the keys into the lock on the interior side of the door and turned them counterclockwise until a metallic sound indicated the tumblers had latched. For good measure he jiggled the door. Satisfied, he extracted the keys and placed them into a metal box mounted on the wall and then descended the single flight of stairs into the cellar.

It was almost a duplicate of his father's study at The Nine Muses. It contained three large, glass-front cabinets that displayed weapons, armor, and family artifacts. His father's desk, which he had had shipped to his house in Asheville, sat prominently against one wall beside a well-stocked liquor cabinet. A sofa and two chairs were arranged over a red Oriental rug.

Chance spread his fingers and pressed his palms forward. One by one the furniture lifted and moved to the opposite wall where each piece returned to the floor gently. Then he turned his attention to the Oriental rug. Raising his hands, he focused on the edge where the fringe fluttered before the carpet rolled into itself, raised into the air, and laid down beside the furniture against the far wall.

Chance swept his hands over the tiled floor as he mumbled an incantation. Soon, tiles lifted and obediently stacked themselves in the corner.

What remained was a gaping six-foot-wide hole in the floor, an entrance to a secret room that Chance had carefully created to hold a priceless relic.

Chance knelt and reached through the opening until he found the light switch and flicked it on. A yellow glow emanated from the tiny room below. He unfolded a wooden staircase and descended into the chamber. With a wave of his hand, flames immediately appeared on torches lining the walls. The small apartment contained only one piece of furniture at the far end of the room where a spotlight illuminated the top of a lectern.

Constructed of reclaimed oak Chance had found at the local lumber yard, the podium was crafted using no nails or screws. All sides were engraved with protection spells consisting of sigils and elemental symbols, which prevented anyone, but Chance, from approaching the lectern. Once completed, Chance had devoted a week to hand-waxing the piece while he sang ancient songs to reinforce the magic.

He approached the podium, pressed his hands together at heart center, and bowed. Walking clockwise, he circled three times before stopping behind it and waving his hands across the top. The platform quietly swiveled to the side, and a large tome rose from the body of the furniture, not by the power of a motor, but by the energy of pure magic. The massive volume hovered mid-air as Chance bowed once again.

"Hi, Sybil," he said as he lightly stroked the outer edges of the leatherbound book. "You have something to show me?"

The book flew open, and pages fluttered back and forth as though blown by ferocious winds. Several moments passed before the shuffling ceased.

The book lay open to a section in the front half of the tome. Because of this, Chance already knew the passage Sybil wanted to share was ancient.

He lightly brushed his fingers across the page, and a trail of miniature sparks licked at his skin. Sybil was alive, a magical entity created a thousand years ago by the first Keeper of the Records and passed on and protected by each generation of Keepers.

Sybil welcomed Chance by gently thrumming in his brain. The internal vibration tickled and produced a crop of goose pimples down his arm. Chance recognized this as her way of urging him to pay attention so he glanced down at the passage.

The intricate drawings along the page's edge began to jump and flash in animation while the text halfway down the page pulsed with a soft yellow glow. In this way, Sybil used her power to direct Chance's attention to an important account from the past.

The script on the page had a flair for curls at the ends of the letters making it difficult for Chance to decipher the words right away. After a few false starts, he finally gained his momentum and read the ancient account by an individual named Genesis aloud.

"Bluestone and sarsen search the heavens for the restorer, but the wheel will turn a millennium before he returns to the ancient shores of Engla land. Bugles blare warnings on Salisbury Plain while armies of magicians and Yfel Brethren clash. Cambria cradles the precious one who slumbers in the Carn's bosom."

Chance read it again and again.

The cryptic passages were difficult to decode. Each author wrote in a different style and utilized references relevant to their time. The messages are clear as mud at the outset, but Chance had since learned to first analyze each word before attempting to understand the meaning.

He began with the first line "Bluestone and sarsen search the heavens..." Since returning home from The Nine Muses, Chance had plunged into researching details regarding his quest, which he knew would lead him to a location in the Preseli Hills located in Wales. As a result, he was already familiar with the terms *bluestone* and *sarsen*, the stones that comprised the monolithic Stonehenge located on the Salisbury Plain near Amesbury, the town in which he was born.

The word *Engla land* seemed self-explanatory to Chance, and he reckoned it stood for *England*. He first considered the writer Genesis may have misspelled the word. But after further research, he found that *Engla land* was an Old English term meaning "land of the Angles" who were one of the Germanic tribes in Britain during the early Middle Ages.

The line "Bugles blare warnings on Salisbury Plain while armies of magicians and Yfel Brethren clash," appeared to be both an event of the past and perhaps a prophetic statement. Chance was aware of the worldwide murders of magicians by the Yfel Brethren, but he wasn't aware of any specific battle near Stonehenge. Unsure of the meaning, he consulted mentally with Sybil.

But she remained mute. Chance interpreted her silence to mean that the detail was specifically relevant to him, and it would be something he would need to experience firsthand.

Battling the Yfel Brethren was not something he looked forward to.

The last sentence stumped him. "Cambria cradles the precious one who slumbers in the Carn's bosom." The words were foreign and made no sense. He had an inkling the words may have been Welsh, but he needed to research more.

Just as he prepared to cross-reference the foreign words, the alarm on his watch sounded, which meant he'd been immersed in the records for almost four hours. It was seven in the morning, and everyone was probably up and getting ready for school.

Chance marked the page with a red tassel that hung from the book's spine and closed Sybil. He ran his fingers along the edges, and she acknowledged him with a shower of sparks. He bowed to the tome and whispered, "I'll be back soon, Sybil."

He waved his hand, and the book descended into the lectern. The top swiveled back into place. He circled it counterclockwise this time, closing the magic he established in the beginning.

He reviewed his work. Satisfied Sybil lay hidden and protected, he headed upstairs into the chaos of his family.

Chapter 2

Janet

IN ONE FLUID MOTION, Janet scurried around the kitchen pouring pancake batter onto the griddle, flipping bacon in the skillet, and cleaning counter spills. Wyatt, her sixteen-year-old son, scrolled through his phone with one hand while absently shoveling cereal into his mouth with the other. A drop of milk rolled down his chin, and Janet swiped it with a dish rag as she set plates of fruit on the table in front of the twins Myla and Maeve. The fourteen-year-old girls chirped at each other in their secret language while they excitedly drew unusual symbols on papers scattered across the table.

Ding.

Coffee was ready. Janet hurried to the coffee maker and poured herself a much-needed cup. She leaned against the counter and sipped while observing her kids over the rim of the mug.

"Mom, something's burning," Wyatt uttered without looking up.

"Jeez, the toast!" Janet cried. She set the mug on the counter and ran to the other side of the kitchen. A waft of smoke slithered out of the toaster oven. She turned the machine off and yanked the door open. "Shit." She stared at the cremains of four slices of bread. She poked a fork into the toaster oven and dragged the charred pieces onto a plate.

"Mom, I think the pancakes are done." Wyatt jabbed at them with a spatula and grimaced. He lifted a blackened flapjack to eye level. "Yep, this one's a little crispy," he advised before dropping it back onto the griddle.

Janet tossed the burnt toast and plate into the sink.

CLANG.

Myla and Maeve glanced up.

Janet raced to Wyatt's side and unplugged the griddle. "Damn!" she screamed. "Can this day get any worse?" Her mood had rocketed from grumpy to seething in seconds.

Thirty minutes earlier, she had found Chance's mug of cold coffee sitting on the floor outside the door to the wine cellar. This had become his familiar pattern: make a full pot of coffee, pour one cup, and then let it get cold while he spent hours consulting with Sybil.

Janet hated to waste perfectly good coffee and grimaced at Chance's cup as she lingered outside the wine cellar door, poised to knock. Chance had made it quite clear that his time with Sybil was sacred and he should never be interrupted. So she decided against disturbing him. *It's my duty to the families, not to just ours, but to all the populations on earth,* he had explained.

She bit her lower lip as his words scraped across her memory. She understood why Chance spent so much time with the book, but the resentment she felt for Sybil, and for magical people, in general, gnawed at her patience...and her sanity.

Six months earlier, before Chance had left The Nine Muses to come home, he called Janet with a request. "Please gather the family for a meeting tomorrow. Around nine. I have a special announcement. Oh, and make sure Chad and Jason are there. No excuses. And Chad needs to come alone, without Mary or the girls. I'll explain later."

Janet assumed he had received a sizable inheritance from his parents' estate. After all, that's why he went to the family home in the first place—for the reading of the will.

Confident a financial windfall would soon be theirs, she didn't ask any questions and quickly agreed to his request. After making him promise to drive carefully back to Asheville, they said their goodbyes and Janet eagerly called their oldest son, Chad.

As expected, Chad argued about the short notice and not being able to bring his wife and babies. Chad was stubborn to the bone, much like Chance. "Your father is sharing news about the inheritance," Janet hinted.

Money was quite the motivator to a nineteen-year-old who had just become a father to twin girls. "Okay, maybe I can work something out. I'll need to stay overnight at your house, though."

"Great. You can stay in your old bedroom." Janet scratched his name off the list and then called Jason who she assumed was in class when she had to leave a voicemail. "Your dad is returning from the will reading and has an important announcement. I expect you to be here before nine tomorrow evening. No is not an option."

When the youngest children, Wyatt, Myla, and Maeve, returned from school that afternoon, Janet announced, "Your father is coming home tomorrow with some fantastic news. I think it has to do with your grandparents' estate. Be ready by nine tomorrow evening."

The girls exchanged glances and giggled. Myla whispered into Wyatt's ear, cupping her hand around her mouth as she spoke to him. Wyatt snorted. Then the teenagers rolled their eyes and marched to their bedrooms.

Janet watched them trot up the stairs and flinched when they slammed their bedroom doors. Although she loved all her kids, there had always been something unusual about her three youngest. The manner in which they interacted with each other, the odd way the girls seemed to know what she was going to say before she said it, and random floating objects. She convinced herself that she was imagining things. But since puberty, the strange occurrences seemed to have escalated.

As nine approached the next evening, everyone assembled in the living room. Chance stood with his back to the fireplace and grinned ear to ear. He was downright jubilant and shifted nervously from foot to foot as he swung his arms back and forth.

Chad and Jason strolled in together and acknowledged their father by jutting their chins at him before they headed to the sofa.

Myla and Maeve entered together and kissed their father in unison, a peck on each cheek, and then playfully winked at him before sitting side by side on the loveseat. Wyatt sauntered in, raised his hand in a casual salute, and slouched into a wingback chair. Janet entered last and quietly closed the door behind her. She hovered by the entryway and nodded at her husband to begin.

Chance cleared his throat. When he finally spoke, the words tumbled out nonstop for several minutes. He told his family about everything that had occurred at The Nine Muses. He described his magical abilities and those of his siblings, and how their powers would assist them on their individual quests. Purposely omitting gory details, he recounted the battle with Stygian, including Hilly's death and resurrection. He defined his role as Keeper of the Records and that he, along with his siblings, would be responsible for banishing the Yfel Brethren and restoring peace to the world.

Janet heard the words *dragon, aliens,* and *supernatural gifts,* which had no relevance to her life. Once Chance stopped speaking, a long silence followed as the wide-eyed family members stared at each other.

Myla broke the lull by jumping to her feet and proclaiming, "Maeve and I have known about Daddy's news for days. We psychically connected with him when Prasad performed his Revelation."

"That's right," Maeve confirmed as she joined her sister. "Daddy has special gifts like us and Wyatt." Maeve whirled and pointed at her brother who scowled at her and sank deeper into the wingback chair.

"Wh-what?" Janet stammered. "You can read your father's mind?" She glanced at Chance and then back to the girls. "What's going on here, Chance? I was expecting you to talk about your inheritance, and you've done nothing but babble about magic and war."

Chance took a step toward his wife. "Hon, this *is* my inheritance. I know it's a lot to process but..."

"Stop!" Janet shouted. "Just stop talking." Her lips twisted back and forth as she tried to find her words. Abruptly, she strode to Chad and Jason and stood behind them gripping their shoulders in a protective embrace. "Are you saying Chad and Jason don't have powers?"

Chance's shoulders slumped. "Janet, I don't know. I'm pretty sure they're Folk like you."

"Folk? What the hell is that?"

Chance sighed. "The ancient families throughout the millennium have always consisted of magical and non-magical members. Those without powers were commonly known as Folk. Though they didn't possess supernatural powers, they were still valued members of the families."

Dread crept up Janet's spine. "That's what we are...valued members?" She clutched her two oldest sons and glared at Chance.

The energy in the room shifted from excitement to uneasiness. Chance's words had inadvertently sliced the family into two groups. Maeve and Myla stood on either side of their father while Janet stood with Chad and Jason.

Wyatt was an island between the two groups. He sank deeper into his chair and stared at his hands fidgeting in his lap. The air was supercharged with magical energy and human emotions.

Wyatt leapt to his feet and extended a hand toward each group. "Enough," he whispered. His words were so quiet everyone tilted their head and leaned forward. "We are a family first. Nothing can divide us.

Nothing *will* divide us." He spoke with a distinct cadence, his words delivered in a calm, easy tone, which had a mesmerizing effect. His next words were inaudible as he moved his hands in gentle circles toward each of his family members.

"...so mote it be." He spoke the last statement in a strong, confident voice and lowered his hands.

He stared at his mother and older brothers then gazed at his father and sisters. Everyone's eyes welled with tears. Maeve and Myla sniffed and swiped at their noses. His older brothers lowered their heads and dabbed at their eyes. Janet studied Chance, her lower lip trembling.

Wyatt was the first to move. He walked behind the sofa and embraced his mother. "I love you, Mom. Nothing will ever change that. Then he tousled the hair of both Chad and Jason. "You'll always be my big brothers, you knuckleheads." A smirk brightened Wyatt's face as he embraced his sisters and father in a group hug.

"You're a healer," Chance said. "You take after your Aunt Fen."

"I guess so," Wyatt replied as he looked away shyly, a tinge of red dotting his cheeks. "It kind of manifested when I found an injured finch in the garden a few months ago. I picked it up and the words just came to me. I couldn't tell you what I was saying. It was like I was on autopilot. A few minutes later the little bird fluttered its wings and flew out of my hand."

Chance went to Janet's side. He gazed into her eyes and gently wiped her tears away. She reached up and smoothed the tears from his cheek as well. "You've raised some amazing kids, Janet."

"We both did," she countered before throwing her arms around Chance's neck and kissing him deeply.

"Eww," squealed Maeve and Myla in unison.

"Listen up, everyone." Chance clasped Janet's hand and walked into the middle of the room. "Wyatt is right. We are a family first and foremost. Today, you've found out that some of us possess extra gifts, but that doesn't make any of us more valuable than the rest. Our powers are our contribution to this family like Jason's amazing brain for numbers and Chad's ability to rebuild an engine blindfolded."

He gazed lovingly at Janet. "And just like your mom who is the most amazing person I know. She has nursed us all through sickness and broken bones while keeping the peace in this house of strong-willed individuals." He tilted her face upward and gazed into her eyes. "Janet, without you I'm half a person. I love you. And I promise this family will remain strong and united."

Janet recalled that tender moment with conflicted feelings. Life as she knew it had been forever altered and although peace had been momentarily achieved, a schism had formed between those with magic and those without. Despite Chance's words, she wondered if he would really be able to keep his promise.

"Good morning!" Chance called out as he burst into the kitchen.

"Morning, Dad!" the girls chorused. Wyatt glanced up from his phone, smiled, and then returned to scrolling.

"Morning, dear," Janet replied as she scraped burnt pancake residue from the griddle. "How's Sybil?"

"She had a lot to say," Chance replied as he joined Janet at the sink. He grabbed her around the waist and kissed the back of her neck. Janet's shoulders tensed. Chance added, "Hard morning?"

"Sorry. Everything seems to be going wrong today. First the toast and now the pancakes..."

Chance placed his hand on hers and whirled her around. "Here, let me help. Grab a fresh cup of coffee and sit down. I'll make breakfast."

Janet relaxed. "Thanks, hon. I appreciate it." She threw out the cold coffee, poured a fresh cup, and joined her children at the dining table.

Chance threw a dish towel over his shoulder and finished cleaning and drying the griddle. Then he poured fresh batter into equal-sized pancakes.

"Anything you can share?" Janet asked.

"Share?" Chance stared ahead. "Oh, Sybil? You mean Sybil."

"Yes. Did she tell you anything interesting?" Janet knew Chance couldn't divulge anything he'd read from Sybil, but asking about it made Janet feel as though she was a part of her husband's magical life.

"Yeah. There's a sale at Dugan's Department Store. Fifty percent off, today only."

Janet paused. For a split second she hovered in that gray area between reality and lie.

Chance turned and wiggled his eyebrows at her.

"Brat," Janet huffed. "I knew you were fooling me."

Chance scooped pancakes onto everyone's plates and joined his family at the table. He grabbed two slices of limp bacon and added them on top of his flapjack before smothering everything with syrup. "Damn, I forgot my coffee. Janet would you, please?"

"Sure." Janet filled the large mug and set it in front of Chance. "I found this by the wine cellar this morning." She smiled gently. "You spend a lot of time with Sybil."

"Jealous?" Chance leaned toward Janet and tucked two strands of hair behind her ear.

She batted him away. "Don't be ridiculous. Now bring that plate of scrambled eggs that's warming in the oven, and perhaps, I'll forgive you."

Chance grabbed the dish and spooned eggs onto everybody's plate. When the girls protested that they no longer ate eggs, he heaped more on their plates and chuckled.

"Dad!" Maeve cried as she picked the eggs off.

"How's football?" Chance asked Wyatt as he sat down.

"Hmm," Wyatt replied as he shoveled food into his mouth.

"Riveting." Chance poked Wyatt in the ribs and repeated, "How's football?"

Wyatt chewed his food, sipped his orange juice, and finally replied, "Now don't get weird, but the coach wants to talk to you."

"What about?"

"Oh, a little matter that happened during practice."

"With you? A little matter is usually a big issue. What did you do?" Chance leaned toward his son.

Father and son glared at each other.

Myla giggled, and Chance shifted his attention toward her. "Aha, you know what's going on, don't you? You're reading Wyatt's mind again. I told you not to do that without his permission."

"I didn't read his mind, Dad," Myla grumbled. "But Maeve and I know that he's in trouble for showing off."

"Shut up, Myla!" Wyatt yelled.

"Hey! We don't say that in this household," Janet scolded. "Calm down, everyone."

Tense moments passed. The kids sulked while Chance and Janet stared at them.

"Okay!" Wyatt barked as he broke the awkward silence. "The coach wants to talk to you about something I did."

"Go on," Chance urged.

"During practice. I got a little carried away."

"He was showing off for his *girlfriend*, Suze," Maeve added.

Wyatt opened his mouth to respond and caught a glimpse of his mother's finger pointing at him, daring him to say what was on his mind.

"Just tell the truth, Wyatt," Chance said gently.

Wyatt picked at the checked pattern in the tablecloth. "I sort of threw the football out of the stadium."

"Okay? What's the big deal? Did you go and get it?"

The girls giggled, and Wyatt scowled at them.

"No. I couldn't get the ball back. I think the ball ended up in the next county." Wyatt looked up with sorrowful eyes. "I'm sorry, Dad. But our quarterback really sucks. He couldn't hit an elephant in the ass with a shovel. I thought I would show him the proper form. One thing led to another, and I got a little...enthusiastic."

"Enthusiastic?"

"Yeah. I forgot about my powers, and the ball soared up and away. Coach watched the whole thing and took me to the sidelines."

A grin wavered on Chance's lips and he asked, "Was he mad?"

"Nope. He wanted to know if I'd be interested in becoming quarterback." Wyatt searched his father's face.

Chance's jaws clenched, then relaxed. His lips trembled and twisted before he broke out in laughter. He shoved away from the table and gasped. "Oh...my...God!"

Myla and Maeve exchanged puzzled looks.

"Son, I should be angry with you, but you just repeated a bonehead stunt I pulled when I was your age." Chance snorted.

"You're okay with this?"

"No, we are not okay with your behavior," Janet interrupted. "Your father has been clear about it. Don't ever display your powers, unless you're at home." Janet narrowed her eyes and swept the table with her steely gaze, including her husband who sat back holding his sides. "Eat."

Wyatt, Myla, and Maeve quietly picked at their food. Janet sat back in the chair and trembled. She couldn't remember the last time she felt in control. She was surprised how great she felt after releasing those emotions, feelings she'd suppressed for some time. She wanted the moment to last. She closed her eyes and relished the peace that confidence provided.

Chance gently touched her shoulder.

Janet jerked then stared at him with wide eyes.

"Sorry, hon," Chance whispered as he leaned toward her. "I didn't mean to disturb you, but I wanted you to know that you're amazing." He kissed her lightly on the cheek. "I love you."

"I love you too." She bopped Chance on the nose and kissed him.

"Eww," Myla and Maeve chorused.

"Time to go to school," Wyatt said as he rolled his eyes.

The kids scraped their leftovers into the trash and then placed the plates into the dishwasher before dashing upstairs.

"Alone at last," Chance said as he gathered Janet into his arms and nuzzled her neck.

She squealed with delight. This was the Chance she had fallen in love with, playful and spontaneous. *I'm so lucky,* she thought as they made out.

But something deep down gnawed at her.

Chance leaned back and held her at arm's length. "What's up?"

Janet avoided his stare. "I still worry about them," she admitted as she began clearing the table.

"Who?"

Janet whirled toward Chance. "Really? You have to ask? Our kids, of course."

"Oh, hon, they'll be fine. We've talked to each of them and explained what they can and cannot do."

"Yes, but the Yfel Brethren still lurk about. They could kidnap Chad or Jason, like they did Curtis."

"I've cloaked their whereabouts. And, for good measure, I add new protection spells every week."

"Hilly did that too, but the Yfel still tricked Curtis." Tears welled in Janet's eyes, and she turned away.

Chance folded his arms across his chest and leaned against the counter. Janet scrubbed the same spot on the counter for a minute before he spoke. "What's going on, Janet? I want to know."

She faced him with her fists clenched. Frustration forced crimson into her cheeks as she glared at him. She struggled to respond.

"Tell me, please?" Chance asked.

Tense moments passed.

Chance was about to speak again when Janet barked, "You're changing!"

"I'm changing?"

"Yes. You are and the kids are—well, Wyatt, Myla and Maeve are. Me, Chad, and Jason are the same old people we've always been. Magic has overwhelmed our lives, Chance. The Yfel, supernatural powers, quests, and Sybil...I can't take it anymore!" Janet crumpled into a chair and cried. "Chance, I'm losing you to something bigger than us. And I can't—no, I won't deal with it anymore."

Chance asked quietly, "What can I do to help you?"

Janet's mind raced. The opportunity had arrived to finally handle the demons that had plagued her since Chance returned from The Nine Muses and yet, as she stared into her husband's eyes, she knew there was nothing he could do.

Chance would continue to transform. Since his memories had been restored, all his powers had aggressively pushed to the surface—strength, speed, telekinesis. She found it endearing, but she'd witnessed other changes as well. Often, she'd found Chance sitting on the roof staring into the night sky. Or he constantly talked about his quest, and his desire to go to England. He'd described the trip as an intense yearning to find something missing in his life. But he hadn't yet explained what was missing.

Janet stared into Chance's dark brown eyes. He waited patiently for her to find her words. He had talked about his intuition so often lately that she wondered if she was finally trusting her own instincts. She loved his calm, nurturing nature. Yet, deep down, she knew she would not be a part of his life in the future. She wondered if Wyatt, Myla, and Maeve would also grow into adulthood with an inexplicable yearning pulling them to different corners of the earth. Would she lose them to magic?

And there it was.

Magic.

She was envious of their extraordinary gifts. Magic united Chance, Wyatt, Myla, and Maeve in a tight-knit bond she would never comprehend.

"I'm the odd person out in this house." She choked back tears. Speaking the truth was freeing but painful. "What will happen to me when everyone leaves on their own journeys?"

Chance gazed at Janet. She hugged herself. Tears flowed freely down her cheeks. He leaned toward her and wiped the wetness off one cheek. "You're right. I am changing."

She looked up.

"I can't stop what's happening. But we can still be a family. The structure and the dynamics will most definitely change, but we're strong. You're strong. This family wouldn't survive without you. I don't say that enough. You will never lose me or the love I feel for you and our children. I can promise that because our love is our own special magic that we created so long ago and that which we celebrated each time we welcomed a new child into our home."

Chance cradled Janet's cheek, and she nuzzled his hand. "We can handle whatever comes our way, Janet. Together, we will see this through to the end, I promise."

Chapter 3

The Triskelion

WYATT, MYLA, AND MAEVE grabbed their backpacks. "Bye!" they shouted as they dashed outside slamming the door behind them.

Chance and Janet wrapped their arms around each other and danced in a slow circle in the middle of the kitchen. Chance nuzzled Janet's neck and hummed a tune.

"What's that tune?" she asked. "I've heard you humming it while you're sound asleep."

"Really? That's interesting. I think it's something I heard when I was young." Chance pushed Janet back and smiled at her. "I love these quiet moments with only you."

"Me too. Reminds me of when we first got married, before all the babies arrived." She pushed her face into his chest. This time she hummed a melody as they slowly twirled together.

"Hm. That sounds familiar. What is that?"

"Jim Reeves song." Janet stopped and gazed up at Chance.

"Ah, yes," he said as he pulled her closer. He kissed her forehead, then her nose and then her mouth."

Chance, you have unfinished business. Sybil's familiar voice poked at his brain.

Janet leaned into him. "Hm," he mumbled. Janet held his head and kissed him back.

Chance. Come now!

"Argh." Chance pulled away from Janet and stared at the floor.

"What's wrong?" Janet tilted his chin and looked directly into his eyes.

"Sybil."

"Oh." Janet marched to the counter. Plates clattered as she dumped them into the sink along with the coffee mugs.

"Janet, I'm sorry," Chance offered. Her shoulders hunched. "It's always urgent when she calls me like this."

"Then go," Janet snapped as she smacked a plate with a dish rag. "Just go."

Chance turned to leave and then looked back. Janet's shoulders trembled. He knew she was crying. He also knew that if he tried to say anything, Janet would be angrier.

Sybil had wedged between them before. And his explanations always got him into more trouble. He made a mental note to make things right later but as the thought passed through his mind, he knew he could never make amends for this lost moment with his love.

He left the kitchen.

As Sybil arose from the lectern, Chance muttered, "We need to work on your timing, Sybil. Janet's furious with me."

When it comes to saving the world, feelings don't matter.

The terse comment accompanied by a dull headache startled Chance. He winced and grabbed his head. He studied the leatherbound tome. Sybil had always been benevolent and tender. She had never meted out pain or harsh words before.

"What's wrong, Sybil?"

It's imperative you begin your quest. We have work to do, Keeper!

The book flew open, and the pages thrashed back and forth until the critical passage was located. The section glowed a soft yellow and the ancient symbols danced around the edges of the page. He found the sentence he struggled with earlier and read it aloud, "Cambria cradles the cherished one who slumbers in the Carn's bosom."

He tapped the edges of the lectern as he mulled over the words. "I'm pretty sure my quest begins in England near where I was born, but these foreign words have me stumped, Sybil."

Chance grabbed a large reference book that lay on a shelf of the podium. The miniature typeface was impossible to read so he swiveled a large magnifying glass over the page and locked it in place. His index finger loomed large and plump under the magnifier as it ran down the page looking for the words beginning with CA. "Aw, here we are. Cambria is another word for Wales, and Carn is a pile of stones."

"Simple. I just go to Wales and look for a pile of stones."

Chance laughed out loud, but the levity was lost on Sybil and her words sliced into his head like a knife. *Keeper. You must prepare. Now!*

Chance grabbed his head. "Dang, Sybil, it was only a joke."

You must find the cherished one and restore her to her seat of power.

"Okay. So, my family stone is somewhere in Wales. Any other details you can share?"

Use your intuition.

Chance had expected that answer. Oftentimes, Sybil had led him to the edge of total knowledge only to leave out the most important details and then demand Chance use his intuition for the rest of the story.

"I'll work on it. Hopefully I can leave tomorrow. Is there anything else I need to know?"

The Yfel Brethren.

"What about them?"

The book suddenly slammed shut.

"Hm. I guess this session is over. Don't worry, Sybil, I always keep my eyes open for the Yfel." He stroked the outer edges of the book, and a shower of sparks swirled around his fingers. Despite her harsh words and demeanor, Sybil's energetic caress of Chance's hand proved that she cared for him.

An ominous feeling shivered up his backbone as he thought of the Yfel Brethren. Genesis' record mentioned a battle with the Brethren. Originally, thinking the words were a reflection of the past, Chance was convinced a fight would be in his future also.

History repeating itself, he mused.

Securing Sybil within the lectern, Chance headed upstairs.

"Can you help with that odd symbol I just emailed you?" Chance hit speakerphone and placed his phone on the table beside the sheet of paper containing a drawing of a three-sided object he'd sketched with a pencil. "It keeps appearing in my dreams. Oddly, enough, it wasn't in last night's nightmare."

"Nightmare?" Fen asked.

"Long story. Not important. I need to know about the symbol."

"I'm looking at it now," Fen replied.

Chance provided more details. "It appears as a green glyph and pulses like a strobe light as I'm waking."

"This is a symbol called a triskelion or triskele. Three spirals connected by a continuous line. While each spiral appears separate, they are, actually, joined as one. It first appeared in Ireland. The triskele means 'three times' and has been interpreted as the cycles of life, the structure of family, and the holy trinity depending on the culture."

"Hm. So why has it been popping up in my dreams lately?"

"You tell me. Was it accompanied by someone or something?"

"Not that I recall. It just appears as a green symbol when I'm waking up."

"If I had to wager a guess, I would say it doesn't represent anything malicious and will present its meaning sometime in the future. Or perhaps it means that you and Janet will take a vacation to England or Ireland."

"Well, isn't that strange."

"What's strange?"

"I'm leaving for England tomorrow."

"Janet must be thrilled!" Fen gushed.

"Um...quite the opposite. I'm leaving on my quest—alone."

"Oh."

Chance frowned at Fen's disappointed reply. He shifted gears. "But we ironed everything out, and once I'm back, we'll take that ten-day cruise in the Caribbean she's always dreamed about."

"That will be nice," Fen replied halfheartedly.

"Thanks for the info, sis. I've got to go."

"Wait!"

"Okay."

"Something's wrong. I can sense it."

Chance cursed silently. "Everything's fine."

"Please, Chance. It's me. Something's bugging you. I can feel the anxiety. Let me help."

Chance glanced around the room, making sure he was alone, then he switched off the speaker and cradled the phone to his ear. "Fen, don't repeat any of what I tell you, okay?" he said in a hushed tone.

"Okay."

"It's about the nightmare I had last night."

"Go on."

Chance recounted his dream nonstop for several minutes. Finally, he paused.

Before Fen could respond, he added, "Why was I soaring over the Welsh countryside? Flying is not one of my powers. Andy why did the dark man call me Hilly?"

"Didn't you mention that Sybil sometimes uses symbolism in your dreams to hint at something important in the records?"

"Yes, but this was different. And Sybil would have revealed her intentions when I met with her this morning. Fen, this nightmare was weird like I was seeing through someone else's eyes. Kai had told me that he had horrific nightmares about Hilly's battle on Denali. They felt very real to him as he battled the Yfel with a broadsword. He explained that the dream was a manifestation of Hilly's psychic connection to him. Do you think that's what's going on with me?

"Do you have a psychic connection to Hilly?"

"No. I'm the odd person out in our family. I can't fly nor can I read minds like the rest of you."

"True. What I believe is that you experienced a future event but not your future. You were given a glimpse of something that may happen to Hilly. Your connection to the records may be so intense, and so interconnected, that your abilities are transforming to a heightened state of awareness even while you sleep."

Chance's lips twisted as he chewed on Fen's suggestion. Since acquiring the Records six months prior, he'd spent every day reading the text and interacting with Sybil. Was that simple relationship morphing? Was he changing? Suddenly, Janet's words from that morning filled his mind.

"That's a lot to absorb." Chance glanced around the room. He wanted things to stay as they were. "If that's true, then Hilly will soon be in trouble."

"Yes. I feel confident about that theory. Whatever the source, Chance, you were given a snapshot so you can prepare for what will come. It's no coincidence that your dream took place in Wales, and today, Sybil advised you to travel to England. Sybil was right. Your quest is urgent."

"I'm sure you're right, Fen. Hilly has completed her task. Kai is halfway through his, and my quest begins tomorrow."

"You will be on my mind. I love you, big brother. My Keeper of the Records."

Chance beamed. "I love you too, Guardian of Peace."

Chapter 4

Amesbury

CHANCE STEPPED INTO THE Heathrow terminal, set his bags on the ground, and stretched his back, which ached from the long flight to England. After several loud pops, a satisfied smile spread across his face. "Much better," he mumbled.

Nearby, a young couple embraced in a passionate kiss, and he thought of Janet.

Earlier that morning, she had dropped him off at Charlotte Douglas International Airport, opting not to join him inside. She stood beside the car, hugged herself, and stared at the ground while he unloaded his bags.

Sadness and fear eked from her pores.

"Everything will be fine," he'd assured her. "I recharged the protection spells around Chad and Jason's homes, and I've added extra security layers for our house."

"Oh? When did you do that?" Janet replied in a chilly tone.

Chance drew in a sharp breath. Janet's emotional simmer was beginning to erode his patience. He exhaled through pursed lips. "I've told you before that I change the protection symbols every week. Plus, Wyatt, Maeve, and Myla will ensure the magic is holding."

Janet narrowed her eyes. The heat from her anger burrowed into Chance's soul. "Nice. I'm glad they can help you," she seethed through thinned lips. "Not like I can do anything to protect my family."

Chance flinched and glanced away, trying hard to calm his frustration. When he looked back, Janet had already walked around to the driver's side. "Janet," he called out, "Let's not part like this."

She stopped at the door fingers lingering on the handle. Chance joined her and gently touched her shoulder. She whirled and buried her face into his chest. "Please don't go," she sobbed.

He hugged her tightly and rested his head into her hair. "I need to do this," he whispered. "Everything will be fine. I've talked to Darrius. He's arranged for a contact to meet me in England."

They held each other as more cars arrived, off-loaded passengers, and departed. Soon, a security guard ambled over to them. "Come on, folks, say your goodbyes and leave. The car can't stay here."

Chance nodded at the guard and pushed Janet back. Her eyes misted with fresh tears. Wisps of hair had become trapped in the moist corners of her eyes, and Chance gently removed them with his thumbs. "I love you, baby girl." He kissed her forehead, then her nose, then her mouth. She threw her arms around his neck and pulled him close.

"Chance Kemp, if you don't return to me and your family, I will never forgive you. Now go. Get on your plane and find your magic crystal." She managed a weak grin before she yanked the car door open and slid onto the seat. Without another word she drove away.

Chance watched her leave.

Honk!

"Hey fella, get out of the lane!" an irritated driver yelled.

Chance stumbled to the sidewalk and shouldered his bags. He peered off into the distance and caught the taillight of Janet's car as she turned the corner and disappeared. He sighed and trudged into the airport.

The flight was uneventful but he couldn't sleep. Something kept pricking the back of his neck. He stood to inspect the headrest but his attention was drawn to the gentleman in the seat behind him. A tanned, dark-haired man with a black eye mask sat snoring softly. His mouth had drooped open, and a string of drool stretched onto his chest. Chance glanced at the passengers on either side of the sleeping man. Wearing noise-cancelling headphones, both individuals were immersed in their laptops and were oblivious to their surroundings.

Chance ran his finger across the headrest. Nothing was out of place, so he assumed a thorn had lodged under his collar. It wasn't unusual to pick up briars while hiking the forests outside Asheville, and despite carefully picking them off his clothes, one pointy thorn would always find its way into the laundry.

He went to the bathroom to check. The tiny room was not built for his large frame, and he slammed the metal walls twice as he gyrated in a circle removing his shirt.

"Is everything okay in there?" a gentle female voice called out to him.

"I'm fine," Chance replied. The last thing he wanted was to draw attention to himself. "The room's a tight fit, but I'm fine." He stood motionless for several minutes and listened to the rumble of the plane's engines, hoping the person had wandered away.

He held up the collar and ran his fingers along the crease. Sure enough, tucked under the back fold, was a tiny brass pin barely a half inch in diameter. Engraved on one side was the three-sided symbol he had seen in his dreams. "A triskele," he whispered. "Janet must have put it there when she hugged me around the neck. But how?"

I never told her about the dream. Maybe Fen said something.

The details didn't matter. He figured that, in one final gesture, Janet had managed to infuse her love and trust by surprising him with the pin. When he had spoken with Fen, she had mentioned that the three spirals could represent family, so Chance latched onto that definition. Family was the only thing that would sustain him on his journey.

He extracted the pin and held it aloft. He gazed at it and whispered, "Thank you, baby girl." Then he gently kissed it before fastening it to the front of his collar. He returned to his seat and slept like a baby the rest of the flight.

Now that he was in Heathrow, the seriousness of his journey weighed on him. The excitement he had felt when leaving Charlotte had dissipated, chased away by Sybil's warning about the Yfel Brethren awaiting him in England.

Shouldering his duffel bag, he grabbed the wheeled suitcase, and headed to the car rental. A first-time driver in England, Chance had never driven on the left side of the road and hoped he didn't cause any accidents while navigating the congested streets of London. *I wish Hilly was with me so she could open a portal and make it easier to get to Amesbury.*

Traffic was horrendous. Chance focused on the road and drove slowly, much to the chagrin of those stuck behind him. Blaring horns and curses were punctuated with finger gestures as angry drivers whizzed passed him. The congestion eased on the M3, allowing Chance a moment to relax as he listened to a classic rock station he'd found on the radio. Meanwhile, the GPS barked orders in a refined, female British accent. Chance smiled each time the disembodied voice spoke. He envisioned it belonged to a female commander in the Queen's Guard sitting beside him in a freshly-pressed uniform and well-placed cap.

The sign for Amesbury flew by. Chance's heart quickened. Finally, after so many years, he was heading to the place in which he was born. He hoped his Cererian contact had located members of his biological family, but with the world's magicians cloaking their whereabouts from the Yfel Brethren, odds were not on his side.

"You have arrived at your destination," his British driving commander announced.

Chance eased the car up a gravel drive and parked outside a stone building. Minutes from Amesbury, the simple farmhouse was one of several ancient buildings in the countryside that had been converted into dwellings. It featured a thatched roof, white stone walls and a bright red door. It appeared like one of those David Winter Christmas houses Janet always set out for the holidays, only there was no snow—yet.

Chance re-read the email he'd received from the estate agent. She had provided specific directions for where the house key would be hidden.

"Just outside the door, hanging from the side of the house, will be three flower baskets with freshly planted pansies. Under the third basket, you'll find a two-foot-tall cement hare. The key will be wrapped in cellophane beneath the bunny."

Things sure are different in England, Chance thought as he snatched his jacket and pushed the car door open. He quickly threw on his jacket and turned his collar against the chilly dampness. An October drizzle hissed as rain droplets brushed against the leaves clinging to the surrounding trees. The rain glistened on the gravel driveway making it a bit slippery as he made his way to the door.

The rain fell steadier.

What the agent had failed to mention was that the statue sat in the midst of a wild and tangled garden, which was bordered by a foot high decorative edging. The incessant rain had turned the patch of ground into a mushy quagmire. Chance took a step over the small fence and his shoe oozed into the mud. Within seconds, his loafer was completely immersed in a cold, sticky goo, and it felt like the shoe could go deeper if he didn't act quickly. He lifted his foot, but the mud sucked at it eagerly, refusing to release its prize. Eventually, Chance won the tug-of-war and stepped onto the gravel with his sodden, filthy shoe.

Time for a little magic.

He glanced around at the neighboring homes. Nobody was out in the misty rain, and the location of the door was such that he had complete privacy from neighboring windows and prying eyes. He drew in a breath and huffed it out. A ghostly curl of condensation drifted into the air.

Raising his right hand, he spread his fingers wide and narrowed his eyes at the cement hare. Several seconds passed without any change until, very subtly, the statue quivered before settling back into the mud. He clenched his jaw and refocused. This time the hare lifted slowly upward before the sucking fingers of the chocolatey mud pulled it back into the mire with a smacking sound.

Chance groaned. He didn't want to damage the statue, but he was going to need to use his strongest powers to yank it from the muck. With both hands directing energy toward the hare, the statue wiggled violently before falling backwards with a sickening *thwack*. The mud quickly encompassed its paws and moved halfway up its chest as the bunny sank deeper into the muck. Chance flicked his left hand and extracted the plastic bag containing the key as the ooze filled the gaping hole.

A coating of black muck smeared the outside of the bag. Chance opened one end, extracted the key, and held it aloft in the rain to clean the goo from the metal. He studied the three-inch skeleton key. It was surprising to see such an ancient method for getting into a house, but he had carefully selected this property because it wasn't a smart home. Like his father, he desired to be free of technology as much as possible to escape detection.

He glanced toward the hare. The greedy mud had swallowed the body except for the eyes, which had been painted a bright blue and now stared at him with a hint of sadness. Extending his right hand, he maneuvered it back into place.

The cadence of the rain quickened, and the trees whispered furiously as the raindrops slapped their autumn leaves. Chance stomped his shoes under the small overhang jutting over the door. He dried the key on his shirt and slid it into the lock. He jiggled and turned it until he heard a *clunk*. Chance grinned, satisfied.

He lifted the latch and stepped into the mud room. The mustiness of ancient times greeted him. A wooden shelf with several metal hooks had been hung on the wall above an oak bench. He set the key on the shelf and sat down to remove his drenched loafers and socks. Cold and thoroughly soaked, he removed all his clothes and hung them on the hooks. In only boxers, he padded barefoot through the home. He entered a tiny snug and immediately bumped his forehead on the low beam above the doorway.

"Damn!" he cursed as he rubbed his head.

He ducked, then moved into the cramped space that featured a window, an unlit fireplace, and dark wood beams crossing the ceiling. It smelled dusty and unused.

He backed out of the cramped snug. The hallway led him into a spacious kitchen diner with several large windows, which offered views of the back garden. Instinctively he went to the sink and turned the faucet. It took a while for the water to become hotter, and he relished the warmth as he cleaned his hands and arms. He snatched a dish towel and dried off as he wandered the rest of the home.

He walked through a formal dining room before encountering a chilled reception room in the back of the house. This one, too, looked over the quaint backyard full of several fruit trees and flower beds. The living room suite consisted of tired, flowered remnants from the 1980s. One overstuffed chair seemed out of place with its medium-blue background and large images of sunflowers. It had been placed by the fireplace and a small footstool. A basket full of yarn and several knitting needles sat nearby. Chance reckoned the owner, when she was using the property, spent time by the fire knitting.

Taped to the front of the fireplace was a note handprinted in blue ink:

Use this fireplace only. Wood is in the bin. More can be found in the garden shed. Enjoy your stay!

The newness of the house had worn away and chilliness poked Chance. Icy fingers raced up his spine while goose pimples ran down his arms and legs. He opened the door to the wood burner, loaded kindling and several logs before poking bits of starter paper into the crevices. Not able to find matches or a lighter, he stood in the twilight shivering as he considered his options.

He snapped his fingers. *Magic.*

He wondered why he didn't think of it sooner. He used his magic on the torches every day when he visited Sybil. So, he waved his right hand in front of the fireplace and yellow flames flickered instantaneously. Warmth soon engulfed the tiny room.

Time to get into clean clothes and socks, he thought. Unfortunately, his bags were in the car. He groaned. His boxers were dry, but the only other clothes he had were sodden and cold and hanging in the mud room. He padded back toward the entry. The chilled flagstones in the hallway shocked his feet and he shivered uncontrollably.

He peered out the door's tiny window. He could see his car parked ten feet away. Between him and the car was wet pea gravel. The rain fell steadily, and a gray mist swirled among the buildings. He looked at his dirty and soaked loafers sitting on the rack and then gazed at his feet. He was going to get wet anyway so why bother putting his shoes or clothes back on.

Ten feet of pea gravel. I can do this.

He clenched his jaw, opened the door, and dashed outside in one movement.

"Ow, ow, ow!" he hollered as tiny rocks bit into the bony parts of his heel. He raced to the hatch, opened it, and grabbed his tote and duffel bag. He slung the bag over his shoulder and hefted the tote before running back to the house.

"Less than a minute!" he proclaimed proudly as he set the case on the ground and lifted the door latch. It wouldn't budge. He wiggled it up and down furiously. The door was locked. "Shit!" he yelled. Then he wheeled and scanned the area.

Here I am, standing in my underwear and screaming obscenities. My plan to remain incognito is out the window.

He peered through the small glass window in the door. The bubbles in the glass distorted his view, but he could see the black skeleton key taunting him from its perch on the shelf. "You bugger," he growled. He stepped back and extended his finger toward the key. He couldn't see the object, so he had to trust his intuition that he was maneuvering it to the keyhole on the other side of the door.

Despite the chilliness, perspiration popped on his forehead. His index finger trembled as if it, alone, was carrying the weight of the key. Finally, he heard a metallic scraping from the other side of the door and realized the key was attempting to slide into the lock. His momentary lapse of focus caused the key to fall to the floor.

"Shit!" he yelled. He no longer cared if anyone saw him standing outside in his wet boxers. He just wanted to get inside. He drew in a long breath, raised his finger, and began the process all over again.

The key slowly lifted from the floor and rose upward until it was parallel to the keyhole. Chance engaged his instincts so he could see and feel the key, which gently poked the hole in the door as Chance guided it backward and forward. At last, the key stuck in the lock and Chance pushed it all the way in. A devilish grin fluttered across his face as he realized the key was turning in the lock.

Clunk.

The door swung open.

"Yes!" he hollered as he thrust his fists into the air.

"Interesting display of magic," a British male voice uttered.

Chance whirled, hands positioned to fight.

Standing beside the car was a man of medium build, wearing a black overcoat, black pants, and shiny black shoes. He held an umbrella over his head and beamed at Chance. He tipped his bowler hat and chirped, "Hello, Mr. Kemp. My name is Alden Stark. I'm your Cererian contact. Darrius sent me."

Chapter 5

Alden Stark

"I APOLOGIZE FOR MY appearance," Chance offered as he led Alden into the home. "You can hang your stuff on the shelf."

"No apologies necessaries, Mr. Kemp." Alden removed the bowler and banged it on his arm to remove droplets before laying it on the shelf. Then he removed his overcoat, shook it, and hung it carefully on the last hook. He smoothed his jet-black hair with both hands. "Darrius told me all about you."

"Oh?" Chance guided Alden to the reception room in the back of the house. "Good or bad?"

"All very fascinating," Alden replied. The Cererian walked into the middle of the room and turned around, taking note of all the furnishings and paintings. "Quaint. Very quaint."

The two men stared at each other.

Alden stood straight, his shoulders square, heels pressed together, and the toes angled out in a V shape. His fingertips pressed together in front of his waist, and he cocked his head to the side as he studied Chance.

Chance frowned, puzzled by Alden's demeanor. "Um, please...please sit while I get changed," he blurted as he backed out of the room. "I've just arrived, so I'll be a few minutes getting dressed." He darted down the hall, grabbed his bags, and raced upstairs.

"I'll make us some tea," Alden called after him.

"I don't think there is any," Chance yelled back. He jumped one-legged around the bedroom while tugging on his jeans. "I haven't been shopping yet."

Fifteen minutes later, Chance had changed, combed his hair, and brushed his teeth. He crept down the hall and peered into the reception room. Alden stood gazing into the backyard. His hands were clasped behind his back, and he absently tapped his palm with a finger.

A tray with a white teapot and two rose-decorated cups with saucers lay on a nearby table.

"You found tea?" Chance asked as he entered the room.

Alden spun around and nodded. "You prefer English Breakfast. Is that correct?"

"I prefer bourbon, but when it comes to tea, I don't like those fancy flavors. I like the basic black."

Alden listened and nodded. His emerald eyes sparkled and danced in the glow of the fire. "So I've been told." He poured tea into both cups. "No milk and one sugar. Correct?" he asked as he added a sugar cube to the cup.

"Yep," Chance replied. He eyed the man suspiciously. "Darrius told you that?"

Alden passed a cup to Chance and held the other. "I, too, prefer English Breakfast but with no milk, nor sugar. Cheers to us."

The men clinked cups. Alden sipped his tea, but Chance held the cup to his lips, unsure about the gentleman before him. They studied each other over the rim of their cups.

"How do you know Darrius?" Chance asked.

"Ah, you're suspicious of me, Mr. Kemp." Alden set his cup on the table. "It doesn't take a magician to understand your body language." Alden ambled to the chair by the fire, sat, and crossed his legs. He smoothed the fabric and adjusted his shirt cuffs before he spoke again. "You're right to be suspicious, Mr. Kemp, especially with the way the world is nowadays. But what do your instincts tell you?"

Chance set his cup on the table and concentrated on the annoyingly polite British man facing him. Sybil's warning about the Yfel Brethren nagged at him, but there was nothing about this man to indicate he was anything but a benevolent Cererian.

Regardless, he took a step sideways so his body was squarely in the doorway, lest he needed to flee at a moment's notice. Though he had brought his broadsword, he had left it in the bedroom. He mentally calculated how long it would take to retrieve his weapon. With his supernatural speed, he could be armed in less than three seconds.

"There's no reason to be alarmed, Mr. Kemp. I mean you no harm." Within a split second, Alden had jumped to his feet and stood inches from Chance.

Chance instinctively shoved him away. Fueled by adrenaline and the unexpected confrontation, Chance's extraordinary strength propelled Alden through the air and slammed him against the far wall. Chance growled and flexed his arms as he prepared for another assault.

A rich chuckle filled the room. "Mr. Kemp, you are everything Darrius said you would be." Alden stood and brushed the dust from his suit. A generous smile filled his face as he glanced up at Chance.

Chance glared back and held his hands at the ready to conjure magic, if needed.

Hands up with palms forward, Alden surrendered. "Enough, Mr. Kemp. As you humans say, I give up." Alden chuckled louder as he grabbed his teacup. He lifted it toward Chance. "To you, Mr. Kemp."

"Did Darrius put you up to this?" Chance lowered his hands but was still cautious.

"Yes, he did. Darrius told me you would be honored if I allowed you to demonstrate your strength. He said wrestling was an activity you had to abandon because your power was too great for your opponents."

Chance's eyes widened. Alden was referencing something that happened when he was in high school, long before he found out who and what he was. He had broken both arms of one of his opponents during a match and the school banned him from sports.

"Darrius followed you on your late-night escapades when you would jump from your second-story window at The Nine Muses and run throughout the surrounding countryside against your father's wishes. Darrius promised to keep you safe." Alden had assumed his rigid stance with his fingertips pressed together in front of his waist.

"You're probing my mind, and I forbid you from doing that!" Chance yelled. He stepped toward Alden and menaced him with a raised fist. "I will not tolerate that behavior."

Alden didn't flinch as Chance drew within inches of his face. "I would never probe your mind without your permission, Mr. Kemp. We are not allowed to do that. I am merely repeating something Darrius shared with me so you can know I am who I say I am."

Chance lowered his hand and stepped away.

Alden rubbed his chin. "Perhaps Darrius' scheme went a little too far. He had hoped it would make you smile."

"I'm very sensitive to anything out of the ordinary. The Yfel Brethren have me on pins and needles."

"You should be on alert. It would give the Yfel no greater pleasure than to capture you or one of your siblings." Alden poured two fresh cups of tea. Handing a cup to Chance, he returned to the chair by the fire. "Come, Mr. Kemp. Let's spend some time getting acquainted. If I am to be your bodyguard during your stay in England, I want to know more about you. You sound like a complicated and most interesting fellow." Alden crossed his legs and sipped his tea.

Chance picked up his cup and sat in the chair opposite Alden. The warmth of the fire felt wonderful against his bare feet. In his rush to get changed, he'd forgotten to throw on socks or shoes. He sipped his tea.

Slurp.

Chance grimaced. "Sorry. I'm not accustomed to drinking tea from these tiny cups."

"Would a ceramic mug suit you more?" Alden asked as he walked to the tea tray and held aloft a black mug.

"What?" Chance stared at the mug, which Alden wiggled at him. "This tea and that mug. They're manifestations, aren't they?"

Alden smiled gently. "They are. As you mentioned earlier, you hadn't been shopping, so I needed to improvise our refreshments."

"Hmm. Can you produce a bottle of Woodford Reserve and two glasses?" Chance's eyes twinkled. "It's my first day in England and I think we need to celebrate the occasion properly."

"Darrius had mentioned your love for that particular bourbon," Alden observed. "And he also cautioned me against your inclinations."

Chance laughed hard, which caused his tea to dribble on the floor. "I guess I did act a little crazy at The Nine Muses. But you have to admit, that was a lot for me to process in one weekend. Don't worry. I won't get out of hand."

"Very well, Mr. Kemp, one bottle of bourbon and two glasses." Without a twitch, the items appeared on the table. The action happened so effortlessly. It was as though they had always been present.

"Excellent. By the way, do you prefer I address you as Alden or Mr. Stark? I call Darrius by his first name, but you've been addressing me as Mr. Kemp, so I wasn't sure if you wanted to keep our working arrangement formal."

"I've never been asked that question before, Mr. Kemp."

"Please, call me Chance."

"Very well, Chance. If it pleases you to use your first name, so shall I. Please, call me Alden."

Chance thrust his hand out. The men clasped hands and then Chance placed his left hand on Alden's back and pulled him in for a hug. "This is how we do it in Asheville." For good measure, he slapped Alden's back twice before releasing him. "How about a drink, Alden?"

"Very well Mist—er, Chance." Alden poured a small amount into each glass. "Ice?"

"Nah. I'll have mine neat."

"Then, I'll do the same." Alden lifted his glass. "I believe a toast is customary."

"To new beginnings," Chance announced. "New beginnings with a new friend."

The two men clinked glasses and gulped the bourbon.

Chance wiggled his glass at Alden who obliged with a second pour for both of them.

The winter storm worsened. Gale winds ripped dead leaves from trees while torrential rains flooded yards. Just outside the farmhouse, a weak light cast an amber glow along a hedgerow bordering the back side of the home. The shrubs thrashed furiously in the unrelenting wind. A dark, hooded figure blended seamlessly with the thick bushes. Motionless, the figure watched Chance and Alden as they drank and chatted.

Chapter 6

The Triskele

THE SUNLIGHT BURST THROUGH the bedroom window and a dazzling display of miniature rainbows shimmered across the walls and ceiling thanks to a row of crystals hanging in front of the window. Chance sprawled naked on his belly across the bedsheet with his head turned to one side, mouth agape. He snored contentedly.

"Chance." Alden called his name softly.

Chance snorted and absently scratched his bare butt.

"Morning, Chance."

Chance opened one eye. Bloodshot, it lolled lazily before focusing on Alden who sat in a chair by the window. "Morning tea?" the Cererian asked as he gestured toward a teapot and two mugs sitting on the table.

"Hm," Chance grunted. He rolled onto his back, slowly opening one eye and then the other. He stared at the ceiling and focused on the dark wood beams stretching from wall to wall. In a corner of the ceiling, a long-legged spider hurried along the silver threads of its web.

"What time is it?" Chance asked in a hoarse whisper.

"Time to get up. There's much to do."

"Um." Chance scratched along his ribs where the pale remnants of a six-inch scar ran from his back to his chest.

"Battle scar? Alden asked.

"What?" Chance answered groggily.

"The scar. On your side."

Chance hefted onto his elbow and looked. "Oh, yeah. Hell of a battle."

"Indeed. Darrius told me you and your siblings vanquished Stygian."

Chance sat on the edge of the bed and rubbed his sleepy eyes. "That was all Hilly's doing. Her plan. Her power. We just helped her with the execution." He stared at Alden. "Of course, you know all that shit, don't you?"

"I found this on your shirt hanging in the mudroom." Alden pinched a small object between his thumb and forefinger.

Chance leaned forward. Alden twirled the object until three tiny spirals were visible. "Oh, yeah. I think Janet pinned that on my collar when we said goodbye at the airport. I didn't even know it was there until I was on the plane." Chance raked his fingers through his hair. "Were you snooping through my stuff?"

"You left quite a mess in the mudroom and the reception room. I did a little tidying while you slept." Alden poured tea into a mug and handed it to Chance. "Drink this. You need to function as soon as possible. You have a lot to do today."

Chance stared at the reddish fluid and grimaced. "Hey, this isn't the usual stuff. What are you trying to pull?"

"It's a tasty hangover cure." Alden sipped his tea and raised his eyebrows. "Nice. Very refreshing."

Chance scowled at the contents in his mug. He sniffed the fluid and jerked with surprise. "Smells like cotton candy. What kind of tea is this?"

"My special concoction. Drink all of it and you'll feel marvelous in no time." Alden leaned back into the chair and straightened his shirt cuffs. It was early morning and the Cererian was outfitted in a freshly pressed black suit and black leather shoes. His black hair was slicked back into finely combed rows.

Chance studied him, peered at the red fluid in his cup, and downed the drink in one gulp.

His face puckered instantly.

"Fuck. That doesn't taste like cotton candy." Grimacing, he smacked his lips while his tongue darted out of his mouth. "Give me something else to take this shitty taste away," he demanded as he brushed his tongue against the bedsheet.

Alden poured more tea.

"Not more of *that* shit. I need something else," Chance barked.

"Look at it, Chance. It is something else." Alden jutted his chin at the mug he had thrust into Chance's hand.

Familiar black tea swirled, and its inviting earthy aroma wafted. Chance downed the steaming fluid in one gulp. "Argh. That was hot."

Alden smoothed the fabric on his trousers. "Feel better?"

"In the rush to get that shit out of my mouth, I didn't notice...but my headache is gone. And my energy has returned. Damn. Good job, Alden. Your nasty cotton candy concoction did the trick."

"Marvelous. Get dressed and meet me downstairs." Alden rose to leave.

Chance slid off the bed and strode to the armoire.

Alden noted Chance's immense thigh muscles bulging with each step. "Darrius had told me that you carry your power in your legs, and it definitely shows."

A jolt of embarrassment poked at Chance as he searched the closet for his clothes. "Thanks...I think..."

"By the way," Alden added from the doorway. "The triskele, the pin with the three spirals is also marked on the bottom of your right foot." He turned and trotted downstairs.

"What did he say?" Chance whispered, staring down at his feet. He launched backward onto the bed. Twisting and contorting his body at odd angles, he grappled for his foot so he could look at the sole. Yanking on his thick leg, he tumbled onto his back and bent his right ankle until it rested on his left knee. Grunting, he grabbed his foot and pulled himself upward so he could inspect the sole. There, in the middle of his heel, was a light brown marking, barely an inch wide.

"Hmm," he mused as he finished dressing. "This is definitely no coincidence. I wager Alden knows more about the symbol." Chance finished dressing and hurried downstairs.

Alden stood at the range. He held a spatula in his hand like a fencing sword and stabbed at the bacon in the skillet. "Take that!"

"Morning!" Chance hailed as he cocked his head at Alden's behavior.

Alden whirled around. "Good morning, Chance."

Chance burst out laughing but quickly covered his mouth with his fist.

Alden had removed his suitcoat, rolled up his shirt sleeves, and wore a bright red apron with white lettering that said, KEEP CALM AND CARRY ON, with a white crown above the lettering.

Chance coughed his chuckle away.

"Something funny?" Alden asked with a quizzical face.

"Nope. Carry on," Chance replied. He forced a rising smile into thinned lips.

Alden turned back to the stove and poked the bacon with the spatula. "Take a seat. Breakfast will soon be ready."

Moments later, Alden placed a plate of bangers, bacon, and scrambled eggs in the middle of the table. "Scones are almost done."

"Scones? You're getting fancy, aren't you?"

"Not at all. I hope you like raisins in yours." Alden moved the teapot to the table and poured two cups.

"No coffee?" Chance asked as he chewed on the end of a sausage.

Alden stopped in mid-pour and stared at Chance. "Sorry, Chance. Just tea today. I'll work on acquiring coffee for tomorrow," Alden replied as he finished pouring the tea.

He held another sausage on his fork. "Wow, this food is awesome!" Chance exclaimed. "What did you call this? A banger?"

Alden chuckled. "Yes. That's a banger."

"Odd name."

"It dates back to World War One. Our food shortages demanded we make our sausages with fillers, which ended up being mostly water. Between the water and the tight casings, many of the sausages exploded while cooking. Hence the term."

Chance held his sausage aloft. "To the humble banger."

Alden raised his as well. "Here, here," he replied.

The men ate in silence. Alden cut small pieces and chewed slowly as Chance shoveled the food into his mouth like he hadn't eaten in days. Between chews, Chance slurped his tea.

Ding.

"Ah, the scones are ready." Alden lifted the fluffy, golden biscuits out of the oven and set them on the range. "I'll let them cool a little whilst we chat."

Chance wiped his mouth as Alden returned to the table. "About that symbol—" Chance began.

"The triskele," Alden affirmed.

"Yes, the triskele. How did you know it was on the sole of my foot?" Chance flicked a glance toward the scones. Alden ignored him.

"When you rolled over in bed, the soles of your feet poked in my direction. That's when I noticed. But full disclosure, I already knew that about your family. That marking is on all within your clan."

Chance kicked off his loafer and removed his sock. He hefted his foot onto the table with a *thunk*. "Everyone in my family has this mark?" he said pointing to the symbol on his heel.

Alden scrunched his face and waved his hand. "Please remove your foot from the table."

"I wanted to show you—"

"I've seen it, and the answer is yes, everyone in your biological family has that mark. Now, please remove your foot." Chance did as he was told. Alden furiously wiped the tablecloth with a wet rag.

"Well, I'll be." Chance re-socked his foot and slid it back into his shoe. "It's going to be damned hard to find other members of my family unless I ask everyone I meet to kick off their shoes and wiggle their tootsies at me." He chuckled to himself.

"Indeed, that would be quite awkward," Alden replied as he draped the rag over the sink.

Chance darted another glance toward the scones. "Are those biscuits ready yet?"

Alden shook his head. "They're still too warm, but I'll get a couple near the edge so you can satisfy your curiosity." He placed three on a plate and set them on the table. "Butter or jam?"

Chance had already taken a huge bite out of one. He looked up at Alden like a guilty child. "Um, they taste great like this." Crumbs fell onto the table with each muffled word.

Alden glared at the table and then Chance. "Goodness," the Cererian began, "you have worse manners than a cow." Alden brushed the crumbs into his hand and marched to the sink where he gripped the edge with both hands and hung his head.

Chance studied his friend. "Everything okay, Alden?"

Alden crossed the kitchen untying his apron. He hung it on the back of the door, sat, and folded his hands into his lap. Chance watched Alden take several deep breaths. "Why are you here, Chance?"

The Cererian's serious tone startled Chance. "Is this about scarfing the biscuit and making a mess. I'm sorry, dude, I didn't mean to offend you. You're right, my manners are atrocious. Everyone one in my family agrees with you."

Emotionless, Alden stared back.

"Um...I want to find my family?" Chance stammered. "I need to find my family's gemstone." He studied Alden's impassive face and continued to babble. "Um...it's my quest. I was compelled to begin my journey like Hilly and Kai. Sybil woke me out of a deep sleep to share all this information about England and Wales and basically ordered me to go."

Silence.

After several moments, Alden sighed. He walked to the large window and glanced into the back garden. With the storm long passed, the bright sun shone high in the deep blue sky. He assumed his ramrod straight stance, but his hands fidgeted behind his back. "Why are you here, Keeper of the Records?" he asked in a low whisper.

Chance turned toward Alden. A puzzled look skirted across his face. "I told you. I'm here—"

"Wrong!" Alden shouted as he whirled and rushed at Chance until there was barely an inch between their noses. "Dead wrong. Dead magician." He spit each word. His lips twisted and his eyes bulged. Suddenly, the benign Brit had turned into a menacing monster. "You are not worthy of the title you carry. You're a bumbler, a buffoon who loves to drink, and you're a comical excuse for a magician. The Prophecy must be wrong. You can't possibly be one of the saviors of this world." Alden shoved Chance with a strength so unexpected Chance tumbled out of the chair and fell flat onto his back. Alden stormed out of the kitchen.

Eyes wide, Chance panted as he scanned all corners of the kitchen for the wild man who had just attacked him. He eased to a standing position and clutched his chest. A severe pain throbbed there, and he tore his shirt open. Two bluish bruises in the shapes of hands formed on each pectoral muscle. Chance gingerly touched one and flinched. A deep purple blotch tinged with red grew around a thumbprint as though it had been dug deep toward his heart.

Damn, Chance thought as he rebuttoned his shirt and looked for Alden. He walked into the hallway and peered toward the front and rear doors.

Nobody.

He crept into the rear reception room, fearing a surprise attack at any moment. As he cleared the doorway, he spied Alden in the garden. Hands raised in defense, Chance eased into the backyard.

"Alden?" Chance squeaked. He cleared his throat. "Alden?" he repeated in a stronger voice.

Alden's voice was low and steady. "Did you see how easy it was for me to overpower you? In less than two seconds, you were on the ground. If I had wanted to, my thumb could have plunged into your heart and stopped it. But, for now, you will wear that bruise as a reminder of what could have been." Alden sidled up to Chance and tapped his chest. Chance winced.

"Who are you?" Chance asked uneasily.

Alden stood tall, straightened his shirt, and brushed his trousers. "I am the one who will teach you how to survive the Yfel. Some have viewed me as a devil and some have claimed I was their angel, but you will never, and I repeat, never forget me."

Alden took a step forward. Chance backed away. "Come now, Chance. We are both on the same side, are we not? Darrius has sent me to prepare you for a most unpleasant encounter. Your schooling begins now.

A twisted grin broke through the seriousness etched into Alden's face.

A shiver raced up Chance's spine. His mission in England had become all too real. This was not a holiday filled with family reunions and cheery get-togethers. He was on a dangerous journey to fulfill a prophecy while avoiding death at the hands of the Yfel Brethren.

Chapter 7

Unlocking a Superpower

"YOU'RE NOT LIKE YOUR siblings," Alden said as he cleared the furniture from the center of the reception room. Like a passionate conductor, he waved his hands back and forth magically commanding the chairs and tables to rise and settle against the wall. "They have the ability to communicate telepathically, fly, cast spells, and—"

"Yeah, yeah. I get the picture. I'm a toad compared to them." Chance hunched against the door frame and crossed his arms. He chewed his bottom lip as he watched Alden rearrange the room.

The Cererian cocked his head at his friend. "Au contraire, Chance. You have only had a taste of the powers you possess. For some reason, which Darrius and I cannot determine, your abilities have not presented themselves as fast as they have for your siblings. Darrius believes it might be tied to Sybil. She is very powerful, and you rely on her too much."

"Has she done something wrong?" Chance scratched the back of his neck nervously. "I *am* her Keeper. We're supposed to do things together."

"Sybil has done nothing wrong. You have done nothing wrong. However, your powers are stuck. They haven't progressed as quickly as expected since your Revelation at The Nine Muses. Darrius believes your interaction with the prophecy book may be delaying your powers a wee bit. That's why your trip to England was fortuitous."

Alden winked.

Chance's eyebrows arched. "Did you or Darrius influence my trip here?"

"In a way. As you know, we cannot interfere with the pace of The Cererian Prophecy. However, we were aware that you would eventually arrive in England, and we encouraged Sybil to expedite that process so I could spend some quality time with you."

Alden scanned the room and announced, "We have exactly two days." He clapped his hands together. "Let's get started."

"Two days for what?"

"To unlock your powers so you can be ready for the Brethren."

"I need a drink." Chance darted toward the kitchen. He opened and slammed the cupboard doors looking for the Woodford Reserve. "Where is that bottle?" he shouted angrily.

"You won't find it." Alden leaned against the doorjamb watching Chance scramble around the kitchen.

"What?"

"You don't need it, Chance. Your strength lies deep within you and not at the bottom of a bottle. Follow me. We have work to do." Alden hurried down the hallway.

"Asshole!" Chance yelled from the kitchen.

Alden's hearty laugh drifted down the hallway. "I'm sure you'll call me that many more times before this day is over. Now, please join me."

Chance kicked the baseboard and trudged to the reception room. He hovered in the doorway. Alden floated above the floor and twirled in a circle with his arms outstretched.

"Your inability to fly is a great weakness for you. But you have something your siblings don't have." Alden stopped spinning and abruptly plunged to the floor with such force the walls quaked, and dust drifted from the ceiling beams.

"What the hell?" Chance rushed into the room.

Alden stood in a six-foot deep hole and reached toward Chance. "Help me up."

Chance grimaced as he hefted the Cererian from the hole. "I'm going to have to pay for this damage."

Alden waved his hand. The hole had filled in, and the floorboards repaired themselves as if nothing had occurred. "There. Good as new. Now it's your turn."

"Puh-lease. I can punch a hole through the floor with my fist. I don't have to dance in the air first." Chance performed a pirouette with one hand above his head and a hand on his hip.

Alden thrust his hands toward the ceiling. A translucent ball of white energy materialized. The mass hissed and snapped as it drifted toward the men. "Observe," Alden urged as he slammed the electrical sphere downward. An immense crack zigzagged across the floor and reached up one of the walls. The depression continued to grow from a stream of white, pulsing energy flowing from Alden's fingers. Eventually the crevasse stretched twenty feet down, and the Cererian halted the flow of energy. With his lesson complete, he stepped aside and pressed his fingertips together in front of his body.

Chance gawked into the depression. "Impressive. But I don't get what you're trying to prove. You're Cererian and have powers I don't possess."

Alden tugged on his cuffs and casually flicked debris off his trousers. "But you are a member of the earth family. Besides your tremendous strength and ability to levitate, you have the gift to manipulate the elements of the earth with such precision that you could direct a shaft straight into the core of the planet without damaging the ground around you."

Chance rubbed his chin. "So, let's assume I do have this power. How would I use it?"

Alden sighed and shook his head. "You have so much to learn, Keeper. It's not a coincidence that Hilly can manipulate sunlight and Kai can alter the weather and winds, and Fen is able to influence the waters of the world. You have an innate ability to restructure mountains and other earthly elements because of your role within your family.

"Each of you belong to clans that represent the four natural elements: earth, air, fire, and water. The day will arrive when all of you will call upon your individual superpowers. Your siblings are almost ready, but you need to work on your skills."

Alden gestured toward the middle of the room and erased all evidence of the cracks and crevasse. "Now, it's your turn. Duplicate what I just did."

Chance loved a good challenge, but he remained unsure. He glanced around the room and then back to Alden. The Cererian observed him impassively. His emerald-green eyes pulsed.

Chance stumbled backward as if shoved by unseen hands. "What the hell was that for?" He raised his fists toward Alden.

"Your hesitancy is a manifestation of your fear, magician."

"I'm not afraid of anything," Chance seethed.

"You are very brave, but your fear of failure prevents you from attaining your potential. Come on magician...Chance...show me the power buried deep inside." Alden poked Chance in his chest, right on the bruise above his heart.

Chance flinched. Angered and embarrassed, he brushed Alden to the side and marched to the middle of the room. "Watch this," he snarled.

Wrinkles furrowed in Chance's forehead as he clenched his jaw and moved around the room calculating the proper approach to his magic. He stretched each arm across his chest. He tugged his head toward the right shoulder and then to the left shoulder. He rolled his shoulders forward and then backward, and bounced on the balls of his feet while flicking the tips of his fingers.

"Enough!" Alden scolded. "Is this how you conjure back in your quaint Asheville?"

"I'm loosening up. I've never used this power, and I don't want to sprain anything."

Alden threw an energy ball into Chance's chest. The powerful punch bowled him over and slammed him against the wall.

Chance crumbled into a tangled heap of arms and legs. "Ow," he whimpered and rubbed his chest. "What was that for?"

Alden kneeled before him, their noses almost touching. "This is not a game, Chance. Your life, and the lives of your siblings, depend on you unlocking your superpower. If you fail, we all fail."

Alden left and faced the garden with closed eyes.

Chance dropped his head. The Cererian angered him, but he knew Alden was right. Since his Revelation, Chance became accustomed to following Sybil's lead. When he did practice magic, it was routine conjuring he had done every day for the last six months when he consulted the prophecy book.

He rolled onto his side and stood. A sharp ache in his chest caused him to double over. "I think you cracked something."

Alden stared outside. His hands fidgeted behind his back.

"Did you hear me? I think you broke something."

Alden turned slowly around and cocked his head to one side. A wry smile slid across his face. "If I had been the Yfel, you'd be dead."

Alden waved his hand, and the ache disappeared. "You will get hurt many more times, magician. But that's the price you will pay to develop your earth power. Do you understand?"

Shame filled Chance's eyes. "I'm sorry, Alden. I guess the only asshole in this room was me."

"I won't disagree with your assessment."

"And here I was expecting to have some fun in my homeland."

"That comes later, magician. Soon, you will meet the family members of your ancient tribe."

Chance's jaw dropped open. "Really? You found my family?"

Alden shook a finger. "But you won't see them if you don't get to work!"

Chance whirled and raised his hands with the palms facing each other. In deep concentration, he bit his lip as he searched for the power source that remained locked deep inside his body. A ripple of energy fluttered between his fingers and immediately disappeared.

He dropped his hands and drew in a long breath to steady his emotions. Then he thrust his hands upward again and stared at the space between his palms. Beads of sweat dotted his forehead. His arms trembled as he focused all his energy into producing a translucent ball. Like a miniature lightning bolt, another ripple of white energy zigzagged between his fingers before quickly dissipated.

"Crap," Chance spat, dropping his hands at his side.

The applause was slow at first, but the tempo quickened as Alden clapped furiously. "Well done, Chance! Well done."

"I didn't do anything."

"Ah, but you did," Alden countered. He crossed in front of Chance and pointed at a black mark on the floor. A tiny pinprick, a hole had been punched into the floorboard.

Chance knelt and ran his finger over the mark. A wide grin spread across his face. "Well, I'll be."

Alden patted his shoulder. "Okay, let's work on your delivery and technique. You want to proficiently channel the earth power. That takes precision and clear focus. Are you ready to begin your next lesson, magician?"

Chance clapped his hands together. "Let's make this happen, Alden. Show me everything you have."

The men worked well into the night pausing, only for dinner. To fine-tune the techniques for parting the earth without destroying the surrounding landscape, they headed into the garden.

"Do not hurt my flowers," Alden cautioned. "If you crimp even one petal, I will be most displeased."

Chance chuckled but coughed the laugh into his fist when he saw Alden's deadpan expression. "Show me how to do that, Alden. Show me the right way."

"Watch me carefully." Alden pointed his index finger toward the ground and rotated his hand in a circle. While there was no visible light, an energy stream like a laser, dug two inches into the sod, leaving a tiny entry point on the surface.

Two hours later, right before midnight, the duo went inside. Chance collapsed into a chair. Alden returned with two glasses of bourbon. "Now, you may have this. You have earned it, Keeper. You've done a most excellent job." Alden handed Chance a glass and then raised his own. "Cheers. Get your rest tonight because tomorrow we work on moving mountains."

A grin spread across Chance's face. "I love the sound of that."

As Alden and Chance chatted in the reception room, a pair of eyes observed them from the branches of a large alder tree in the backyard. Motionless, the dark figure hunched on one giant limb and watched the men. "I'll be damned," the male voice whispered, then he snapped his fingers and disappeared.

Chapter 8

Moving Mountains

"You'll be fine," Alden reassured. "You may feel a little disoriented since it's your first time teleporting." He patted his leg, gesturing for Chance to stand beside him. Chance inched toward the Cererian, unsure of what might happen.

Like a human lariat, Alden's arm whipped around Chance's waist and pulled him close.

And they vanished.

Moments later they appeared atop a small hill in the countryside. Chance bent over and dry heaved. "My head is spinning," he moaned.

"Take a few deep breaths," Alden encouraged.

Chance sucked in a breath and hacked up phlegm. Another breath caught in his throat as the urge to vomit kicked his insides. He fell to his knees, gripped his stomach, and panted.

Alden studied the countryside painted on the surrounding hills with reds, oranges, and pale greens. "The Preseli Hills are beautiful this time of year."

Chance retched into the grass and fell onto his side. Alden glanced briefly at him and continued musing on the landscape. "These ancient lands are important to you, Chance. This is where your original family found their beginnings."

"Fa—family?" Chance eked in a hoarse whisper. He rolled onto his back and stared up at Alden. "Where did you say we were?"

"We're in Wales. The Preseli Hills to be exact."

"Wales? A passage in Sybil indicated I'd be coming here." Chance struggled to stand on wobbly legs. He swiped his mouth with the back of his hand. "Teleporting with you is like strapping myself onto a tilt-a-whirl for an all-nighter at the county fair." He rubbed his stomach. "No offense, but I'm not looking forward to the return trip."

"No offense taken. Teleporting is a very efficient form of travel." He looked Chance over and added, "For those who are accustomed to its nuances."

"Why are we here?" Chance asked surveying the surrounding area.

"To move mountains," Alden chirped.

"I thought that term was your way of bolstering my confidence. I didn't realize you meant I was literally going to move a mountain."

"It's the final step in unlocking your hidden powers. If you don't practice your gift, it will retreat into the darkness like it did before. Believe me, this ability will come in handy one day." Alden slapped his hands together. "Shall we begin?"

"Won't we be seen?" Chance peered into the distance and pointed. "I see people over there."

"Our presence will not be detected. I have cloaked us to anyone that may happen by."

"But if I'm blowing up mountains, don't you think people may notice?"

Alden laughed and slapped Chance on the shoulder. "You can be quite funny, sometimes, Chance."

Chance narrowed his eyes at the Cererian. "Are you crazy? People will notice big chunks of dirt flying around."

"The earth shifts every day. Your little ripples will not be noticed." Alden gestured for Chance to follow him. "Walk with me." The duo hiked to the bottom of the valley between two round hills. Along the way, they passed piles of flat rocks abutting large boulders.

Alden stopped at one pile and picked up a stone. "This is bluestone." He passed it to Chance. "This one has been cut in two. Notice the white speckles? Interesting characteristic for this rock. Slabs of bluestone from this area were used in the formation of Stonehenge."

"Genesis wrote an account in Sybil about bluestone. It doesn't look blue."

Alden spit on the rock and rubbed the spittle across the surface. "See. The blue comes to life when it's wet. Now, put your talents to the test. Move that pile of stones from the hill on the left to the hill on the right, and you'll move that pile of rocks from the hill on the right to the one on the left at the same time."

"Jeez, they're about half mile away from each other."

"Distance doesn't matter, precision does. You're already familiar with levitating a single object. But in this exercise, you'll move two groups of items simultaneously. This method will keep the energy in balance."

"What energy?" Chance peered into the distance to where Alden was pointing.

"You *feel* the energy. Energy is everywhere. When you move a large object, the energetic flow of the space it occupied is disrupted and causes a ripple effect that can be felt far away. Somewhat like throwing a stone into the middle of a pond. Ripples travel outward from the displaced water. So, to avoid causing potential harm, you move two objects at the same time."

"I'll demonstrate." Alden took two steps away and raised his hands, one toward each pile of rocks. A breeze raced through the valley. Chance shuddered in the chilled blast and hugged himself. A low rumble snatched his attention as two groups of boulders passed midair and settled on the opposite slopes from where they originated.

The entire process took less than two seconds.

"I'll be damned. That was really cool."

"Your turn, Keeper. You practiced making holes in the backyard yesterday. Now, let's see what you can do about maintaining balance when moving mountains." Alden took Chance's elbow and guided him to the exact spot where he'd conjured his magic.

"Take cleansing breaths and calm your mind," Alden instructed as he backed away allowing Chance ample space for his attempt.

After taking three deep breaths, Chance raised his hands toward the rock piles like Alden had demonstrated. A gust swept by him. Despite the chill, sweat dripped down his face.

"You're trying too hard, magician. Calm down. It should feel second nature and unforced. Drop your hands and begin again."

Chance shook his arms and rolled his head from side to side. He drew in a long breath and slowly exhaled through pursed lips. Then he raised his hands toward the two piles of stone. His biceps trembled slightly as he stretched toward the two hills. Finally, a gentle breeze washed over him, and the piles lifted into the air. His eyebrows arched with surprise, but he gritted his teeth and pressed forward until he had he successfully transferred the rocks.

"I did it!" he yelled, jumping up and down and pumping his fists into the air. He grabbed Alden around the waist and twirled him around. "I did it!" He set his friend back on the ground and pumped his hand. "Thank you, Alden. Thank you for teaching me how to do this."

"You possessed this ability all along. You just needed to be shown how to bring it forward. But this is not all you can do with this power."

Chance abruptly stopped shaking his hand. "Oh?"

Alden chuckled. "This is only the beginning. You *can* move mountains with this technique. But remember that transference of objects must be done simultaneously to avoid a catastrophe that could result from an imbalance of energy."

He led Chance to another spot on the hill. "Now, let's try your skills by manipulating two hills. This is trickier because you must move an entire community and all its resources—rocks, soil, insects, microorganisms, animals, and plants. You must engage your powers to find the natural boundaries of each community and then scoop them up in their entirety before switching them with a compatible community."

Chance stared at Alden with his mouth wide open. "What? How would I possibly do that and not harm something?"

"Daunting, is it not?" Alden teased. "But it can be accomplished with such finesse, that not even a speck of dirt will linger in the air once the transfer has been completed."

"I've doubted you before, Alden, and you always proved me wrong. But this lesson seems far-fetched. Show me how to do this right because if there's a way to screw it up, I'll find it."

Alden nodded. "Okay. Let's begin." He demonstrated the technique while carefully noting the specific stages of magic so no injuries or fatalities would be sustained.

The sight of two hills and their communities passing by each other in midair tugged at Chance's sensibilities. The movement was so swift only a blurred shimmer hinted of the transfer. "Hilly would never believe this. Hell, I'm witnessing it, and I'm not sure I believe it."

"Your turn, Chance." The men switched places.

Chance's lips thinned as he focused. Then he closed his eyes and raised his hands while engaging his intuition to locate the natural boundaries of the communities.

"Breathe, Chance," Alden reminded. "You're holding your breath. Remember to breathe and relax."

Chance dropped his arms and gasped. He leaned forward and panted. "Damn this is hard."

"Try again," Alden said gently.

I've got this, Chance told himself. He planted his feet and pushed a hand toward each hill. This time he kept his eyes open as his instincts probed for the individual groups of organisms. He rotated his hands, and the mounds of earth slowly lifted, passed each other, and settled into place on the opposite ground simultaneously. An earthy aroma hung in the air.

"Excellent!" Alden praised. "Now switch them back."

Sweat soaked Chance's shirt and ran down his arms. "This is harder than my workouts. I'm drenched."

"You'll reach a point when your magic will be second nature and effortless. Practice, practice, practice."

"I don't see the benefit of this magic, Alden. Why not maintain the natural order of things? You know, not mess with Mother Nature."

Alden nodded. "It is best to allow the environment to flourish in its own peaceful way. But, sometimes, we must disturb that tranquility to prevent unnatural catastrophes."

"What do you mean?"

Alden's eyes twinkled as a corner of his mouth jerked upward. "One day, you'll understand, magician. The Cererian Prophecy has plans and you must be ready when that day arrives."

"Ah, yes. That mysterious prophecy that's messing with me and my siblings' lives." Chance sighed. "It's maddening for you and Darrius to share snippets of its information and lead us to the edge of awareness, only to claim that one day all will be revealed." Chance spit on the ground. "It's crazy, Alden."

"It's not easy knowing so much about your future," Alden explained as he jabbed a finger at Chance. "The details I know—like who will live and who will die—are quite a burden. But that was the design of the Prophecy. It was constructed with the intention that individuals would receive information *only* when the time is proper for them to understand it."

Alden held his hands in front of his chest, the fingertips lightly touching. "I don't possess all the knowledge, Chance. Like you, I'm at the mercy of the Prophecy's timeline. So are all the other Cererians, magicians, Folk, and magical entities of this world." He paused and studied Chance. "I dare say, your mind would implode if all the details of your future suddenly revealed themselves." Alden's hands flew out to either side of his head as he pursed his lips. "Bang."

Chance looked at the hills in the distance. "I get it, Alden. I'll never get used to the Prophecy's annoying process, but I understand what you're saying."

"Friends?" Alden asked.

"Yeah, we're friends. I suppose I'd better practice moving those hills before the Prophecy gets angry with me." Chance jabbed his elbow in Alden's side.

"Excellent, magician. Excellent."

They worked into the night until Chance successfully swapped the hills four times under five seconds. After the final attempt, Chance collapsed to the ground. Every muscle ached but a satisfied grin remained on his lips as he gazed into the night sky. With no light pollution to ruin his view, thousands of tiny stars filled the blackness with a dazzling display. "What a wonderful feeling," he uttered.

"What is?" Alden asked. The Cererian sat cross-legged on the ground with his hands on his knees.

"Knowing I can accomplish something big like this."

"Having the ability is one thing, wielding the magic is another. The true power comes from understanding when to employ it and when to restrain yourself."

Alden sighed. "Looking at the stars and galaxies above us makes me feel small, but I know I possess the same amazing magic as all living things." He glanced at Chance. "You may not understand this now, Chance, but you and I are equal in our power...our magic. You are only limited by what you know at this moment in time. But, one day..." Alden gazed into the darkened sky.

Chance stared at his companion. Alden's words had piqued his curiosity. "What were you going to say?"

"Nothing, Chance. Nothing." Alden closed his eyes and began humming. The hypnotic melody soon lulled Chance to sleep.

The first blush of morning stretched across the horizon. "Wake up, Chance. Time to go home." Alden stretched his arms above his head and then bent low to the ground.

Chance rolled into a sitting position. "That was some of the best sleep I've ever had." He stood and sidled up to Alden. "I've been dreading the return trip."

"There is another way."

"What?"

"It's another gift you possess. It's unique to your earth family but is akin to portals or teleporting. To many it's more direct, but there is a drawback. You can only use this mode of traveling if you know the exact spot to which you are traveling. The locals call it 'flicking'."

"So, since I've been to my Amesbury cottage, I should be able to transport back there with no problem?"

"Yes. But if I asked you to go to the North Pole, where you've never been, you wouldn't be able to flick there.

"I see. So how do I 'flick'?"

"The method is quite simple. You envision the location you want to travel to and then you snap the fingers of your dominant hand." Alden snapped his fingers as a demonstration.

"Really? That's it?" Chance closed his eyes and imagined sitting by the fire in the reception room, then he snapped the thumb and forefinger of his right hand. When he opened his eyes, he was sitting in the comfy chair by the fire in his cottage. "Well, I'll be," he whispered in awe.

"Welcome home, Keeper."

Chance jerked.

"Did I surprise you?"

"Well, I didn't expect you."

"I had a way to get back, you know. You're not the only one." He shoved a glass of bourbon toward Chance. "To your success."

Chance raised it toward Alden. "To an exceptional teacher."

The men sipped and gazed at the roaring fire. Alden placed a hand on Chance's shoulder. "Since you worked through the night, take time to rest and recover today because I have a surprise for you later tonight. You'll finally meet some of your family members."

Chance beamed. "I can't believe this is finally going to happen."

Chapter 9

Gabriel

"WHAT HAPPENED HERE?" CHANCE asked as he and Alden strolled along a cobblestone path leading toward town. The moon illuminated the pair in a gray spotlight as they passed darkened structures whose roofs had collapsed. Charred and broken beams punched into the night sky like gnarled fingers curling out of foundations of white stone.

"The weather was not kind last year," Alden explained. "Heavy snows crashed through roofs. Fires erupted all over town. Despite the destruction, no lives were lost."

Lilting music drifted toward them. The bright light of the town's center glowed ahead.

"Where are we going?" Chance asked.

"A local haunt I think you'll enjoy," Alden replied.

The main road curved into the countryside, but a footpath, its entrance lined with five large metal stanchions, wound deeper into town. Alden pointed down the walkway. "Let's go down there."

Loud laughter and singing floated down the alley. "Ah, we're near," Alden said.

"I sense a pub ahead." Chance quickened his pace, anxious to have a little fun and excited to meet family. He left Alden behind as he trotted to a white-washed, two-story building accentuated with black wood. A bright red sign hung over the doorway. Emblazoned in gold lettering was the name: Flanagan's Irish Pub.

Awesome, Chance thought. He stood on the lane and took in the sights. Three overcrowded picnic tables sat outside where members of two soccer teams sang bawdy songs and danced on the tabletops to the cheers of their mates. Loud singing burst through the front door every time someone exited or entered the establishment. Couples linked arms and sauntered down the alley before disappearing into the night.

"Quite a sight, isn't it?" Alden noted as he joined Chance in watching the crowd's antics.

"The building looks like it's literally going to burst if anyone else goes inside," Chance exclaimed.

"Let's put your theory to the test." Alden pushed Chance toward the door.

A man and a woman staggered out as Chance pulled on the handle. "Scuse me," the woman said as she giggled and gripped her partner's arm. They hurried off into the night amid rolling laughter.

Chance pulled the door open and peered inside. A mob of bodies milled around every inch of the building. "Looks stuffed, Alden. We'll have to find some place to sit out here."

Alden shoved Chance inside. "There's someone I want you to meet." Once through the door, Alden led Chance through the crowd and yelled above the din, "After all your hard work, I thought you would appreciate a surprise!"

Alden muscled his way to a corner booth in the back, pulling Chance behind him. The simple wooden table with two benches had ample room for four bodies, but one person sat alone, hunched over a pint. A black fedora skimmed his dark eyebrows. He wore a brown windbreaker over a graphic T-shirt. Visible were the stylized letters A, S, S.

"Chance, meet my dear friend, Gabriel Telfer." Alden grinned wide and gestured toward the man at the table.

The dark figure sipped his beer and then glanced up. His dark brown eyes floated in a tanned face. Chance squinted. A glimmer of recognition tapped against his brain. "Hello. You look familiar. Have we met before?" Chance pushed his hand toward the stranger.

The man shifted his gaze from Chance's hand to Alden and raised an eyebrow. Alden covered his mouth with his hand hoping to hide the smile forming on his lips.

Gabriel slammed his glass to the table, seized Chance's forearm, and yanked him off balance. Chance tumbled forward across the table and into the man's open arms. Before Chance could react, Gabriel planted a juicy kiss on his cheek and shoved him across the table toward the opposite bench seat. Chance crashed against the back and grunted.

"Welcome to Amesbury," the man bellowed.

Chance righted himself, his hands snapping forward in a defensive posture. He would have retaliated if Alden hadn't immediately scooted in beside him and gently lowered Chance's arms before he threw a defensive spell at Gabriel.

"Gabriel has a sense of humor much like your own," Alden noted.

"Sally, three pints!" Gabriel shouted to a young, dark-haired woman pushing through the crowd, scooping empty glasses from tables.

"Aye, Gabe," she responded as she neared their table. She batted her pale blue eyes at Chance. "Who's your mate, Gabe?" She grinned and winked. "You're new here."

"Easy, Sally," Gabriel cautioned. "He's taken. Got himself five young'uns, he has."

She looked Chance over from head to toe. "Pity. You're a looker, you are."

Chance blushed.

"Off with you, Sally. My throat is like the Saharan desert." Gabe clenched his throat and gasped a strangled cough.

"I'll be back in two shakes of a lamb's tail," she chirped as she plowed into the sea of humanity. "Move! Coming through!"

Chance followed her departure. Gabriel studied his gaze. "Don't let Sally lead you astray magician."

The use of the term *magician* in public caught Chance by surprise. He hunched low and gestured with his hands for Gabriel to keep his voice low. "Aren't you concerned about the Yfel?" he whispered.

Gabriel hollered. "Mates! Are we afraid of the Yfel?" The dull roar of animated chatting quieted, and the men and women blinked at Gabe. Several seconds passed before everyone yelled in unison, "No!" Then the patrons erupted into laughter and continued their conversations.

Chance eyed the crowd and then looked at Gabriel.

Alden interjected. "You're right to be concerned about the Brethren, Chance, but they will never find this pub."

"How's that possible?" Chance threw his arms wide. "With this noise, anyone from outer space could find us."

Gabriel sipped his pint and wiped the foam mustache from his upper lip. "You've been away from your homeland too long. Alden caught me up on the situation with your memories being erased and then recently restored. That must have been tough not really knowing who you are and then having The Cererian Prophecy kick you in the butt, being that you're one of four who will restore peace on earth."

Chance stared at Gabe.

"No wonder you're nervous about the Brethren, Chance. If I had a target on me back, I'd be looking over me shoulder, too!" He downed the remnants of his pint and yelled into the crowd. "Sally, three more!"

From deep in the bar a female voice cried out, "Right-o, Gabe!"

Gabriel shoved the glass to the side and leaned toward Chance. "The Yfel will never find this pub because it is enchanted. To them it looks like another boring seventeenth-century cottage with a burned-out attic. But to magicians and their Folk, this is a rollicking getaway where we can drink, dance, and sing without fear of being discovered.

Chance cast a sideways glance at Alden. "How is Alden able to see this place for what it is? He's Cererian like the Yfel."

Sally strode up to the table and thumped three glasses on the table before whirling and answering a shout from the other side of the room. "I'm coming, Clancy. Keep yer shirt on."

Gabe watched her leave and replied, "Alden had to be granted special access." Gabe pointed at Alden. "We tweaked our cloaking magic to include our friend here."

Alden nodded. "Even Darrius wouldn't be able to find this pub."

Chance rubbed his chin. "Interesting. So, what about people coming and going? That would attract unwanted attention."

Gabriel shook his head and huffed. "We definitely have work to do on this one, Alden."

"Hey," Chance protested. "Don't talk about me like I'm not here."

"Easy, magician. Don't get your knickers in a twist." Gabe sipped on his beer before continuing. "You need to be around your people for a while and then things will make sense. As for the Yfel not noticing our comings and goings, when people leave the pub, they flick home." Gabriel snapped his fingers. "Just like that and you're home. Understand?"

Chance nodded. "Yeah, I understand. Hiding the pub in plain sight is like me cloaking my house in the States."

"Exactly," Alden replied. "With the help of your family, you'll learn so much more about your powers." Alden extended his hand toward Gabriel.

"Family? Gabriel?" Chance stared across the table. "Wait, now I know where I've seen you before. You were wearing a sleep mask, but that hair and your skin...you were the man sitting behind me on the plane, weren't you?"

A toothy smile filled Gabe's face. "Guilty!"

"Did you put that pin on my collar?"

"Guilty, again," he confessed.

"Why?"

Gabriel glanced at Alden. "We decided to add another layer of protection during your travels." He leaned forward and tapped the pin on Chance's collar. "The triskele, when worn, will protect you against the Yfel. It not only contains magic from your earth family, but Alden added a wee bit of his Cererian charm as well."

Chance glared. "You sat in your seat, pretending to sleep, while I went crazy looking for the thing pricking my neck?"

"Yep. That poor flight attendant was so worried. All the noise you were making in the loo did make me wonder what you were actually doing." A quick chuckle escaped Gabe. "Great entertainment for a few minutes."

Chance absently touched the pin and shifted his scowl to Alden. "You acted so innocent when I told you about finding it on my shirt, and all along, you had a hand in its design."

The Cererian touched his fingertips together in front of his chest and bowed his head. "Some things must reveal themselves when it is their time to be known."

Gabe roared with laughter and slammed the tabletop. "There you go again with your Cererian babble speak. Perhaps you've had too much beer." Gabe grabbed Alden's mug.

Alden jerked his head at Gabe. "As you can see, Gabriel shares a lot of your family traits."

"How, exactly, is he related to me?"

"I'm yer cousin," Gabriel blurted. "Our mums were sisters. I'm head of the family in this locale." He spread his arms wide. "There's a way to prove our connection." Gabe leaned back and slammed his left leg onto the tabletop. He grinned as he untied the laces of his boot. "I'll show you mine if you show me yours, magician."

"What the..." Chance arched is eyebrows.

"The mark on your foot," Alden added.

"Oh, the triske..., trikilaylay, tricuitley..."

"Triskele," Alden uttered.

"Yeah, that thing," Chance confirmed. Alden slid off the bench so Chance could swing his right leg onto the tabletop and untie his laces. Gabe had removed his boot and placed the mud-encrusted shoe on the floor. He watched Chance with interest.

Chance groaned as he worked through the double knot on the lace. Finally, he pulled off his sneaker and let it drop to the floor and whipped off his sock."

"On the count of three, we show our feet," Gabe instructed. "One, two, three!"

Both Chance and Gabe swung their feet toward each other. The marking on Gabe's foot had a purplish quality to it like a deep bruise but the triple spiral symbol was prominent on his heel.

"I'll be damned," Chance said with a mix of awe and excitement.

"That's not all," Gabe teased as he gestured toward the crowd where many had already removed their shoes and dangled their foot at Chance, displaying the triskele marking imprinted on their heels.

Chance gawked from person to person. One by one they nodded and shouted "Welcome!"

"Welcome home, Chance," Gabe said. "We've waited a very long time to have you on English soil again."

The loud deep voice of the pub owner rang out. "All right, you mangy lot. 'Tis time to close 'er down for the night." Chaos filled the pub as people scooted their chairs under tables and deposited their empty mugs on the counter. Five men stood in a circle and downed their brews while bystanders encouraged them with song. Then slowly people disappeared as they snapped their fingers and flicked back from wherever they came.

Only Gabe, Alden, and Chance remained. "Wow," Chance said. "That was a crazy exit." He turned toward Gabe. "Is the pub open every night?"

"Every night," Gabe replied.

"And I find it by picturing it and snapping my fingers?"

"Aye. It's as simple as that. We'll always be here for you." Gabe winked, snapped his fingers, and disappeared in an instance.

"It's time to go," Alden said as he stood. "I'll teleport while you practice your new skill. Let's see who can get back to the reception room first."

Chapter 10

Family

ALTHOUGH THE MEN HAD exited the pub at the same time, when Chance materialized inside the reception room, Alden was already by the fire with two bourbons. He dangled one toward Chance. "Welcome home."

"How'd you get back here so quickly?" His words carried the sting of disappointment as he snatched the glass from Alden.

"As I mentioned before, teleporting is quite an efficient form of travel. Here's to us," Alden toasted.

Chance sneered. "Yeah, to us." He clinked glasses and turned his back on the Cererian. While his emotions simmered, he sipped his bourbon. Then, he whirled. "Sorry for my behavior, Alden, but I've been doing so well with my magic and thought I'd beat—"

"You're competitive, magician," Alden interrupted. "As such, you expect perfection. No. You demand perfection from yourself."

"I do," Chance agreed.

"I like that."

"You do?" Chance's eyebrows arched.

"Yes. Magicians should constantly challenge themselves to sharpen their skills. But failures await you on your path to perfection, waiting for you to give up. The source of your magic is what compels you to stand and keep moving forward." Alden tapped Chance's chest near his heart.

"The source of my magic." Chance repeated. "What is the source of my magic?"

"Oh, Keeper, we have a lot of work to do." Alden patted Chance's shoulder. "The source of magic is the same for any living entity. The energy generates behind your heart and circulates throughout your body. There are some individuals who can see the rays of this energy emanating from a figure. Some call this brilliance an aura. I like to describe it as a magical glow."

Chance placed his hand over his chest and closed his eyes. With each thump of his heart, he imagined a bright white stream of energy zipping through his veins and arteries. He nodded. "I understand."

The men drained their drinks and placed the glasses on the table.

"Meeting my family was a great surprise," Chance remarked. "Thank you for that. You're a wonderful mate."

Alden beamed. "You've been here four days and you're already using your natural English jargon."

"Really? I didn't realize it."

"I dare say, more memories will step forward since we've shattered the logjam, so to speak." Alden gestured toward the stairs. "Time for you to go to bed. Tomorrow, Gabriel will take you to Stonehenge. You need to be rested because he has a big day planned."

"I'm still wound up from meeting my family. I'm going to sit by the fire a while." Chance collapsed into the stuffed chair and yawned. He gazed into the fire with sleepy eyes. *I had no idea returning home would be like this,* he thought.

Seconds later his raspy snore filled the room.

Alden waved his hand and Chance lifted upward from the chair and hovered above the floor with his arms dangling downward. With Alden directing from behind, Chance floated up the stairs and into his bedroom where Alden gently undressed him and placed him into bed.

"Until tomorrow, Keeper," he whispered.

Intense sunshine stabbed into Chance's eyes. "Argh," he grunted as he cupped his hand over his face.

"Morning, Chance!"

Chance bolted into a sitting position. "Gabriel?" Raking his fingers through his hair, he rubbed consciousness into his brain. "Where's Alden. How did you get in?"

"Alden is away on urgent business. As for me, I let myself in. I've been here before so I can flick in and out as I please."

Chance peered curiously at him with bloodshot eyes. "Flick in and out?"

"Yeah. I'll tell you more later. Get up. We've got a lot planned today."

Chance swept the bedspread aside and threw his legs over the edge of the bed. He yawned and rubbed his eyes. "Where did you say Alden was?"

"Had to leave early. Said he had an appointment. It's only me and you, mate." Gabriel grabbed the shirt and pants lying on a nearby chair and threw them at Chance's chest. "Get dressed. I'll meet you downstairs."

"I need coffee," Chance moaned.

"You'll have a cup when you get cleaned up and come downstairs. Oh, and wear hiking shoes. You're going climbing today." A huge grin spread across Gabe's face as he quickly turned and loped downstairs.

Chance stood in front of the window and stretched. His mind was silent. It was odd not to hear Sybil calling him insisting he visit her in the wine cellar. It had been almost a week since they last interacted, and he didn't miss her. Something else demanded his attention here: magic.

These stirrings were a new experience for him. He yearned to flex his magical muscles, test his newly discovered powers, and explore his familial homeland. As he stared at the distant meadow, several white sheep meandered about grazing.

You're changing, Chance. Janet's words drifted through his mind, and he sighed.

He turned away from the window and stared at the clothes on the bed. Gabe had promised coffee if he got dressed and went downstairs, but he wasn't quite ready. Not yet.

He padded barefoot around the bedroom and studied the pictures and curiosities decorating the room. Two portraits, one of a man and one of a woman, loomed above the mahogany dresser. The couple faced each other with serene expressions. Though one hand rested in their laps, the fingers of their right hand extended upward as if in a gentle acknowledgement. Decades of dust coated the oil paint causing the brilliant hues to appear drab and gray.

Chance leaned closer and carefully dabbed at the dark-gray dust with the lace doily from the top of the chest. Brilliant colors appeared as he revealed the woman's emerald gown and the gentleman's dark blue suit. Both had sandy blonde hair and dark eyes. Chance studied their characteristics. *I wonder who they are.*

"Chance!" Gabriel's shout yanked him out from his musing. "Time's a-wasting."

"Coming!" he shouted back as he padded across the hall and into the bathroom.

Freshly scrubbed and sporting new clothes, Chance bounded down the stairs and into the kitchen. Gabe sat at the table and shoved a forkful of eggs into his mouth. "Finally. I thought I might have to eat all this food myself!" He jabbed his fork in the direction of various platters of sausages, eggs, bread, and potatoes lining the countertop.

"Damn, this is some spread," Chance exclaimed.

"Grab your coffee and come sit with me, cousin."

Chance filled a large mug of fresh coffee and sat across from Gabriel with a plate heaped with all the offerings. He shoved a slice of bread into his mouth and chewed off a hunk. "What the hell?" he said as he stared at the crusty slice.

"What's wrong?" Gabriel asked.

"I've never had bread like this. It has an incredible flavor, and the crust is so chewy..."

"Ah, it's fresh made," Gabriel explained nonchalantly. "Me sister is a marvelous baker, and I brought you one of her sliced loaves."

"Wow. It's like I've never had bread before." Chance finished the slice, grabbed another, and spooned some eggs on top.

Gabe observed Chance as he forked food into his mouth in one continuous movement. "Aye, you've got the family enthusiasm for all things culinary, that's for sure." His hearty chuckle filled the kitchen.

"Yep." Chance muffled through a mouthful of food.

The two men ate in silence for several minutes interrupted only by them getting up to refill their mugs.

"Hey, Gabriel, I have a question."

"Gabe. Call me Gabe."

"Gabe. The portraits in my room. Are those family?"

Gabe stopped eating mid chew and stared at his cousin. A drop of butter trickled down his chin, which he deftly caught with a piece of bread, and then shoved into his mouth. "Hmph," he mumbled as he chewed and nodded.

"What?"

Gabe swallowed hard and blurted, "Aye, they be kin."

"Who are they?"

Gabe sighed. "They be your parents." Gabe tilted back on the chair's back legs and interlaced his fingers behind his head.

"My parents?"

"Aye." Gabe watched Chance's face transform from the paleness of shock to the pink flush of acceptance.

Chance thumbed his chest. "My...folks."

"Aye."

Chance gripped the edge of the table as a wildness ripped into his eyes. He glanced briefly at Gabe before sprinting up the stairs to his bedroom.

Gabe found Chance standing before the portraits with tears streaming down his cheeks. Chance hugged himself and rocked slowly. Occasionally he'd sniff and swipe his cheek.

"Somethin', eh?" Gabe mentioned as he strode into the room.

"Their names. What are...were their names?

"Chauncey was yer dad's. Jane was yer mum's."

"And their surname?" Chance whirled to face Gabe. "What's my real last name?"

"Drury. Your full name is Chance Easton Drury."

Chance glanced at the floor and silently repeated the names. He faced the portraits. "My parents." He raised his hand toward each face and hovered inches from the paint. "I wish...I wish they were here. Do you have any photographs?"

"Alas, no. All was destroyed in the fire."

"Fire?" Chance faced his cousin.

Gabe sat on the bed and fidgeted with a loose thread on the comforter. "I was a wee baby," he began in a low whisper. "I'm the same age as you, so I only know what me kin told me. But the Yfel attacked yer home with ferocity and keen purpose as if they knew exactly where everybody would be."

Chance sat on the edge of the bed and leaned toward Gabe. "Go on," he urged.

Gabe gazed at his cousin with sorrowful eyes. "My family had left your house minutes before the Brethren arrived...just minutes. They heard an explosion as we walked the four blocks home. A huge blue fireball lit up the sky, and they knew...felt it in their hearts...that everyone had perished." Gabe's eyes watered. "Oh, Chance. Me mum said that blast of energy was unnatural with frenetic pulsing and electrical charges snapping and hissing as tendrils of bright light zigzagged in all directions as if searching—no, hunting for its prey." Gabe paused and licked his lips.

"Dad, along with several other magicians, ran toward your house while Mom gathered me and me sister up and flicked us to a safe house in Wales." Gabe turned away and wiped at the tears running down his cheeks.

"What happened, Gabe?" Chance placed his hand on Gabe's shoulder and squeezed gently. "Please tell me what happened."

Gabe coughed into his fist and cleared his throat. "Me dad was killed along with three of our best soldiers." Gabe halted and swallowed hard before continuing. "They died fighting to save you and yer ma, pa, and yer sister from the fire, from the Yfel.

"The benevolent Cererians arrived too late to save everyone, but they did manage to pull you from the wreckage. The energy ball the Yfel created propelled your crib into the cellar and covered you with flames and heavy beams. While the Yfel killed your parents and sister and consumed their life forces, they didn't know where you had disappeared to. That small amount of time allowed the benevolent Cererians the time they needed to fight off the Yfel and locate you.

"Alden found you in the cellar burned head to foot. Your body had been broken from a smoldering wooden beam, which he'd lifted off of you. You were seconds from dying in his arms."

"What happened?" Chance pressed

"A Cererian named Prasad cradled you in his arms and breathed a new life into you."

"Prasad," Chance whispered the name and looked up at the ceiling. *Thank you, dear friend.*

"Alden and Prasad spirited you away as Darrius and the other benevolent Cererians ensured all the Brethren were gone."

"Do you know who attacked my family...who killed your father?"

"I only know what others have told me. They said Stygian announced he had come to kill the earth warrior and his family."

"Stygian," Chance hissed as he pounded his fist into his hand. "He's caused a lot of grief for my family and yours as well."

"Look, Chance. Alden wanted to tell you about your family. I mean, he was involved in finding you and all. But when you asked about the paintings, I needed to let you know. You deserved to know." Gabe drew in a long breath and continued.

"You asked about me earlier about flitting in and out of this house. Well, this was my home. I grew up here. Me mother was a renowned artist in these parts and painted those portraits of yer folks as a surprise for their wedding anniversary. A huge party was planned and—" Chance's eyes welled with tears.

"I'll let Alden know I told you about yer parents. He won't be mad, but he can fill in the gaps and provide other information. I'm sure he can better answer many of yer questions." Gabe sighed as though he'd been holding his breath for minutes.

"Let's finish breakfast and then head out to Stonehenge," Gabe said. "There's more to discover about your family." Gabe darted down the stairs.

Chance stayed on the bed. He gripped the bedspread so hard his knuckles blanched bone white. He glanced toward the paintings and relaxed. The images of his parents softened his emotions, and he rose to join them.

The likeness of his father was like looking in a mirror—the brown hair, the strong jawline, the dark eyes peering back at him as though he was searching his soul. He tried to imagine a time when this man might have held him as an infant. Chance closed his eyes and tried to envision his mother and sister alive. But he was only a baby when he lost everyone and any memories, if any, didn't survive the trauma of the fire.

"Chance?" Gabe stood in the doorway. "Come on, mate. Let's get going before we lose this day altogether." A mischievous but unsure smile darted across his lips before he dashed down the stairs again.

"Mom and Dad. One day I'll make things right again." He blew a kiss toward the pictures and then raced down the stairs after Gabe.

Gabe peered up when Chance strode into the kitchen. "Thanks for telling me, Gabe. I appreciate my kin sharing that kind of news. It's personal that way." A smile wavered across his face before he exited the kitchen.

"Where ya going?" Gabe called after him.

"I'm getting my jacket. Didn't you say it was time to go to Stonehenge?"

Chapter 11

Stonehenge

"WE'LL TAKE ME LORRY," Gabe said as he led Chance outside. He zipped up his windbreaker and scanned the bright-blue sky. A few wispy clouds drifted overhead. "Gorgeous day for exploring Stonehenge."

The small, white service vehicle sat in an outbuilding across from the house. Stacks of firewood crowded the left side of the vehicle making it impossible to open the passenger door. "Hang on, Chance. I'll back 'er out so you can get in."

The miniature truck coughed black smoke as it eased from under the overhang. Gabe pushed the door open. "Come on in. It's a bit cramped, but she's a good little work truck."

Chance folded himself into the tiny front seat, which was barely big enough for a person half his size. His spine curved along the headliner while he wrapped his arms around his legs drawing them close to his body until his knees jutted into his chest. Then he laid his head on his knees and faced Gabe. "Comfy," he mocked.

Gabe chuckled. "Good thing we don't have far to go. I'd hate for you to get stuck in that position."

Chance strained to examine as much of the interior that he could. The aroma of motor oil wafted and black stains splashed the fabric high and low. Miscellaneous car parts littered the dash, the floorboard, and the small cargo space behind the seats. "Let me guess, you're a mechanic?"

"Ha!" Gabe barked. "I do a little bit of this, a little bit of that. I'm good with me hands." He held up his left hand, which had thickened fingers with black-stained nubby fingernails.

He shifted down as a slow farm vehicle appeared over a hill. The lorry bucked and squealed from the unexpected maneuver. "Come on, Amos. Move 'er aside," Gabe shouted out the window as he squeezed between the combine and a thick hedgerow bordering the narrow lane. Branches scratched and lashed the side of the vehicle as it passed.

An angry curse from the farmer faded in the distance as Gabe shifted into a cruising pace and left the combine far behind.

Chance arched his back and shifted his legs, but he couldn't move out of his cramped position. Forced to stare at his cousin, he studied his physical traits. Unruly dark curls filled Gabe's entire head. Some wispy strands had fallen across his tanned face, which was clean and smooth from a recent shave. A prominent bump in the middle of his nose hinted of having once been broken, but not recently.

"Why don't you live in the cottage now?" Chance asked.

Gabe smirked but didn't answer.

"There was a lot of yarn and knitting needles by the chair in the reception room. I assumed the owner was a woman," Chance added.

Gabe's lips thinned then relaxed. He cast a quick glance at Chance and returned to look at the windscreen.

"Not that I'm prying, but—"

"But you are." Gabe interrupted.

The men drove on in awkward silence except for the occasional whine from the engine when Gabe shifted.

"I lost me mum recently," Gabe began in a soft voice. "We lived together in that house. I took care of her in her final years. She was so sick, but she loved sitting in that blue chair by the fire. She'd fiddle with her knittin' needles, but her eyesight had become so bad she couldn't really make anything beyond a long strand of yarn with wonky knots." A tear streaked down his cheek and fell onto his jeans. "I still can't sit in that chair. It's too painful."

A thick, sad energy swirled in the cab causing tears to well in Chance's eyes. "I'm sorry, Gabe."

Gabe gulped his emotions. "Ta. It's been six months, but the pain is as keen as if it happened yesterday." He peered into Chance's eyes. "That's why I was so excited when Alden told me you were coming. Me cousin finally coming home..." The shift in Gabe's demeanor switched from melancholy to cheery within a few words.

Chance stretched a hand toward Gabe's arm and patted it. "I'm glad you're in my life, Gabe. I mean that."

Gabe cleared his throat. "I watched you and Alden for two nights," he admitted.

"Whatcha mean?"

"Alden told me to stay away while you got adjusted, but I was too excited to see you. I wanted to see what ya looked like and what powers you had."

"You've been spying on me since I arrived?"

"Aye. I hung around in the backyard. Alden found me and tried to shoo me away with his energy."

"So, that's why Alden kept staring outdoors."

"Aye. It were our little game: where's Gabriel?" Gabe chuckled. "When you perfected your earth magic that one night in the backyard, I was there keeping a watchful eye on you. Very impressive, cousin."

Chance beamed. "Thank you. Thank you, kindly. I was pretty pleased with myself."

"We're not far away," Gabe called out as he shifted down. The truck squealed in protest. Stonehenge was only three miles from their country cottage, but the Amesbury morning traffic slowed them to a crawl. Thirty minutes later, Gabe pulled into a gravel lot.

"We're here!" he announced as he pushed the door open and exited in one movement. He walked toward a fence line, stretched his back, and gazed across a field.

Chance unfolded from the lorry. Hunched over, he crab-walked toward Gabe. "A little help standing, please."

"That looks a wee bit uncomfortable," Gabe chuckled as he positioned himself behind Chance. Crossing each arm in front of Chance's chest, Gabe pulled them back and up. Several snaps and cracks later, Chance stood erect. Gabe resumed his position at the fence.

Chance sighed with relief. He followed Gabe's view across the grassland. "Whatcha looking at? I don't see Stonehenge."

"Aye." Gabe continued to gaze across the field. "'Tis tricky to visit our ancient site with all the visitors snapping their photos and jockeying for position to get the best selfie with the sacred stones. We wait here until the site closes. It'll be dark by the time you get to cavort with the sarsens."

"Dark? That's about three hours away. What do we do until then?" Chance scowled.

"Hold that thought," Gabe uttered, holding up a finger. He trotted back to his truck, opened the café doors in the back, rummaged around the interior and then slammed the doors. He returned toting a large cooler and two camp chairs, which he handed to Chance. "Set those up whilst I set up lunch. Under that tree over there is best."

Chance unfolded the canvas chairs while Gabe withdrew a slim table from the side of the cooler and placed it between the chairs. "What's yer pleasure? Ham or roast beef?" Gabe chirped.

"I could eat either."

"Fine, both it is." Gabe thrust two thick sandwiches at Chance, then grabbed his own and sat down. He withdrew two bottles of beer and handed one to Chance. "The opener's on the side of the box," he instructed. "Here's a package of crisps." Gabe tossed potato chips into Chance's lap.

"Have you done this a lot?" Chance asked as he hid the beer from view. "I mean, set up in a parking lot and picnic?"

"What's wrong with it?" Gabe replied as he bit into his sandwich. He chewed loudly and smacked his lips. Then he took a long guzzle from the bottle.

"The police would frown on this in the States." Chance cast a worried eye toward a car passing by them on the roadway.

Gabe watched him. "Oh, I see what ya mean. Don't worry. Nobody can see us."

"Oh?"

"Magic." Gabe wiggled his fingers in the air. "I set up me psychic markers around this vacant lot. If people pass, they'll only see gravel and weeds."

"Nice. Very nice." Chance stroked his chin. "I look forward to learning how to do that."

Gabe stopped eating. "You don't do magic?"

Chance's cheeks flushed. "I do. Well, I can weave protection spells, levitate items, and things like that. And I learned how to perform earth magic and flick."

"I see," Gabe replied.

Chance grew quiet and fidgeted in his seat.

Gabe felt the heat of embarrassment rising from Chance's body. "I'm sorry, Chance. I meant no slight."

"That's okay. There's a lot I need to learn." Chance took a bite of his sandwich, chewed slowly, and swallowed hard. "I feel like I'm back in elementary school learning all the basics."

"Aye, that you are. 'Tis better late than never." Chance turned away and faced the field. "There's no need to be embarrassed about what you don't know. We know your story. We know the importance of your presence in the world."

Chance stared at Gabe while contemplating his words. "My story? Everyone knows?"

Gabe tousled Chance's hair and then playfully shoved his shoulder. "We've known for years, but we needed to be patient. We knew you would come home. The Cererian Prophecy likes to leave out details and feed us snippets of information at a time." A wide grin spread across his face.

Chance frowned and stared back across the field. "This is hard, Gabe."

"What is?"

"All this. You, the family, learning who I am. This is the second time in six months that I've learned I'm not who I thought I was. Sometimes I wish I could go back in time and live my simple, non-magical life with Janet and the kids." Chance gulped the remaining beer in his bottle and burped loudly.

Gabe finished his beer, grabbed two more bottles from the cooler and shoved one into Chance's hand. "When I was a boy and I'd get cross about something that was beyond my control, me father would share his wisdom."

"Oh? What did he say?"

"You can lead your horse to water—"

"But you can't make him drink," Chance interrupted.

"Nope. That's not it. You can lead a horse to water, but he'll still bite you in the arse if you turn yer back." Gabe snorted. "Me dad had a weird sense of humor."

Chance mulled over his cousin's words. He clinked his bottle against Gabe's. "Yep. Your dad was right. I feel like my ass has been bitten too many times recently, and I need to change that. I need to change my attitude."

"Thar you go, Chance. That's the ticket." Gabe slapped his cousin on the back.

The men ate and drank and chatted about family until night fell and the stars filled the black sky. "New moon, tonight," Gabe said as he threw the empty bottles and trash into the cooler. "Time to go meet Stonehenge. Help me pack up the van and then we'll strike out across the field."

They stood at the fence and gazed across the land. With no moon it was difficult to pinpoint the location of the stones but headlights moving along the border road helped establish the boundaries.

Gabe pointed into the distance. "They used to have these huge spotlights all over the stones and like moths to a candle flame, people started driving off the road lured, by the brightness of those lights. Too many accidents, so they took the spotlights down. I'm not complaining. I thought it tainted the energy of the stones. Don't forget, Chance. Once you've visited, you'll be able to flick back and forth at will."

"That's right. I keep forgetting about that. There's a lot of things I need to get used to."

"Are yer ready to run off some steam?" Chance nodded excitedly. It had been a long time since he'd used his powerful legs in an all-out sprint.

"Ready. Set. Go!" Gabe yelled as he leapt the fence and sprinted into the darkness. Chance kept pace with him. Their legs and arms pumped furiously.

"You call this a sprint?" Gabe teased as he pulled ahead of Chance, swiveled around, and ran backward while maintaining the same pace. "Come on, cousin, kick it into gear." After uttering the last word, Gabe zipped out of sight.

Chance ran as fast as he could. When he arrived at the large sarsen stones, he found Gabe leaning against the monolith. Neither man was out of breath.

"Nice of you to join me," Gabe teased.

"That was some fancy footwork," Chance noted. "I need to work on my speed."

"You'll have plenty of opportunity. We have foot races all the time. There's fellas and gals much faster than me." Gabe pointed into the distance. "Let's start over there. There's plenty to explore."

The men walked to one of the large boulders that formed the outer ring of the circle. Gabe crouched low, sprang thirty feet into the air, and landed on top. He motioned for Chance to join him.

Once Chance was on top of the stone, Gabe instructed, "Tell me what you sense about this rock. The energy is different up here. I reckon too many visitors have left their negative energy all over the base of these stones."

Chance moved to his hands and knees and slid his hands over the smooth surface. "I'm seeing a ton of mental images but none of them make sense."

Gabe nodded. "The ancients are with us. Their energy is always swirling high above the monument. Sometimes, from the corner of my eye, I catch a glimpse of hooded figures standing by the stones watching me."

"What are those rocks down there?" Chance pointed toward the center of Stonehenge where several thirteen-foot boulders clustered together.

"Bluestones. Let's check them out." Gabe jumped to the top of the closest one and Chance leapt to the neighboring rock.

Upon landing, Chance wobbled sideways and held his head. "I feel like I'm caught in Alden's teleporting energy. I feel so dizzy."

Gabe quickly joined him on the rock and steadied his arm. "You okay?"

"I feel odd, like I'm standing with a foot in the past and one in the future. The air around me is shimmering as if I'm in water." He gripped his head. "Argh. My brain is being split apart." Chance suddenly fell out of Gabe's grip and tumbled to the hard dirt thirteen feet below.

Gabe quickly jumped to the ground. "Are you okay?" He helped Chance to his feet.

"I'm still a little woozy."

"Hello, Chance!" an unfamiliar male voice hailed.

Chance and Gabe whirled with their hands raised ready to fight.

Four figures stood ten feet away, their faces darkened by the shadowy night.

"It's time, Chance," one of the figures hissed.

"Time for what?" Chance growled. Sensing a battle, he focused his strength energy into his arms and hands. Muscles bulged while a white glowing mist swirled around the surface of his skin. Gabe also engaged his battle magic.

"Time for the past to meet the future!" The stranger declared.

Gabe took a step forward and snarled as he narrowed his eyes at the figures. "Friends of yours, Chance?"

"Nope. I smell Yfel," Chance replied as he reached into his pocket and withdrew a small slender knife with a translucent edge.

"You'll need something bigger than that," Gabe remarked.

Chance pressed a button on the hilt, and the blade extended six feet while the handle lengthened in Chance's palm. The translucent blade shimmered. "Like this?" A sinister grin spread across Chance's face as he hunched low and swung the blade in front of him. The motion caused the sword to sing in the chilled night air.

Gabe reached into his back pocket and withdrew a folded weapon made of bronze. Flicking his wrist, the metal separated into three curved blades like a triskele. Each blade had a jagged point that curved backward. "Now you'll see why this symbol is so important to us."

"Enough of this posturing," one man growled. "You will soon be dead. Two magicians against four Brethren. The odds are not in your favor." The man sniffed the air. "I can smell your sweet power from here. What a delight it will be to consume the energy of the earth warrior."

A light breeze kicked gravel against the boulders. Suddenly, two men materialized near Chance and Gabe. "Darrius!" Chance exclaimed.

"This is my friend, Benedict," Darrius said as he stood beside Chance and Benedict stood on the other side of Gabe. Alden appeared in front of the magicians and joined their ranks.

The dark man growled. "You think this improves your odds, magicians? Darrius, Benedict, and Alden cannot interfere. They are forbidden by The Prophecy." A deep throaty laugh echoed off the boulders as the Brethren stepped closer. The leader raised his hands toward Chance. "I promise you won't suffer." Another maniacal chuckle rose into the air.

"We may not be permitted to fight you," Darrius said. "But we can thwart your advances." Darrius and Benedict marched up to the Brethren until mere inches separated them. "Aaron, you disappoint me," Darrius rebuked as he slowly stared into the faces of the other three men. "This is a battle that will not be won today. Leave!"

While Darrius engaged the Yfel, Alden pulled Gabe and Chance further away. "This is a battle you will not win," he cautioned them. "You must leave now."

"We can take them," Gabe seethed. "We don't run away from fights."

Alden gently placed his hands on Gabe's shoulders and stared directly into his eyes. "Not today. Not now. Use your power and go home."

Chance leaned toward Gabe. "Cousin, let's go," he whispered. "We'll head home and fight these idiots another day."

Alden glanced toward the Brethren who glared in their direction. "Now!" he shouted.

Gabe and Chance snapped their fingers and disappeared.

"No!" Aaron wailed as he pushed by Benedict and Darrius. He jabbed his finger toward Alden. "You interfered!"

Unmoved by Aaron's anger, Alden stood his ground, his fingertips touching together in front of his chest. "I have not interfered. I have only performed the actions allowed me by The Prophecy."

Benedict clamped a hand on Aaron's shoulder. "Aaron, it's time you went back to your prison." A bright white energy grid discharged from the tips of Benedict's fingers and raced down Aaron's arm rendering the Cererian helpless.

"Lord Aaron!" Aaron's two soldiers bounded toward Benedict. One gripped Benedict's neck and the other pulled his hand away from Aaron's shoulder. Their swift action broke the flow of energy paralyzing Aaron and allowed him to move away while they wrestled Benedict to the ground.

Darrius didn't move. He impassively watched Benedict fight with the two Brethren while Aaron retreated into the darkness.

"I'll be back, Darrius," Aaron sneered. "Balor. Cary," he barked at his soldiers. "We leave, now!" All three Yfel vanished leaving behind only the cool draft from their teleporting.

Then there was one. The fourth figure lurked in the darkness where he had first arrived. As Darrius, Benedict, and Alden slowly advanced, a menacing growl erupted from the blackness.

"That is no Cererian," Alden stated. "But his power is more intense than a magician."

"I sense a dark void," Benedict observed.

Deep laughter rolled toward them and echoed off the boulders. Without warning, a ball of blue fire shot out of the darkness and whizzed by Darrius' head. "Consider that you're only warning, Darrius," the figure threatened. "I will find the Firewalker. She will be mine."

A blast of bright light filled the sky momentarily blinding the three Cererians. When the illumination retreated, an eerie calm swirled among the stones.

"Who...what was that?" Alden asked.

"That was Ryan Pierson," Darrius replied. "Jake's father. He has consumed so much magic throughout the decades, he is no longer human."

"Who is Jake?" Alden asked.

"The man who will save this world," Darrius replied.

Chapter 12

Homecoming

WHEN CHANCE MATERIALIZED IN the reception room, he was all alone. Had he misunderstood Alden's message to return home? He searched the house upstairs and downstairs but couldn't find Gabe. He ran outside and spied a lone figure standing under the outbuilding's ramshackle roof. A red pinpoint of light glowed from something in his hand.

Chance flipped his collar up against the frigid, still air and approached the shelter. "Gabe?"

The end glowed brightly as it became clear the figure was sucking on a cigarette. "Aye."

"Why are you out here? It's safer inside."

"That was me first time," Gabe whispered.

Chance joined him under the overhang. Even in the darkness, Gabe's face appeared drawn and tired as though he had aged twenty years. The cigarette trembled in his hands. "I didn't know you smoked."

"Gave it up twenty years ago." After a long drag, Gabe blew the smoke into the rafters and ground the butt out on his palm. He didn't flinch. "Haven't touched one again until today."

Chance shivered in the freezing temperatures. "Come on, cousin. Let's go inside and warm up." He placed a hand on Gabe's shoulder, but Gabe shrugged him off and stepped away.

"That's okay. I'll stay out here." He leaned against a stack of firewood and pulled out another cigarette. He struck the match, and it flickered violently in his jittery hands. Chance wrapped his hand around Gabe's and guided it under the cigarette.

"Your first time with the Yfel?" Chance asked.

"Aye." He dragged on the cigarette and coughed. "I'd heard stories from me family and, of course, knew the legends of what me father and friends did. But, until tonight, I had no idea what it was like to face pure evil. The Brethren's energy was like a tidal wave crashing down on me. His reddened eyes searched Chance's face. "I was so scared."

"Is that why you snarled?"

"I did? I don't recall doing that." Gabe managed a weak smile.

"I couldn't believe that noise was coming out of you, and it scared the bejesus out of me. When you stood beside me and withdrew your weapon, that was a calculated move only a trained warrior would make, not the nervous reaction of a frightened magician. You never hesitated. If you hadn't told me, I would never have guessed that was your first time."

"Humph." Gabe sucked hard. "Me insides were quaking like jelly. I'm surprised I didn't shat myself."

The men stood in silence as Gabe finished his cigarette.

"I need a warm drink," Chance announced as he started for the house. He stopped and turned around. "Stay out here if you like, but I'm going in." In the warmth of the kitchen, he pulled the bottle of bourbon and two glasses out of the cabinet. As he finished pouring the second drink, he felt a presence beside him. Without looking up he asked, "Care for one, Gabe?"

"Aye."

Chance handed him the drink, and the men clinked glasses.

"Have ye been in battle before?" Gabe asked as he collapsed into a chair.

Chance wasn't sure how to reply. Based on Gabe's question, he assumed his cousin didn't know about his battle against Stygian. He wanted to support him in his angst, but to relate the epic battle on the beach, which had been *his* first fight against the Yfel, would be like throwing salt on Gabe's open wound of battle fear. "I've used my broadsword before, but I also had my siblings with me. It was four against one." He sipped his drink and avoided eye contact, hoping his answer satisfied Gabe.

"Is that where you got the scar?"

Chance cleared his throat. "Scar?"

"The one along yer ribs. I saw it yesterday morning when I woke you."

"Oh, that. Yep, that's where that came from." Chance poured another drink.

"Hmm. You said you were with your siblings. Were they hurt?"

Crap. I knew he was going to keep asking questions. How do I explain about Hilly? "Um..." Chance struggled for the right words.

"Hi everyone!" a female voice shouted.

The men whirled toward the sound. "Hilly!" Chanced shouted as he scooped her up, twirled her around, and set her back on the ground. "It's great to see you. What are you doing here?"

"We're all here," Fen said as she strolled into the kitchen. "Kai and Jake are with us too." Everyone pushed into the spacious room. Gabe stepped back against the counter, eyes widening at the sight of the people pouring in.

"Darrius messaged me the location, and I opened a portal for all of us," Hilly said as she hugged Chance.

Gabe quietly crept toward the door. Just as he got one leg across the threshold, Hilly noticed him.

"Hi! Who are you?" she asked as she shoved her hand out. "I'm Hilly Kemp."

Gabe accepted her hand and gazed into her bright green eyes. "You're a Firewalker."

Hilly cocked her head to the side with a half grin on her face. "Yes. Yes, I am. And you are?"

Chance jumped forward. "Hilly, meet Gabe Telfer. He's my cousin. My *actual* cousin."

"Nice to meet you, Gabe." Hilly turned and pointed toward the others. "That's our sister, Fen, our brother, Kai, and our friend, Jake Pierson."

"Hi Gabe," Kai and Fen said in unison. Jake jutted his chin in acknowledgement.

"This calls for a round of drinks." Chance collected more glasses.

Hilly held up her hand. "Darrius is not far behind. Perhaps we should hold off until everyone's here."

"I'll have one," Jake responded as he pushed past Fen and Kai. He took the drink and clinked glasses with Chance. "Good to see you again, brother." They embraced and slapped each other's backs.

"Brother? You two are brothers as well?" Gabe asked.

"Bourbon brothers only, Gabe. Jake is a great friend of mine." Chance wiggled a glass toward Kai. "Care to have a little nip?"

Kai glanced at Hilly who grimaced her dissatisfaction. "Yes," he responded. "I think I'll join you."

"Don't say I didn't warn you. I'll keep an eye out for Darrius," she said as she marched out of the kitchen.

While Jake, Chance, and Kai drank and caught up on the news in their lives, Fen sidled up to Gabe, who still hovered near the door with his hand on the jamb ready to bolt. "Overwhelming, isn't it?" she said softly.

"A wee bit," he replied as he studied her from head to toe. "You're different. Your energy is odd."

"You certainly know how to make someone feel welcome," Fen replied with a smile.

"Sorry. I meant no disrespect. But I can't help noticing the peace and calm that surrounds you." He pointed his finger at Chance and the others. "Their energy is literally bouncing off the walls."

Fen glanced at the men. Chance smiled and winked at her. She nodded back as she looped her hand through the crook of Gabe's arm. "Nothing is ever as it appears. Wouldn't you agree?"

"Um..." Gabe hesitated. Fen stroked the back of his hand as she led him toward a couch against the far wall.

"We all have unique energies," she continued while she brushed her finger along his hand and then his arm. "Let's sit on the couch. I would love to hear more about you and your family."

Kai, Jake, and Chance chattered nonstop between toasts and laughing. "I suppose I should wait until Darrius gets here, but..." Chance glanced around the kitchen and then continued, "but Gabe and I just got back from squaring off against the Yfel Brethren at Stonehenge."

"Really? Who showed up?" Jake pressed.

"It was dark. I never saw their faces. Gabe and I were getting ready to fight and then Darrius, Benedict, and Alden intervened."

Gabe tensed at the mention of the Yfel. Fen whispered, "I detest fighting." He shivered as she lightly traced a vein with her fingertip. "You have strong hands. These hands have seen action."

She flipped his hand over and gazed at his palm. "There are sensitive people who know how to read the roadmaps printed in our hands." She glanced up and Gabe stared at her. "I'm not one of them, but I sense an intense caring and compassion deep inside of you that few people have a chance to witness."

"Who are you?" Gabe said, ripping his hand out of Fen's embrace.

"She is the Guardian of Peace, Gabe," Chance interrupted. "My baby sister is a shamanic healer. She's been working with your energy while you two chatted."

Gabe searched Fen's face and then Chance's before he bolted off the couch. "Bloody hell!" he shouted. "Ganging up on me? Poor old Gabe is a coward and needs counseling...that's what you're thinking?" He jabbed Chance's chest with a thick finger. "You have no idea what I'm capable of, cousin!" He shoved Chance aside. "Get out of me way!" Gabe raced out of the room.

The front door opened and slammed shut.

"That's an odd reaction to your emotional magic." Chance observed.

"His emotions run deep," Fen noted. "There's something inside of him—doubt or sadness—a remote feeling that he wouldn't let me penetrate."

"He's hiding a secret?"

"Not in the sense you're meaning. I think there's something he wants to tell you, but there's pain wrapped around the words, and the trauma that caused that pain prevents him from saying them."

"Hmm. He's been straightforward until now. He's already shared so much with me."

"Has he?" Fen replied.

"Hi Gabe," Hilly greeted as Gabe marched toward the front door.

"Out of me way," Gabe barked.

Holding her hands up in surrender, Hilly backed against the wall and watched Gabe yank the front door open and slam it shut.

Moments later, Chance hurried down the hall. "Based on your expression, I'm guessing Gabe just passed by?"

"Yeah. What's got him all wound up?"

Chance was already out the door. Hilly stood in the entryway and watched as her brother trotted toward the dark outbuilding.

"Gabe? You out here?" Chance peered into the blackness, using his psychic instincts to sense if his cousin was hiding. A metallic sound near the back of the structure snatched his attention. "Gabe?" Chance muscled his way past firewood, boxes full of heavy items, and discarded tires. While shoving the junk aside, he didn't see the low beam and slammed into it. "Shit!" he hissed as he rubbed his forehead. "Dammit, Gabe. I bet you think this is funny."

Silence.

"Fuck you, cousin!" Chance yelled as he turned toward the house. "My head hurts and I'm cold. If you want to sulk, that's your privilege." Chance huffed into the chilled air. A burst of steam swirled around his head.

"What's up?" Hilly asked. She stood outside hugging herself.

"Nothing, Hilly."

She peered into the darkness just past the corner of the house and grinned. "That's a lot of swearing for nothing."

Chance lunged for the door handle, but Hilly blocked him. "Come on, Hilly, I'm cold," Chance protested.

"What happened?"

Chance sighed sending another cloud of condensation into the air. "I screwed up. I poked my nose into something I shouldn't have, and I got Fen in trouble as well."

"Aye, that you did."

"Gabe?" Chance turned at the sound of his cousin's voice.

Just beyond the corner of the house, a figure emerged from behind a plump evergreen. "Aye. Yer sister knew I was thar the entire time, didn't you?" Gabe said nodding toward Hilly.

"My work is done," she responded as she opened the door. She paused and looked back. "The two of you have work to do." She flashed a grin and closed the door behind her.

The two men faced each other but stared at the ground. Chance sighed while Gabe shifted his feet in the dirt. Finally, Chance broke the awkwardness. "It was my idea," he admitted. "I asked Fen to work with you." He glanced up and found Gabe staring at him.

"Me father had a saying for what you did."

"Oh?"

"Don't go poking a sleeping pig with a stick."

"Or what?"

"That's all. You should never poke sleeping pigs with a stick. That get mighty testy, especially if they have youngins."

"Hmm." Chance scratched his chin. "I'm sorry."

"I reckon ye thought ye was helpin'. I'll give ye that. But, next time, ask first."

"Deal. Friends?" Chance extended his hand.

Gabe slapped it away and grabbed Chance in a bear hug. "I couldn't stay mad at ye for long."

"It's freezing. Let's go inside," Chance gestured as he opened the door.

"Welcome, gentlemen," Darrius hailed as the men stomped their feet in the mudroom. "You're just in time for the debriefing. Please join me in the reception room."

Chance and Gabe exchanged puzzled expressions before they obediently followed the Cererian. Gabe hovered in the doorway as Chance joined his sisters on the sofa. Kai lounged in a chair, and Jake leaned against the fireplace, the sole of his boot against the stones.

"You can sit over there." Darrius pointed toward the stuffed blue chair near the fire.

"Um, if ye don't mind, I'll just stay here," Gabe responded as he nervously gazed around the room.

"Here, sit beside Hilly," Chance offered as he stood. "I'll sit by the fire. I'm still pretty chilled from the night air."

"Thank you," Gabe mouthed as he passed his cousin, who winked in return.

Benedict and Alden stood near the patio doors observing the proceedings. Gabe nodded at them as he passed. Taking his seat beside Hilly, Gabe continued to sneak peeks at the Cererians.

Darrius addressed the crowd. "Hello everyone. I believe all of you have met Benedict, so let me introduce the newest member of our team, Alden. He's been working with Chance since his arrival in England." Alden raised a hand and nodded.

"Alden, let me introduce the Kemps—Hilly, Fen, and Kai—and our friend, Jake Pierson." Darrius pointed at Gabe. "And Kemps, this is Gabriel Telfer. He's an important addition to our group. In addition to introducing Chance to local family members, Gabe has been assisting Alden with Chance's protection." Gabe nodded stiffly.

"Now that introductions are complete, let me recap what has occurred and why you are all here. Aaron Aningan escaped his prison with the help of two new Yfel converts and a rogue magician." Jake shifted uncomfortably and cleared his throat. "The psychic marker of their teleport from Ceres showed them moving toward southern England, near Amesbury. Since Hilly has already united her crystal with the Guardian boulder, the Yfel have been quite motivated to find and kill the rest of you before you can locate your crystals and unite them to their seats of power.

"When we received news of Aaron's escape, Fen advised me that Chance had departed for England around the same time. We were concerned the Brethren had planned to attack Chance. Since he is not able to receive our telepathic transmissions, we were not able to warn him, so I asked Alden to look after him.

"Tracking Aaron and his accomplices has been difficult because they deploy numerous psychic roadblocks to thwart our attempts. However, we have detected a pattern in their movements, which indicted Aaron would be at or near Stonehenge earlier this evening. When Alden advised that Gabriel and Chance also planned to visit Stonehenge this same night, we schemed to intercept Aaron and his Brethren at the monument."

"Thank you for that," Chance said. "We weren't relishing a fight with four Brethren."

"Our pleasure," Darrius replied. "As you are aware, The Cererian Prophecy prevents us from engaging the Yfel directly in battle, but we were hopeful our distraction would allow you and Gabriel time to find a safe place.

"Since I was aware you and Gabriel would return to this home, I telepathically informed Hilly so she could bring the others via a portal." Darrius paused and tapped his fingertips together in front of his chest. "We were able to delay the battle this evening. But Aaron will try again. That is a guarantee. We have two critical missions while in England: Kai must unite his crystal with its Guardian boulder, and Chance must locate his family gemstone.

"Our journeys will take us in two different directions. Jake knows the location of the Guardian boulder but is forbidden to share the coordinates, so he must lead Kai to it. Additionally, Fen must accompany Kai as she is the reader of the symbols that will unlock the Guardian. I have chosen to accompany them as an observer.

"The other group will be focused on finding the earth family crystal and will consist of Chance, Gabriel, Benedict, and Alden."

"What about me?" Hilly cried. "You haven't assigned me to a group."

"You get to choose, Hilly," Darrius replied. "Your skills will be a welcome addition to either party."

"I choose helping Chance."

"Great. I suggest all of you get as much rest as possible. We'll embark on our respective adventures tomorrow evening. Be ready by ten o'clock. Benedict, Alden, and I will return before then."

"Where are you going, Darrius?" Hilly asked.

"We have business to attend to. But Alden has secured this house against the Brethren. You'll be safe if you stay inside. Yfel scouts may detect your magical markers if you venture outside. Now that Aaron knows Chance has returned to his birthplace, he'll be aggressive about using his confederates to search the area for him."

"Until tomorrow evening, my friends." Darrius nodded and, one by one, the Cererians disappeared.

Chapter 13

Family Reunion

CHANCE RUBBED HIS HANDS together. "Now that they're gone, I've got a surprise for everyone. Join me upstairs in my bedroom." Chance hurried down the hallway to the staircase. "Come on guys. You'll love what I'm going to show you."

One by one they mounted the steps and filed into his bedroom. Kai and Hilly flopped onto the double bed while Fen wandered to the window and gazed at the star-filled night sky. Jake leaned against the doorjamb, and Gabe lingered on the landing outside the door.

"Are you ready?" Chance's eyes danced with excitement. "Meet my mum and dad." He gestured toward the paintings hanging on the wall above the dresser.

"What?" Hilly jumped off the bed. "You have a picture of your real parents?"

Kai and Fen joined Hilly as they huddled around Chance craning their necks to peer at the serene couple who stared impassively back at them.

"How do you know they're your parents?" Kai wondered aloud.

Chance jerked his thumb toward the door. "Gabe's mum painted them for my folks as an anniversary present the year I was born. But Mum and Dad never saw them because the Yfel got to them first."

"I'm sorry, Chance," Fen consoled as she rubbed his back.

Hilly faced Gabe. "Your mother painted those?"

"Aye, me mum painted them." Gabe's nervous gaze darted between Hilly and the floor.

"They're very good. Very authentic." Hilly flashed a gentle smile.

"She was known around these parts as a bit of an artist. She preferred painting flowers and birds, but she wanted to surprise her sister with something special. Took her a month."

"Did she work from photographs?"

"Naw. She worked from the images in her brain." Gabe pointed to his head.

"Wow. That's impressive."

"Agreed," Kai added as he inspected the portraits. "Your mother's technique was unique. I don't see brush strokes. It looks like she used a blunt tool to blend the colors together, but I can't figure out what instrument she would have used."

Gabe stared at the floor, fingers twisting nervously in front of him.

"Please forgive my brother's curiosity," Hilly said. "He's a professional artist." She gestured toward Kai. "Paintings fascinate him, especially techniques. Isn't that right, Kai?"

"Hilly's right," Kai agreed. "Do you know what tools your mother used? I'd be interested in seeing them."

"I don't have them anymore," Gabe whispered.

"Pity. It's such an unusual style. The shadowing around the faces really brings them to life."

"Do you have family photographs or video you can share?" Hilly asked.

"Everything was burned in the fire," Gabe responded.

"What fire?"

Gabe gazed beyond Hilly and found Chance looking at him. "'Twas the fire the Yfel started when they attacked Chance's folks."

"Oh." Hilly dropped her head and turned around. "Sorry. I didn't mean to bring up bad memories."

"I have no memory of that day, Hilly," Chance said softly. "But now I have these amazing paintings to help build new ones." He nodded toward Gabe. "And my cousin has already introduced me to other family members."

All eyes swiveled toward Gabe.

"Really?" Hilly exclaimed. "Can we meet them?"

"Yeah," Kai added. "We could have a family reunion within our family reunion."

"That would be lovely," Fen remarked.

Gabe's eyes darted back and forth while their questions pelted him like sleet. He peered over their heads at Chance, his eyes imploring his cousin to intervene.

"Be patient, you guys," Chance gently admonished as he pushed his way toward Gabe. "My cousin has only known you for a few hours. He needs a little time to get accustomed to your weirdness."

"Sorry, Gabe," Hilly offered. "I'm super excited Chance has found his biological family. Fen and I haven't been that lucky yet."

"You mean Kai met his birth family? C'mon, Kai, what are the details?" Chance excitedly probed.

"That's a long story."

"Well, I think this is a tale that must be shared," Chance proclaimed. "Gabe and I haven't eaten since yesterday afternoon, and I'm starving. Let's head downstairs to the kitchen." Chance shepherded Gabe in front of him as they headed down the stairs. Kai and Fen quickly followed.

Jake grabbed Hilly's arm as she passed and stopped her. "Gabe is hiding something. I don't trust him."

"Darrius trusts him, otherwise he wouldn't have allowed him to be with Chance."

"Be careful what you say around him."

Hilly placed her hand atop Jake's. "What's going on, Jake? You've been quiet since we arrived. Is it about your father?"

Jake stared at Hilly several seconds before averting his gaze. "Nothing. I guess I'm tired." He pushed away from the doorjamb. "I'm hungry. Let's head down to the kitchen."

Raucous laughter exploded in the kitchen.

"Imagine my surprise when a bigfoot opened his mouth and spoke to me. To me!" Kai exclaimed. "He was my proctor for the second test to gain access to Shasta."

"A talking yeti? Shasta sure is different than Asheville," Chance uttered over his shoulder as he and Gabe bustled around the kitchen. The savory aromas of sausage, eggs, and fried potatoes mingled with the bitter notes of fresh roasted coffee.

"The dude was huge," Kai continued as he stretched his arms wide. "He acted all gruff and mean. And he ripped a huge tree in half before he demanded I do the same. I thought I was going to crap myself."

"Whatcha do?" Chance asked as he placed platters of meat and eggs in the middle of the table. Gabe added a bowl of fried potatoes and a basket of bread.

Kai squared his shoulders and smiled smugly. "I did what any child of the air element would do. I conjured a massive storm. I'm not strong enough to break a tree in half, and I didn't want to kill a tree to prove anything, but if I was going to see Shasta, I had to sacrifice one."

"Hilly, you were there," Chance said as he set the coffee carafe on the table. "Is this all true?"

"It does sound far-fetched," she said batting her eyes at Kai.

"Cut it out, Hilly. Jake was there. He knows what happened."

Jake held up his hands. "I'm staying out of family business."

"It's the truth," Hilly admitted. "Hell, Jake and I almost got Kai kicked off the mountain because we stumbled past the sacred circle. Axel intervened on our behalf, otherwise I think Toby would have ripped us both in half."

"Axel? Toby?" Chance's brow furrowed.

"Toby is my bigfoot friend," Kai replied nonchalantly. "And Axel is a coyote—my spirit guide."

"What kind of a spirit guide tears out your throat?" Hilly blurted.

Chance stopped chewing. A sausage protruded from his mouth and gravy dribbled onto the tablecloth. He spit the meat onto his plate. "Axel ripped out your throat?"

"Hilly makes it sound so dramatic," Kai dismissed.

"Dramatic? Please. Jake and I watched Axel shred you to pieces and then tear out your throat."

Chance reached across the table, grabbed Kai's head, and twisted it side to side. "I don't see any scars. You guys are making this up!"

"It's true," Jake said. Tilted on the chair's back legs, he clasped his hands across his chest and rocked slowly back and forth. "It's magic."

"Magic?" Chance squinted at Jake. "Are you telling me magic rebuilt my brother after being torn apart by a coyote?"

"Yup." Jake smirked. "Pale blue magic."

"I should have asked Axel to tighten up my jowls at the same time," Kai interjected as he patted the skin under his chin.

Fen covered her mouth with her hand.

Hilly snorted.

Kai burst into laughter.

"You're lucky you didn't emerge looking like a Smurf," Hilly chuckled.

"I'm fortunate I emerged at all. I've never experienced pain like that in my life."

"Why did Axel do that to you?" Chance asked.

"It was my first test. A test of bravery. I had to pass three tests to penetrate the veil and see Shasta." Kai sighed. "I almost didn't do it. But the unusual dreams I had and that visit from Shasta herself...I couldn't throw away my only chance to find my family."

Chance heaped more eggs onto his plate. "And did you find your crystal?"

"Yes."

"Congratulations, bro. When can I see the gem?"

"That's an interesting request..." Kai began. A cockeyed grin slowly spread across his face prompting Hilly to giggle. "It's not really something to share at the dining table."

"Oh? What makes it so mysterious? Hilly's crystal wasn't weird."

"Well..." Kai hesitated.

"Good grief," Hilly cried out. "Just show him."

"Okay. Here goes." Kai leaned back and slowly unbuttoned his shirt. He teased his shirt open exposing his left breast. "Ta-da."

"What the?" Chance reached toward the bright blue image shimmering within the shaman's eye tattooed on Kai's chest. He hesitated to touch it, unsure of how the marking might react. "I thought it was supposed to be a gemstone with facets and edges."

"Oh, it is," Kai assured him. "My people are the Leohts, and, in our natural form, we exist as energetic balls of light."

"What the hell?" Chance said in disbelief. "You belong to a family of light bulbs?"

"Chance!" Hilly scolded. "That's not nice."

"But he just said his family were balls of light."

"Chance, I know it's hard to believe. But my biological family comes from the magical world in Shasta's realm."

"So, you're not human?"

"I'm kinda both. My parents were Leoht, but I was born in the realm of man and raised a human." Kai sighed. "My parents ventured into this world to help the magicians fight the Yfel. Unfortunately, the Brethren killed them as they traveled back to Shasta. They died on her slopes. I was saved by Darrius who spirited me away to The Nine Muses. And you know the rest of the story."

Kai fiddled with the food on his plate. "Shasta expects me to make a decision on whether I'll stay with my human family or return across the veil and be with my Leoht family."

"You need to make a choice? That's bullshit!" Chance yelled. "Of course, you'll stay with us. Right?"

"I'm not sure...yet."

Stunned by Kai's remark, Chance glared at his siblings and Jake. "Is this what we signed up for?" he exploded. "We get ripped away from our families and transformed into beings destined to battle evil just to satisfy a prophecy none of us had anything to do with? Bullshit!"

"Chance, there's no need to get upset," Fen soothed.

"Just wait until it's *your* turn, Fen, then let's see what you have to say." Chance shoved away from the table, forgetting to rein in his supernatural strength, and slammed hard against the cooker. The chair disintegrated, and Chance crashed to the floor.

Kai hiccupped a chuckle.

A smirk spread across Hilly's face.

Fen hid her grin behind a napkin.

After several seconds, Jake slammed the table and roared.

The room filled with uncontrollable laughter, including Chance who rolled around the floor howling. "Stop," he gasped. "I'm going to bust my gut."

"I think you busted enough already," Kai joked. His comment sent everyone into more fits of laughter.

Gabe assisted Chance to his feet and gathered up the splintered chair remains. Then he brought another chair. "Try not break this one," he teased, a twinkle in his eye.

"If that's your crystal," Chance said poking a fork toward Kai's chest. "How do you unite it with its Guardian boulder?"

"I'm still figuring that out. To cross the magical veil separating Shasta's world from the human plane the gemstone had to fuse with my body. I'm not sure how to reverse the process, but Shasta assured me the crystal will know what to do when the moment arises. I just hope it's not as painful as when it became attached to me. On a scale of one to ten, it was a twenty."

"I can attest to that," Hilly said. "He was in agony."

"Sorry you had to go through that."

"Thanks, Chance. Me too!"

Chance cleared his throat. "I have some more news."

The room quieted.

"I learned to fly."

"What do you mean by 'fly'?" Fen asked.

"It's not exactly flying. But I can zip from one place to another with a snap of my finger."

Gabe softly groaned. "Not now, Chance," he uttered under his breath.

"However, I can only flick to a location I've been to before."

"Flick?" Kai asked.

"Yeah, that's what we call it. Flicking. Isn't that right, Gabe?" Gabe stared at the table and didn't respond. "Oh...and I can move mountains."

"I don't think you should be sharing family secrets," Gabe whispered from the side of his mouth.

"We are family," Hilly said raising her voice. "We don't keep secrets." Gabe shrunk lower in his seat. "What's this about moving mountains, Chance?"

"Alden helped me unlock my superpower. That's what he called it...my superpower. He said I'll need to use it one day."

Jake leaned forward. "You mean you can actually move a mountain?"

"Well, there are conditions... To preserve the dependent communities living on the mountain, I can only move a patch of ground with a compatible section of ground so the energy balance is maintained. It sounds complicated, but the process takes seconds."

"Earlier, you said you met some of your family," Fen interjected. "Where?"

Chance clapped Gabe on the shoulder. "I met Gabe at a local pub...Flanagan's Irish Pub. It was there that I met many of my clan." He paused. "Actually, I think everyone in the pub was kin one way or another. Is that right, Gabe?"

Everyone's stares burned into Gabe's forehead. He cleared his throat and answered with a throaty, "Aye."

"When will we get a chance to meet them?" Kai asked.

"Won't be possible," Gabe responded quickly. "Only kin allowed."

"We're Chance's kin, so we should be allowed," Hilly reasoned.

Gabe peered at Chance, his eyes pleading for help.

"Hilly, it's not that easy," Chance began. "Yes, we're family," he said as he gestured around the table. "And now I have family here in England. The difference is the meeting place...the pub. You will never be allowed in because it's magical and only accessible by members of our clan...the earth family. All others, including Darrius, are not allowed entry."

"I don't believe there's a bar anywhere in this world I can't get into if I set my mind to it." Jake narrowed his eyes and studied Chance and Gabe. "I smell a challenge."

"Jake, it's not that way," Chance cautioned. "It's nothing personal, but you're not welcome at Flanagan's Irish Pub."

"Wow. That's a pretty harsh statement." Jake tilted back in his chair and eyed Chance. Slowly he rocked backward and forward as he tapped his fingertips together.

"I might be able to arrange something." Gabe's comment caught everyone off guard.

Wide-eyed, Chance stared at his cousin. "What are you saying?"

"Hilly's right. Family is family. I'll need a little time, but I might be able to work out a scheme to make everyone happy."

"Thank you, Gabe." Hilly patted his hand.

A weak smile fluttered across his lips.

"I hate to be the bearer of bad news," Fen began, "but we've been chatting for hours and it's already five in the morning. I need some rest if I'm going to be hunting a Guardian boulder tonight. I suggest we all try to get a little sleep."

"I'll take ye to yer rooms," Gabe offered as he rose and headed for the doorway.

"I'll clean up down here." Chance collected the plates and scraped remains in the waste bin as water filled the sink. Fen and Hilly kissed him on the cheek and followed Gabe.

"Chance, we need to talk," Jake said in a hushed tone.

"Not right now," Kai interrupted as he looped his arm through Jake's and tugged. "Leave Chance to his domestic duties. You two can chat later."

Chance plunged his hands into the water and began scrubbing plates. "Kai's right. We can talk later after we're all rested." He nodded at his friend. "I promise."

Chapter 14

Jake's Secret

THE AUTUMN LEAVES SPARKLED like gold coins in the early morning sunshine. Cows mooed contentedly as they ambled toward the milking shed of a nearby farm. Sheep bleated and ran before a black and white border collie that steered them toward a pasture.

Chance stood at the window and slurped his coffee.

Just outside the cottage's kitchen window, warblers and wrens scavenged seeds from the wild grasses and declining flower heads. They flitted from branch to branch unaware they were being observed.

"Isn't this where I left you last night?" Jake asked as he strolled into the kitchen and rummaged for a mug. "Fresh?" he asked pointing at the coffee.

"Yep. Get any sleep?"

"Are you kidding? Gabe snores like a hoard of bees, and the continuous creaks and groans of this old house made me wonder if it would remain standing through the night. I've had better naps tucked inside Lola flying through a blizzard." Jake sipped his coffee and licked his lips. "How about you?"

"Seriously? Look at me." Chance pointed to his face. "I have so many bags under my eyes, a small family could go on vacation."

"You do look a little disheveled." Jake frowned at his coffee. "This is a little weak. I'll make a new pot."

"Wait." Chance withdrew a silver flask. "Add a little of this."

"Bourbon, this early?" Jake held his mug out.

"Consider it a little sunshine to start your day. Cheers."

Chance poured another cup of coffee, added some bourbon, and slumped into a chair. "Help yourself," he uttered, setting the flask in the middle of the table.

Jake leaned against the sink and studied his friend. Chance was changing. It had only been three months since they had last seen each other, but Chance's muscles had gotten bigger and his neck was thicker. Chance was almost sixty, but his skin appeared tight and the tiny laugh lines that usually popped out around his eyes were no longer visible.

"You look pretty good for a man your age. Been working out?"

"Not more than usual. Sybil consumes my time nowadays." Elbows on the table, Chance leaned over his mug and allowed the steam to bathe his face. He closed his eyes and breathed deeply.

Abruptly, he sat back and gazed at Jake. "You wanted to talk last night...er, earlier this morning—" He looked at his watch. "Shit, that was only two hours ago." He grimaced.

"Yeah." Jake set his mug on the counter and crossed his arms. He chewed his lower lip and stared at the floor as he gathered his thoughts. "I need to tell you something."

"Oh? By the look on your face, it's something that is really bothering you. Are you still pissed I said you weren't welcomed in the pub?"

Jake waved his hand. "No. I don't give a shit if I ever set foot in Flanagan's."

"Then what is it?"

Jake snatched his mug and sat opposite Chance. He grabbed the flask and poured a good measure into his mug.

Chance's eyebrows arched. "That bad, huh?"

Jake nodded as he sipped and grimaced.

Chance took the flask from Jake and poured more into his mug. "Okay, get it off your chest. What's gnawing at you?"

Jake sighed and stared at his friend. "It's about my father."

"I thought your dad was dead."

Jake held up his hand. "Let me say what I've got to say...okay?"

"My lips are zipped." Chance slid his fingers across his lips and twisted them at the corner.

"Remember when Darrius mentioned Aaron escaped with the help of a rogue magician?"

Chance nodded, his lips pursed tightly together.

"That magician is my father, Ryan Pierson."

Chance's eyes widened and his jaws clenched.

"I know you want to say something so just spit it out."

Chance exhaled as if he had been holding his breath. "Holy shit! How? When?"

"The how and when don't matter, Chance. What you need to understand is my father is a serious threat. He's been with the Yfel so long he's like a magician on steroids. His powers have increased exponentially, and he can overpower you despite your new abilities."

Chance hurried to the coffee maker, grabbed the carafe, and retrieved the Woodford Reserve from the cabinet. "I'm going to need more of these," he said as he sat down. "Are you saying he's Cererian? Has he turned into one of the Brethren?"

"Not yet...I don't think."

"What does he look like so I will recognize him?"

"You've met him already."

"What? When?"

"He arrived with Aaron and the other two Cererians in Stonehenge yesterday. You were lucky Darrius, Benedict, and Alden intervened."

"It was dark. Everything was black. I don't recall what any of them looked like."

"Frankly, I don't know what my father looks like anymore. He betrayed his family and joined the Brethren when I was only five. My grandfather raised me." Jake pushed a creased snapshot of his family toward Chance. "Once the Sentinel boulder revealed the sordid history of my father, my grandfather gave me this family photograph." Jake tapped the sepia image. "My grandfather mesmerized me and my sisters so we wouldn't remember the treachery my father committed. Our memories were altered to believe Dad had died in the plague with Mom. That's him in the middle, holding me."

"Shit, Jake. You're the spitting image of your dad."

"That's not a compliment, Chance."

"Sorry." Chance handed the photo back to Jake. "After all these years, I'm sure your dad looks much different."

"Darrius advised me that since Dad...er, Ryan has been feasting on the souls of the magicians he had killed, his physical and mental states will be altered. I figured kin will know kin regardless of how they look. If our paths cross, I'll know him. I'll recognize his energy."

"Tonight, we're splitting into two groups. What do you think he'll do? Chase after me and Hilly while I'm searching for my crystal or hunt for you?"

Something rapped at the window, both men turned.

A bird hopped along the stone sill, pecking at fluffy seed heads stuck to the outside of the glass. Jake followed the wren's movements as he responded. "Ryan would love to snag Hilly." He turned to Chance. "He'll want to kill her to impress Aaron."

"We both know nobody can beat Hilly when it comes to magic."

"Perhaps. But if enough Yfel join forces, they may be able to subdue her." Jake grew pensive and stared at the table. "Promise me something, Chance," he requested.

"Anything, brother."

"Protect your sister at all costs."

"Done. Do the others know about your dad...um, Ryan?"

"Fen, Hilly, and Kai know about his deception. I'll leave it to you to inform Gabe. Everyone should be aware of what Ryan is capable of."

Chance grabbed the flask and portioned out the remaining contents into both mugs. "Sounds like tonight will be extraordinary. Here's to us and to all the magicians who wage a good fight."

Chapter 15

Gooey Dog

AROUND TWO IN THE afternoon, Fen and Hilly strolled into the reception room and found Chance and Jake snuggled together on the couch. Jake clutched a cushion to his chest and leaned against the arm of the sofa. Chance's head lay on Jake's shoulder while his arm reached in front and gripped the same cushion.

Dual throaty snores buzzed loudly.

The women looked at each other.

"I can guarantee you liquor was involved." Hilly giggled. "This is not the first time I've found them huddled together after some serious drinking."

"They look...almost angelic," Fen observed. She gently touched Chance's knee. "Wakey, wakey."

Chance's eyelids rolled up displaying the whites of his eyes. "Yikes," Hilly exclaimed. "That's not a good look." Jake snorted, shifted, and grabbed Chance's arm, pulling it further across him like a blanket.

"Morning, sisters!" Kai shouted as he burst into the room. Jake and Chance jerked, and their eyes shot open. In a stupor, the two men blinked slowly and looked at Kai, Fen and Hilly.

"Well, now. What's going on here?" Kai teased.

With the drowsiness chased away by Kai's intrusion, Chance realized he was hugging Jake and pushed him away. "Morning," he grumbled as he smoothed his clothes and raked his fingers through his hair. "What time is it?" He glanced at his watch.

Jake rubbed his face. Drunken sluggishness consumed him. He swiveled his head first to Chance and then back to the Kemp siblings. "Humph," he greeted. He tried to stand but couldn't get off the couch. Finally, with Chance pushing from behind, Jake launched onto his feet. "Morning," he mumbled as he shuffled by the stunned group scratching his backsides.

Hilly glared at Chance accusatorily. "Let me guess, Chance Kemp. Instead of getting rest, you guys stayed up and drank bourbon."

"Me?" Chance protested. "How can you accuse me of such a thing?"

Hilly reached forward and lifted a nearly empty bottle of Woodford Reserve from the fold of the couch. "Because this was stuck between the two of you."

"For once I'm not the one being caught in a compromising position!" Kai exclaimed. He whirled and hurried into the hall. "I'll check on Jake. He didn't look so good."

"Hilly, it's not like it looks," Chance explained. "I couldn't sleep. Jake couldn't sleep. We stayed up talking and drinking coffee." A sheepish grin popped onto his face. "At some point we may have started to add bourbon to the coffee to make it taste better." Chance mulled over his words before adding, "I guess it is very much as it appears." He dropped his head. "I'm sorry."

"As you should be," she admonished. "Thank goodness we have enough time to sober you guys up before Darrius and the others arrive. Darrius would be furious!"

Chance struggled to stand but fell back into the cushions.

Hilly grabbed an arm. "Fen, help me get Chance into the bathroom so we can clean him up."

"Here you go," Chance said waving his free arm. Fen grabbed it, and, together, the sisters hefted their brother to his feet. They manhandled his more than two-hundred-pound body down the hallway. Steadying

Chance against the wall, Hilly opened the bathroom door and found Kai hovering over Jake whose head was halfway in the toilet.

"Taken. You'll need to drag your drunk upstairs," Kai directed.

"Ugh," Hilly mumbled as she hefted Chance against her body. "I'm not taking the stairs."

"Oh?" Fen replied. "What other options do we have?"

"I'll open a portal and shoot us upstairs."

"Have you ever done that in a small space before?"

"Nope. So, it could be interesting. Hang on, Fen."

The swirling maw opened at the foot of the stairs. The gateway's breeze sucked in newspapers that had been sitting on the bench near the front door. "Let's get in before it sucks other debris in with us," Hilly cried out as they struggled in with their brother.

The portal closed.

Seconds later, they appeared at the top of the stairs. A tangle of papers shot out with them and swirled about their feet.

Awakened by the commotion, Gabe raced out of his bedroom and gawked at Hilly and Fen struggling with Chance. "What happened?"

"Please help us. Chance is a little drunk and we need to get him sobered up."

"Here, allow me." Gabe gently shouldered his way under Chance's armpit. "I've got me cousin. You go back downstairs. I'll have 'em right as rain in a tick."

"That's very kind of you. Are you sure you don't want our help?" Hilly asked.

Chance belched loudly and acid fumes wafted.

"Uh-oh," Gabe warned.

Before they could react, Chance vomited all over Hilly. "Whoopsie."

"Chance!" Hilly bolted into the bathroom, ripped the shower curtain aside, and jumped in fully clothed.

Fen ran behind her hollering, "Hilly, let me help you!"

Gabe stared after the girls and then looked at his cousin. "Jeezus, Chance, what the hell have ya been eating?" He fanned the air with his hand. "This is a fine mess you've gotten us into. With the women in this loo, I'll need to get you downstairs. Hold tight. I'm gonna try to flick us downstairs together."

Gabe snapped his fingers.

They appeared in the shower and Kai stared at them. "Where the hell did you come from?"

"Uh-oh," Chance uttered.

"Clear the way, Kai, Chance is gonna spew!" Gabe warned.

Kai pulled Jake from the toilet as Chance leaned over and vomited. "Oh, I feel like crap," Chance moaned.

"Urp," Jake gasped.

"Out of the way, Jake's gonna hurl!" Kai shouted.

Jake and Chance held onto the toilet bowl and puked while Gabe and Kai sat on the rim of the bathtub.

"I didn't imagine starting my day like this," Kai mused.

Gabe chuckled. "Neither did I. You should see Fen and Hilly."

"Oh?"

"Chance threw up all over Hilly. Fen's helping her in the upstairs loo right now. That's why I brought Chance down here."

Kai sighed. "Welcome to our dysfunctional family, Gabe."

By the time nine o'clock in the evening rolled around, both bathrooms had been scrubbed cleaned, Hilly had showered twice, and Gabe had mopped the upstairs landing. Unfortunately, the small Oriental rug that caught the fallout of Chance's purge was deemed beyond salvaging and was disposed of in the outdoor bin.

"Don't get accustomed to me alleviating your headaches whenever you get drunk," Fen scolded. Chance and Jake sat in the kitchen while Fen stood behind them and cradled the backs of their heads, applying her healing energy. "This is your final warning."

"Sorry," the men said in unison.

Kai shredded lettuce and diced vegetables for a big salad, and Gabe heaped deli slices of turkey and ham on a row of bread slices that had been slathered with a spicy mustard. Then, one by one, he added the tops and cut them diagonally.

"I doubt they'll be hungry," Kai whispered to Gabe, nodding toward Jake and Chance.

Gabe glanced at the men. "I don't care. I could do with a wee bit of food, and I know the girls are famished."

"Right you are, Gabe." Kai toted a large bowl of salad to the table and set it down in front of Jake and Chance. He frowned at the two men.

"Blech," Chance complained as his eyes roamed over the fresh cut veggies.

"Not up for discussion, Chance," Kai countered. "If you and Jake don't like the offerings, I suggest you go elsewhere. Are you done with these two clowns, Fen?"

"Sure am. I'm hungry, and that salad looks scrumptious." She patted Jake and Chance on the tops of their heads. "Okay, fellas. I'm done with you."

Gabe carried a large tray of sandwiches to the table. "There's water and pop in the fridge. "Everyone grab a plate and help yourself."

"Everything looks tasty," Hilly noted. "Thank you, Gabe, for fixing our dinner." She smiled warmly at him.

"Hey, what about me?" Kai whined.

"Yes, yes. You did a great job, too," Fen added as she hugged him.

Despite his protest against the salad, Chance grabbed a sandwich and handed Jake another. The two buddies ate slowly and quietly, pausing in between bites to ensure the food stayed in their bellies.

Buoyed by the kinship he had formed with Kai and Hilly, Gabe felt bold enough to ask a question. "I was just wondering…"

Everyone ceased eating and stared at Gabe who looked back with frightened eyes.

"Wondered what?" Kai asked with an encouraging smile.

Gabe shifted in his seat. "Um…I was wondering which direction everyone is heading tonight?"

Jake and Chance chewed their sandwiches.

"Guys," Hilly barked, "he's talking to you. You *are* the ones leading the groups, right?"

"I can't tell you," Jake replied curtly.

Gabe flinched as though Jake's words had slapped him across his face. He drew in a deep breath and spoke again. "Darrius mentioned yesterday you were leading Fen and Kai to the Guardian boulder."

"That's right," Jake responded as he grabbed another sandwich.

"So, you know where it's located?"

"Yup."

"Great. So which direction are you heading?"

"I can't tell you."

Kai leaned over and touched Gabe's arm. "Give it a rest, Gabe. Jake can't tell *anyone* where we're going."

"Why?"

Jake sighed. "It's a Prophecy security layer to prevent the Yfel from finding out details regarding the Guardian boulders. We—Fen, Kai and me—have specific duties to perform. No one else can do the ritual that unlocks the boulder except for Fen and Kai, and no one else knows where the Guardians are located around the world, except me. We are all forbidden to speak the words. When we do, our words come out like annoying static electricity."

Gabe rubbed his chin. "Interesting." He turned toward Chance. "Is it the same for you? Are you the only one who knows where the family crystal lies?"

"Not exactly. I have hints from Sybil who maintains the family records, but I have to figure it out on my own. I have to use my intuition to home in on the gemstone."

"What direction are we heading?" Gabe cast a sideways glance at Jake expecting Chance to respond in the same curt manner.

"We're heading into the Preseli Hills."

Jake's eyebrows hitched up.

"Pembrokeshire?" Gabe exclaimed. "I've visited the area before."

"You have? Do you know where Carn...hm, Gooey Dog is located?"

"Gooey Dog?" Gabe looked at Chance with a perplexed face. "Oh, you mean Carn Goedog. I've never been there but I've been to other carns in the area."

"Carn go dog? What's that?" Hilly asked.

"A heap of rocks," Chance explained.

"Folks in other areas may know them as cairns," Gabe added.

"Oh, yes. I've seen cairns on hiking trails in North Carolina where people have stacked flat rocks to show others they've passed. Sometimes they paint words and symbols on the rocks."

"Carns in the Preseli are more substantial and feature rocks from large pillars to slabs to small boulders," Gabe explained.

"The Gooey Dog is significant," Chance continued. "Rocks in this area were used in the formation of Stonehenge. Sybil hinted at my crystal being cradled in the bosom of the carn that had a connection to bluestones."

"But there's other carns that are thought to have provided bluestones for Stonehenge. Carn Menyn and Carn Breseb are two I know of. How do you know it's this one?" Gabe pressed.

Chance paused and pondered all the information Sybil had provided within her pages. "Well, at least Gooey Dog is a start. If it's not there, I'll search the other two. As I mention before, I'll use my intuition to find it."

Hilly and Fen began clearing the table. "Kai, you must be excited about uniting your crystal with its Guardian boulder," Hilly remarked.

"Yes and no. I'm not looking forward to the crystal's separation from my chest, but I'll be happy when it's on its seat of power Then we'll have two crystals in place and two to go."

"I'm nervous about reading the symbols in the proper order," Fen said. "It's only been a few months since Hilly united her fire crystal, and there were so many firsts associated with the ritual. Thankfully, the Sentinel boulder gifted me the sight to easily understand the symbols, so I won't struggle through their interpretation like I did with the markings on the Sentinel's surface."

"You'll be fine, Fen," Kai consoled as he patted her hand. "In Alaska, you went straight to work without hesitation as though you had always known the proper words. I was like your sidekick."

Pink flushed Fen's cheeks, and she bowed her head. "Thank you, Kai. But you and I know we couldn't have done it without each other's help. We complete each other."

"And we'll do it again, sis," Kai said as he hugged her. "We're the only act on earth that does what we do."

"Good evening!" Darrius hailed as he strolled through the doorway. The Cererian wore a navy-blue suit, black shoes polished to a high sheen, and a green and blue striped tie that spilled down the front of his bright-white shirt.

Alden and Benedict followed him.

Holding his ever-present bowler hat, Alden sported a black-on-black striped suit, fresh-pressed white shirt, and a deep purple tie. Benedict appeared relaxed and informal in his brown robes that hung loose on his lanky frame.

"Do they always dress so posh for a hike on the moors?" Gabe whispered to Chance.

"Always," Chance replied in a low voice. "It's a Cererian thing."

"Did I overhear someone is going to the Preseli Hills?" Darrius asked.

"You have good ears, Darrius," Chance responded. "I made that claim."

"That sounds logical, considering your family's connection to Stonehenge and the bluestones. What's your strategy for finding your crystal?"

"I know I'm looking for a specific carn."

"And?" Darrius asked.

"And what, Darrius? That's it. Sybil provided cryptic passages for where I should start. At a place called Gooey Dog."

"Carn Goedog," Gabe corrected.

Darrius raised his hands in front of his chest and tapped his fingertips while staring at Chance.

Uncomfortable by the accusatory gaze, Chance blurted, "Why do I need a strategy, Darrius? I go to the carn, I find the crystal, and I'm done."

Darrius' brilliant emerald eyes flashed, and the air thickened as though the kitchen had been plunged underwater. The Cererian scowled at Chance.

Those around the table shifted uneasily in their seats. Fen clutched Kai's hand and squeezed.

Fingertips still pressed together, Darrius circled the table. His eyes darted from person to person until he reached Chance.

His eyes swirled dark with flashes of gold.

A breath caught in Chance's throat.

"Let me be succinct," Darrius began as he placed a hand on Chance's shoulder. "While you eat and drink and tell your jokes, Aaron and his associates are planning your deaths. Aaron knows you're in Amesbury because you and Gabe were foolish enough to visit your family's monument without cloaking your whereabouts."

"But—" Gabe began.

"Unacceptable behavior!" Darrius bellowed.

Gabe shrank into his seat.

Chance winced as Darrius dug into his shoulder. "Once Hilly united her crystal with the Sentinel boulder, a message thundered across the globe informing the magical populations and nature's spirits that the Prophecy was in motion. That message was also detected by the Yfel causing them to escalate their plans to prevent the four of you from completing your mission.

"Yet, you're sitting on your laurels in a quaint country kitchen." Darrius' stern gaze swept those gathered at the table. "Unlike you, Aaron has not been complacent. Despite being sealed in his prison on Ceres he crafted a strategy for revenge. Now, he prowls this country using the information his confederates have unearthed about you. Make no mistake, Chance. He *will* find you." Chance groaned under Darrius' tightening grip.

Darrius released him and placed his hands on the table. Leaning forward until their noses almost touched, the Cererian continued, "But *you* have no strategy. This is not the way of a warrior, Chance."

Chance trembled and peered back with fearful eyes. "Darrius, it's only been six months since I found out I was a warrior. And only recently did I heed the call to find my crystal, and—"

Darrius slammed the table. "Enough excuses!" He stood and calmly tugged at his shirt cuffs. Clearing his throat, he spoke again in a calm voice. "It's time to own what you are—each of you." He pointed at each person including Jake. "You are the ones the Prophecy has identified. Millions of lives await the day you restore peace to the Earth.

"Forgive my brusqueness, but I have grown impatient with your progress. The Brethren are hungry, and the Prophecy prevents Alden,

Benedict, and me from interfering. You *must* be ready...you *must* have a strategy for success."

Darrius rejoined Alden and Benedict. After drawing in several deep breaths, his face relaxed and his eyes returned to their tranquil green. The atmosphere immediately felt lighter.

A wry smile spread across Darrius' face. "So, I ask again, what is your strategy?"

Chapter 16

The Strategies

"I've never seen Darrius so angry. He scared the shit out of me—and that's not easy." Chance leaned back on the sofa and stretched his legs onto the coffee table.

Jake looked out the window into the darkened garden. "You're lucky Darrius granted you the time. He's aware of Prophecy details that we may never know. He carries a huge burden on his shoulders, ensuring the crystals are united with their Guardian boulders while preventing our untimely deaths. I've learned to be nimble when it comes to anything concerning the Yfel or the Prophecy. It's why I have contingency plans on top of contingency plans."

"C'mon Jake, you've lived with your powers much longer than I have." Chance crossed his arms and pouted. He glanced at the closed door to the lounge, faint voices and laughter drifted from the kitchen. "I wish I was with them."

"Darrius was clear," Jake said. We need to have our strategies in thirty minutes and be ready to rock out of here by ten o'clock, so stop whining."

"That's harsh, Jake. I might complain, but I don't whine."

"You're stalling. Jeez, Chance. Focus!"

"Do you have a plan? And don't say you can't tell me."

"I had a plan before I arrived in England. Not only do I have a plan for you, but I have a strategy for when Fen goes on her quest as well."

"Shit. Seriously? How can you have plans for something you're not aware of?"

"Who said I wasn't aware?" A hint of a smile lingered on Jake's face.

Chance peered around the room and lowered his voice. "Are you saying you know things before they occur?"

"Who are you looking for?" Jake asked as he followed Chance's gaze. "It's just the two of us here. And you don't need to whisper. Look, Chance, let's just say that I receive privileged information from time to time."

"You mean like how Sybil shares important details with me? Or how Darrius knows what's going to happen because of The Cererian Prophecy?"

"Yes and no. I don't mean to be vague, but I can't tell you any more than that I'm occasionally made aware of future events."

"That's clear as mud." Chance sat back, crossed his arms, and studied his friend. "And I suppose you would have to kill me if you *did* tell me."

Jake smirked. "Something like that. Look, brother. I know you've only recently strapped on the warrior mantle, but you need to think like a soldier. There's no turning back. Not for you. Not for Hilly. And not for Kai or Fen either."

"That's easy for you to say."

"Not at all. None of this is easy. We were thrown together within months of your family's battle with Stygian. We all possess magical powers, and we're all driven to unite the crystals so peace is restored to Earth. What's easy about any of that?"

Chance glanced away.

Jake cocked his head. "Why are you resisting all of this?"

The question punched Chance right in his heart. He softly replied, "Janet and the kids."

Jake hung his head. "I thought so. I don't know what to tell you. But you need to make a decision. Either you commit one hundred percent to being a warrior or you walk away and go back home to Asheville. But, if you choose the second option, you will always be looking over your shoulder for the Brethren. Peace will never be restored to the world and millions of magicians will perish, including members of your family."

Chance rolled his eyes. "Thanks for that heap of guilt."

"You can't have it both ways. Either you're in or you're out. My life depends on you. The lives of your siblings depend on you. I need to know right now. What do you choose? Warrior or family man?"

The men stared at each other.

Chance bowed his head and whispered, "I choose warrior."

Jake slapped his friend on the back. "I know it's not easy. Janet and the kids will be fine. All you need to do is find that friggin' crystal and restore it to its seat of power. Easy, right? And once that's done you can go back home and be the family man."

"Easy," Chance scoffed. "I'll hold you to that."

Jake cracked a smile. Even though the words came out of his mouth, he didn't believe them. Nothing in his life had ever been easy. Now that his father was in England, Jake's thoughts were constantly on Ryan's whereabouts. Unaware of his father's supernatural powers he had to be prepared for anything and suspicious of everything.

"Earth to Jake."

Jake shook his head. "Did you say something?"

Chance's brow furrowed. "Everything okay?"

"Yup. Now, about our strategies—"

"You're beginning to sound like Darrius, my friend," Chance teased. "I have an idea, since your plan is done, why don't you share yours. You *are* the experienced warrior in this room."

"Fair enough, asshole." Jake paced the room as he recounted his plan. "First things first—transportation. Since Hilly is traveling with your party, she can open a portal and take you and Gabe with her. I'm sure Alden and Benedict will want to teleport themselves since they're accustomed to that mode of travel. But, if they choose, they can also join everyone in the portal."

"That sounds logical," Chance agreed.

"As for my group, traveling is more complicated because I'm forbidden to tell anyone where we're going." Jake shook his head. "That secrecy aspect is frustrating, so I have to employ one of my contingency plans.

"What will you do?"

"I'll provide Darrius the coordinates of a nearby landmark where he can teleport with Fen. Kai and I can fly, so I'll lead him to the agreed upon location. Once we all meet up, we'll trek the rest of the way in."

"Aren't you concerned about being spotted?"

"Nope. We'll use cloaking magic. Nobody will spot us unless they have the preternatural sight. Plus, it will be dark."

Jake paused and considered his next statement. "As for the rest of my strategy, I'm afraid I can't tell you anything else because it contains specific information about the location of the Guardian boulder. Your turn." He jutted his chin at Chance.

"Gabe is somewhat familiar with the Preseli Hills. Although he hasn't been to Goedog, he's been to some of the other carns in the area. I plan to start at Carn Goedog. If my crystal's not there, then I'll check the other two Gabe knows about. I plan to use my intuition to locate the gemstone. I'm sure Darrius wants something more concrete than that, but it is one of my more reliable powers."

"Once you find your gemstone, how will you get back here?"

"Gabe and I can flick back to the cottage or we can join Hilly in a portal. As you mentioned before, Alden and Benedict can manage what they want. I'm not worried about them."

"Good. What about contingencies?"

"Why do we need those?"

"Things always go wrong. It's best to plan for those moments for when your plan backfires. For instance, what if you can't find the crystal no matter how much you've searched? How much time do you allow yourself before you give up and head home?"

"I thought I would keep looking until I found it."

"There's a reason we're going during the night, Chance. We're heading into public areas and the chance of civilians hanging around is less than during the day. If we're challenged by the Yfel, we don't want innocent lives taken, do we?"

"I see your point. Then if I haven't located the crystal by five in the morning, then we abandon our mission and come home."

"Make sure to erase any evidence that you visited the area so the Yfel don't pick up the scent. And don't forget the Brethren utilize a vast network of associates who get paid handsomely for any information they dig up on you and your family. Those people are not just Cererians. They can also be disgruntled magicians and Folk looking for extra money or powers."

"I'll be on alert at all times." Chance glanced at his watch. "Our time is almost up. Did we cover everything?"

"I think so. Just remember, even though you have this plan, something will always occur that forces you to the next plan."

Chance stood and stretched. "Okay, let's go see Darrius and reveal our strategies."

Darrius sat at the dining table with Hilly, Fen, and Gabe while Alden and Benedict stood with their backs toward the door leading into the garden.

"We have our plans, Darrius," Chance announced as he entered the kitchen.

"Well done," Darrius responded. "Let's prepare for our departure."

"Don't you want to hear my strategy?"

A grin fluttered across Darrius' face. "Do you believe it's a solid plan?"

"Yes."

"Did you cover all contingencies?"

"Yes."

"Then, we can prepare for our departure." Darrius gestured at Alden and Benedict who exited the kitchen.

"I spent thirty minutes on a strategy and you don't want to hear it?"

"The important thing is that you have a plan. Now that you know how to create a strategy, you will know to expect the unknown." Darrius paused before he added, "I knew you had it in you. You just needed a little prodding." Turning toward the others in the kitchen, he added, "Assemble in the lounge in ten minutes." As he left the kitchen, he nodded at Jake who dipped his head in return.

Chance noticed the exchange. "What was that?" he asked Jake.

"What was what?"

"Cut it out, Jake. Did Darrius have a part in you and me getting together?"

"Nothing personal, but Darrius knew I stood a better chance at getting you to pound out a plan than he did." Jake shrugged. "Who cares how we got the end product, right?"

"I feel so used."

"Don't feel bad, Chance," Fen consoled as she patted his arm. "Darrius grilled each of us while you were away with Jake. He wants to ensure we're prepared for anything the Brethren may throw at us."

"This is serious business," Hilly added. "Our destinies were activated when we battled Stygian on that beach. And as we each find and unite our family crystal with its Guardian boulder, the Yfel grow more desperate to stop us. We must plow forward. There is no going back."

"Gee, where have I heard that before?" Chance said as he winked at Jake.

"C'mon, everyone." Kai waved from the doorway. "It's time to get this show on the road. Take small children by the hand and follow me to the lounge."

"Leave it to you to lighten the mood," Fen said as she took his hand.

As they entered the lounge, Alden greeted them by the open door to the garden. "This way, please. We'll assemble outside before we depart."

"What about Aaron's associates snooping?" Hilly asked.

"We've made special arrangements in the garden. No one will be able to detect a thing." He swept his arm toward the backyard. "If you'll please join Darrius and Benedict outside."

Except for the dim glow from a streetlight near the front of the house, the garden loomed dark and surreal. Trees and bushes were shapeless shadows appearing much like camouflaged predators awaiting their chance to pounce from the darkness.

Alden closed the door and applied magic around the door frame by signing sigils in each of the corners. As he joined Darrius and Benedict, he said, "All is secure."

Jake, Fen, and Kai assembled in their group. Hilly looped her arm through Chance's arm and joined Gabe near Alden and Benedict.

"In a few minutes we begin our journeys," Darrius began. "While we depart in our separate groups, we must maintain constant connection with each other via telepathy. The Brethren *will* find you, so be prepared for that eventuality. When you run afoul of the Yfel, alert everyone. Remember Chance and Gabe cannot receive telepathic transmissions. Benedict, Alden, and Hilly will always be with them, so if there's trouble, they'll let them know."

"Your siblings have the gift of telepathy?" Gabe asked Chance in a low whisper.

Chance responded softly, "Yeah. It's one of those things that make us different."

"But you and I will be able to flick, and they can't." The two men nodded.

"One more thing," Darrius added. "Remember that Benedict, Alden, and I cannot assist you if there is a confrontation with the Yfel. The

Prophecy prevents us from battling our brothers. But we can use distraction techniques, if required."

Darrius studied Jake, Gabe, and the Kemps. "I have faith in each of you," he said as he lightly tapped each person on the shoulder. "I've watched you embrace your powers and assume your responsibilities even though the tasks are daunting.

"Expectations are high, and the rewards are low. The threat of death is ever present, yet you willingly press forward to complete your mission."

Darrius paused. "I am in awe of each of you, warriors. Prepare yourselves, for the time has arrived for us to depart." Darrius turned to his colleagues. "Be well, Alden. Be well, Benedict. Until we meet again."

Alden and Benedict bowed their heads as they responded together, "Be well, Darrius."

"I have the coordinates, Jake," Darrius confirmed. "Fen and I will teleport and meet you and Kai at our predetermined location." Darrius wrapped his arm around Fen and disappeared while Jake and Kai shot into the night sky and soared west toward their destination.

"Hilly, we have decided to join you in your portal," Benedict announced. "That way, Alden and I can ensure everyone remains together."

"Excellent decision," she replied. Peering into the night sky, she invoked the elementals. "Spirits of the north, the east, the south, and the west, assist me now as we journey into unknown lands." A swirling gateway appeared. "Please stay together," she cautioned. "I wouldn't want to lose anyone."

The group stepped across the threshold and the portal closed with a hiss. Seconds later they emerge atop a mound in the Preseli Hills.

"Welcome to Wales," Gabe said, sweeping his arms wide.

Chapter 17

The Guardian Boulder

JAKE AND KAI DESCENDED from the darkened sky and landed softly on the grass. "Nice to see you again," Darrius hailed. He and Fen emerged from the shadows as the men touched down.

"Welcome to Llyn Cau," Jake said sweeping his arms wide. "This is a glacial lake within the crater of Cadair Idris."

"I imagine this lake is quite beautiful in the daytime," Fen said as she gazed across the inky water surrounded by a shadowy landscape.

"Like a deep blue marble," Jake replied. "That's what I thought of when I first saw Llyn Cau on a sunny day." He stared at the dark cliffs high above them. "This land is steeped in magic. We are within the protective hands of an ancient mountain shrouded in myths."

"Will we encounter any mysterious beings on our journey?" Fen asked.

"Perhaps. One never knows what spirits will reveal themselves. It is rumored that giants once roamed these rocky cliffs."

"How far away are we from the Guardian boulder," Kai asked. He absently scratched his shirt on the left side of his chest.

"Not far," Jake replied, grinning. "You know I can't tell you exactly."

"You can't blame a guy for trying." Kai rubbed his shirt harder. "Man, something itches."

"What's that blue glow?" Fen asked.

Kai tugged at his shirt and strained to see what his sister was pointing at.

"Open your shirt," Jake suggested.

Kai undid some buttons and peered under the flap. "That's weird."

"C'mon you tease," Fen said as she grabbed his shirt and pulled it open. "Oh, my."

The shaman's eye brand on Kai's chest glimmered a soft luminescent blue, pulsing in rhythm with Kai's heartbeat.

Jake stepped closer to inspect it. "Does it hurt?"

"Thankfully, no. But it itches...a lot." Kai gently tapped his finger on the marking careful not to damage the family gem that had fused to the shaman's eye.

"Your crystal senses the Guardian boulder is near," Darrius observed. "Very curious."

Kai rebuttoned his shirt. "I hope the itching is how it behaves when we finally arrive at the Guardian. I don't want a repeat of the pain it caused when it merged with me."

Jake slapped Kai on the back. "It'll be fine. No worries."

"I'll hold you to that." Kai managed a weak grin.

"How was the flight here?" Fen asked changing the subject.

"Unbelievable," Kai replied. "Jake and I flew over farmland that looked like a patchwork quilt of blacks and grays. Then we flew over town centers that were lit up like beacons in the night gloom." He paused and rubbed his chin. "You know, this is the first time I've flown since the battle on the beach."

"Now there's a memory I wish I could forget," Fen commented. "But I must admit, there were some wonderful moments during our reunion at The Nine Muses."

"We should journey to the Guardian boulder," Darrius reminded everyone. "Time is of the essence. Benedict has just informed me his group will soon embark to Carn Goedog to search for Chance's crystal."

"Our destination is not far," Jake reiterated. "But it will be a challenging trek. In addition to the steep ascent and loose rocks, there may be snow and ice at the higher elevations. Stay close, step where I step, and we'll be okay."

"I'm glad I wore my hiking shoes," Fen replied. "But, Darrius, I think it was a mistake wearing your Italian loafers for this excursion." She pointed at the tips of his shoes, which gleamed in the dim light.

"I appreciate your concern, but I'll be fine," the Cererian replied.

"Follow me," Jake instructed as he followed a worn path around the edge of the lake that snaked up to a rocky outcropping at the base of the cliff. Kai fell in behind Jake, then Fen, and then Darrius. As the group trekked along, the Cererian dispensed cloaking magic to hide their footprints.

"Should take less than thirty minutes," Jake called over his shoulder as the trail wound upward steeply. "Careful along here. Go slow. We'll be walking along a thin ridge for several yards."

Kai walked slowly with his hands out to either side as though he was on a tightrope. Fen followed close behind him, her hand gently touching his back. As they rose up the side of the mountain, a fast-moving cloud engulfed them in a fine drizzle. Kai slipped on the slick pebbles and fell into Jake who tensed and held his footing. Kai fell to the ground behind him.

"Easy, Kai," Fen called out. Her fingers gripped the back of his shirt. She lurched forward but kept herself on her feet.

The rain cloud rushed away carried by swift winds.

"Is everyone okay?" Darrius asked

"Banged my knee, but I'm okay," Kai said as he righted himself.

"Just a reminder, Kai," Jake began. "If you fall off the side of the mountain, *you* can still fly, but don't pull your sister down with you. Fen, place your hand on the rock wall for support as we follow the trail upward."

"Good idea," she agreed.

Once the group crossed the ridge, the path snaked through a wide, grassy area. "Stay on the trail," Jake called out. "We're almost there."

"Hold up!" Fen cried out. "I need a short break."

"You okay, Fenny?" Kai asked.

"I'm fine. I hike back home in Georgia, but we don't have steep paths like this. I feel like my nose is going to touch my kneecap with each step."

"Would you like me to carry you?" Darrius asked. "It would be my pleasure."

"That's very sweet of you, but I'll manage. I just need a short rest." A sudden gust pushed Kai into Fen. "Wow, the weather is really unpredictable up here, isn't it?"

Jake stared into the darkness, narrowed his eyes, and grimaced.

"Everything okay, Jake?" Kai asked as he followed his gaze.

"Yep," Jake replied bluntly. "We need to move—now." Without awaiting an answer, Jake trudged up the trail.

"C'mon, Fenny, break's over," Kai joked. "Back to the grind." The pathway threaded through a rocky outcropping and then dropped down another wide slope before the trail broke into two paths.

Jake stopped at the junction.

Kai stepped beside him. "My instincts are telling me to turn right." Kai absently scratched his chest.

"Agreed," Fen said. "I'm pulled that way as well. We must be close to the Guardian boulder. We're both feeling it's energy."

"Perhaps," Jake responded. He looked to the left and then scanned the area to the right. "Sometimes, things are not as they appear. Darrius, stay with Kai and Fen. I'll be right back."

"Is there cause for concern?" Darrius asked.

"I'm not sure. I'm going to check." Jake launched into the air and vanished from sight.

Fen stared into the night sky. "Wow. It was like he was shot from a cannon."

"His speed and agility are inspiring," Kai added. "On our flight to Wales, I did all I could to keep up with him."

"All is okay," Jake announced as he emerged from the blackness and rejoined the group.

Fen jumped, surprised by his sudden appearance. "Good grief, Jake. Warn a girl, will you?"

Jake strode past Fen and Kai and whispered into Darrius' ear. The Cererian nodded.

"What's going on?" Fen asked.

"All is okay," Jake said.

"Why don't I believe you?"

"Let's take the path to the right. We're almost there."

"Told you!" Kai shouted. "I knew the Guardian was in that direction."

Jake whirled on his friend. "Shut up, Kai." Kai looked wounded, and Jake added, "I'm sorry. We're entering a treacherous area. We need to proceed with caution." He turned and continued on the path.

A thick mist descended on the group as they passed a collection of giant boulders that towered over their heads.

Jake stopped and pointed. "Over there. In the middle of the clearing."

Kai and Fen peered where he pointed, but the dense fog moved like a milky soup and distorted all objects. A shadowy form about ten-foot-tall drifted in and out of their vision, and the swirling cloud undulated up the sheer cliffs that surrounded the clearing on three sides.

"Is that the Guardian?" Fen asked.

"Let's use our minds," Kai suggested.

The siblings gripped each other's hands, closed their eyes, and reached out telepathically. *I am Fen Kemp, Guardian of Peace. This is my brother, Kai Kemp, Keeper of the Keys. We have come to restore the crystal of air to her seat of power.*

Welcome my children. The male voice drifted through their heads like a gentle breeze. *Come closer. I'll light the way.* A bluish glow pulsed from the dark object, barely visible in the middle of the clearing. A luminescence emanated from the ground and encircled the clearing. *I've created the sacred circle. Once you step across, you must not leave until the ritual is complete.*

"We've been acknowledged," Fen announced and turned around. Darrius stood alone behind them. "Where's Jake?"

"He had an important matter to handle," Darrius replied.

"Oh? I thought he wanted to be a witness like he was for the crystal of fire."

"C'mon, Fen, we need to get to work," Kai said as he tugged at her elbow.

"I'll stay on the pathway outside the sacred circle," Darrius advised them. "Good luck."

The siblings disappeared into the damp, chilled mist. Fen assumed the lead. She inched toward the dark shape with her arms stretched in front of her. Kai closely followed her with his hand on her back. Once they arrived at the boulder, the glow pulsed a brilliant electric blue before it gradually returned to a gentle throbbing.

"How will you remove your crystal?" Fen asked.

"The Leoht Elder, Bromus, told me the gem would let me know. But all it's done is itch like crazy."

"Well, let's get to work and see what happens."

The siblings gazed back toward Darrius. The dense fog had erased all evidence of the pathway as well as the Cererian.

"This is spooky," Kai said. "I feel like we've been whisked into another world."

Welcome my children. A pulse of warm energy engulfed the siblings, causing the mist to billow gently. *I was told of your arrival. My brother, the Sentinel, was most impressed with your kindness and skill when uniting the crystal of fire with him. Please stand before me.*

Fen and Kai walked around the glowing blue boulder until they faced a side where ancient symbols were carved into the surface. They glowed rhythmically. Time and weather had worn down the sharp edges of some markings. Lichen filled the crevices of others.

Holding their hands at heart center, they bowed toward the boulder. Fen knelt at the base and stretched her hands toward the pillar until she contacted its cold, rocky surface. A chill raced up her arm. "Kai, stand behind me and place your hands on my shoulders," she instructed.

A cold blast of wind swept through the clearing and knocked the siblings to the ground. "Ugh," Fen said as she struggled to her feet with Kai's help. "The weather up here is nasty. With each blast of those gales, the chill goes deeper into my bones."

She knelt on the ground once again. "Once the boulder is open, you'll be able to break contact with me so you can deposit your crystal. Is it talking to you yet?"

Kai placed his hand over his left breast. "Nothing. Not even a vibration." He unbuttoned his shirt and exposed his chest. Goose bumps covered the skin in the damp air. "Do you see any change, Fen?"

She studied the shaman's eye brand. "There's a slight luminescence about it. Look there." She pointed to the dot in the middle of the marking."

"Owww!" Kai yelled as he clutched his chest and fell to his knees.

"Kai!" Fen wrapped her arm around his shoulders. "Is it the crystal?"

"Shit! It's more painful than before!" He whimpered.

Fen pried Kai's fingers away from his chest. The entire Eye pulsed a violet blue. She glanced at the Guardian boulder and then back at the marking. "They're syncing their pulses," she uttered. "They're recognizing each other." She hugged Kai who squirmed in her arms.

"Fuck!" Kai screamed.

"Kai, take your hand off the brand!" Fen yelled. "It needs to communicate with the Guardian."

"It's not your fucking chest that's on fire!" he screamed back. The marking blistered and pulsed rapidly maintaining cadence with the Guardian boulder.

"Kai, I know it hurts, but we've got to open the boulder so the crystal can join with it. Please try to focus." Fen knelt on the ground and guided Kai behind her. Whimpering, Kai placed one hand on her back. "Kai, you must use both hands!" she cried out. "We must have complete contact between us and the Guardian."

Kai sniffed back tears as he placed both hands on her shoulders. Fen reached forward, connecting with the glowing symbols on the face of the pillar and mouthed inaudible words. Both the pillar and the brand pulsed faster and faster as her conjuring advanced.

Kai clenched his teeth and groaned.

A shower of pebbles rained down on them from the cliffs above. With Fen in a trance and Kai in extreme agony, neither noticed the dark figure float down and land outside the magic circle. The figure slowly walked toward them with something gripped in one hand. The moment the person crossed the sacred circle the Guardian boulder and the marking ceased pulsing.

Danger is at our door, the Guardian warned Fen and Kai.

Fen broke away from the pillar and stood. Kai joined her. They strained to see anything in the thick swirling fog.

"What danger?" Kai whispered. "I can't see a damned thing."

"There." Fen pointed into the mist. "Something shadowy is coming."

"I've come for the crystal," the male voice growled.

Kai grabbed Fen and pushed her backward toward one of the cliff walls. He withdrew his blade and assumed a protective stance in front of her.

"I didn't know you were armed," she said.

Kai raised his sword and demanded, "Who are you?"

A wicked laugh echoed off the cliffs.

"I don't see him anymore," Fen said.

"Neither do I," Kai replied.

A cold wind pummeled them from above. With the gales came the sting of sleet on their faces. They lifted their arms to ward off the ice crystals while trying to maintain their gazes on whoever stalked them.

Abruptly, the wind died down.

Stillness.

"Boo!" a dark figure shouted from Kai's left.

Blindly, Kai slashed his sword toward the sound. He pushed Fen further into the wall.

"Too slow, magician," growled the voice, this time from the right side. "I smell the sweet magic of two powerful shamans." Evil laughter chuckled all around them.

Stay still. The thought drifted through Fen and Kai's brains. *I won't let him hurt you.*

Jake? Fen replied telepathically.

Suddenly the figure raced up in front of them and menaced them with an immense sword. "You're mine!"

"No, they're not." Jake jumped between the siblings and the figure. "Your fight is with me, Dad."

"Dad?" Kai whispered.

"Ah, my lovely baby boy," the figure mocked. "You're the spitting image of me when I was your age."

"And I hate that!" Jake pounced forward, tackling the figure to the ground. The thick fog enveloped them, and they disappeared.

"Where'd they go?" Kai asked.

Return to the Guardian. Darrius' calm voice commanded. *Jake has given you time to complete your mission. Hurry!*

"C'mon," Fen ordered. She grabbed Kai and pulled him through the mist. The Guardian loomed dark at first and then the blue light pulsed as they drew near.

Kai screamed. He dropped his sword and clutched his chest. "Not again!"

"Assume the position, Kai!" Fen yelled as she fell onto her knees.

In agony, Kai doubled over and moaned.

"Now, Kai!" Fen screamed as she reached for him and yanked him to her side. "Focus, Kai. I need your help!"

Kai placed both of his hands on Fen's shoulders. Immediately, vibrations rippled between the Guardian and Fen and Kai, completing the circle of energy. Fen resumed her soundless incantation as the Guardian pulsed faster and faster in time with the marking on Kai's chest.

Fen's lips stopped moving.

Clunk.

The loud thud was followed by high-pitched grinding as two rocky slabs slid across each other. The granite sections slowly moved apart, creating a gaping hole in the Guardian boulder. Rock shavings showered the ground as the cavity widened to expose an obsidian recess with a notched cavity under ten inches high.

"Look, Kai," Fen whispered. "A keyhole."

The crystal, still fused to the shaman's eye, had burned through Kai's shirt and flickered like blue fire. Agony consumed Kai, and he gasped his response. "I...know...what...to...do." He withdrew a small ebony box from the bag slung around his shoulder. Holding the ancient relic in his left hand, his right hand slid along the edges of the box in a clockwise motion as he recited a sacred spell. After several moments, the lid of the tiny box popped open and revealed four skeleton keys.

"Excellent," Fen whispered.

Kai studied the keys in the box, using his intuition to guide him in selecting the proper one to use on the Guardian Boulder.

"Hurry," Fen urged.

"Shh," he responded. "The key must choose me." He held his right hand over the set of keys and closed his eyes. As his hand hovered, a gentle vibration poked his palm. Taking care not to disturb the other keys, Kai pinched one between his thumb and forefinger and gingerly lifted it from the box. After placing the case on the ground, he leaned toward the black chamber and guided the skeleton key into place.

He turned it to the right.

Click.

The key vanished from Kai's grip and reappeared alongside the other three in the ebony case on the ground. The box slammed shut.

A deep grumbling like rolling thunder issued deep within the ground. The sound of rock on rock pierced their ears as the obsidian layer dropped away and exposed a smaller chamber of white selenite. The crystalline walls pulsed azure in cadence with the pillar and the brand on Kai's chest.

A soft melody floated within the sacred circle as the Guardian boulder sang its welcoming song. Barely audible at first, the humming, which sounded like a million honeybees, rose and fell like a comforting breeze. The hairs on their arms rose as electrical charges raced through the clearing.

Tears formed as they listened to the Guardian's words that were both joyous and sorrowful. Happy that the crystal of air would soon be reunited with it and sad they had been apart for a millennium.

The humming ceased.

"Do you hear that sweet sound, Fenny?" Kai asked.

"I don't hear anything."

"It's lovely."

"The Guardian is communicating only with you," Fen said. "Like with Hilly, the boulder is ensuring you are the proper person to unite the crystal."

The Guardian telepathically spoke to Kai:

> *Within this granite, an entity lies waiting,*
> *Awaiting the one who will remove the barrier,*
> *Embracing the one who will provide the soul,*
> *And breathe life into the element of air.*

Tears rolled down Kai's cheeks as emotions swept through his body. The intensity of the Guardian's message not only touched his heart, but the words also revealed Kai's importance in the world and his spiritual connection to all living things.

My son, this holy text is meant only for you. As I speak the words, your crystal will respond and yearn to be reunited with me. You may step forward with your offering.

The shaman's eye glowed a steady electric blue in sync with the constant light illuminating from the pillar. Kai separated from Fen, removed his shirt, and stood in front of the pillar.

I am ready to receive your message, Guardian, he announced as he lifted his hands toward the boulder.

Very well, my son. The Guardian shared his message, which only Kai could hear.

> *I stand alone, one of four,*
> *United the four will be one.*
> *The breath inside you carries the life.*
> *The world awaits your air from the heavens!*

Upon the Guardian's last word, complete stillness filled the air as though the world, and everything in it, had momentarily stopped.

Kai reached for Fen's hand. The moment she gripped it, a searing pain exploded in his chest. His head wrenched back, and his mouth opened wide to scream, but only silence filled the ether. Tears streamed down his face as he clenched his sister's hand with such force, she bent forward and gritted her teeth.

A delicate blue orb pulled away from the shaman's eye and hovered in front of Kai's face. At the moment of separation, all pain ceased, and Kai opened his eyes. The ball of light flashed a myriad of colors, and it reached out. *Thank you, Kai Kemp, Keeper of the Keys, Shasta's trusted ambassador, and member of my Leoht family.*

Kai gasped, and though there was no more pain, tears trailed down his cheeks as he watched the crystal drift toward the cavity and position itself upon its seat of power. The minute the orb joined the Guardian, a light-blue flame flickered within the receptacle. Instantaneously, granite slabs growled and screeched as they slid toward each other on their arduous journey to close the opening and make the boulder whole again.

Once the slabs reached their destination, a shower of rock shavings fell to the ground.

Silence.

Then the Guardian boulder sighed sending a shockwave coursing around the world. Carried in the rolling vibrations was its joyful message audible only to the magical populations of the world: *Air has been restored. The second marker is secure!*

Kai collapsed to the ground.

When Fen rolled him over, she found a gaping wound in the left side of his chest. "Oh, Kai," she cried as she quickly covered the bloody hole with her hand. "I'll make you better." She called upon her shamanic ancestors and healing wisdom as she chanted over Kai.

With each magical word, clots formed and fine strands of fibrin knitted along the border of the injury. Healing hairs joined with the outside edge and bridged toward the middle of the wound like a spider weaving a silken web. Soon, a golden mesh appeared as though honey had been drizzled, and it had formed a latticework over the injury.

Your words carry power, the Guardian boulder observed. *Your brother will heal nicely. Already the crystal of air has reached out to the crystal of fire that lives within my brother, the Sentinel. Their energy has connected.*

With Kai's laceration protected by her healing, Fen laid his head on the ground. He snored softly and mumbled as he rolled onto his side and drew his knees to his chest. Fen turned to the Guardian boulder and placed her hands upon the granite. *You worked so hard to separate your slabs for the crystal. May I offer you healing magic?*

Ah, yes. The Sentinel mentioned your generosity at healing our wounds after such a torturous process. I will gladly accept your healing.

Fen slid her hands up and down the pillar and softly hummed as she dispensed healing energy into the Guardian. When she finished, she stepped back and bowed.

How can I repay you? the Boulder asked.

That is so kind of you, but there is nothing I need.

You are a powerful shaman. I shall bestow upon you a gift that will keep you safe.

The Guardian's blue glow faded away and murkiness returned to the clearing. Kai whimpered and turned over, knocking against Fen's leg. When she looked down at him, she noticed something fluttering around her neck. It was a necklace with a dangling pendant.

Wanting to see it more closely, she removed the cherished item and gasped. The charm was a miniature dream catcher fashioned from white feathers and bluestone beads. She smiled, placed it around her neck, and patted it.

Thank you, she said to the Guardian.

The mist dissipated, and Kai's eyes fluttered open. "Hi Fenny," he said, staring up at his sister.

"Did you have a nice nap?" she asked.

"I remember blue pulses...and pain—" He touched his chest. "Hey, it's almost healed. You?"

"Yes," she responded as she helped Kai to his feet.

"Thanks. Hey, what's that around your neck?"

"A gift from the Guardian boulder."

They walked back to the pathway and found Darrius standing in silent meditation, his eyes closed, and fingertips pressed together. When they drew near, he opened his eyes.

"I hear you were successful," he stated. "The Guardian's message has already circled the Earth five times."

"Has Jake returned?" Fen asked with hope in her voice.

"No. And Benedict advised me the Yfel Brethren just arrived in the Preseli Hills."

Chapter 18

The White Stag

CHANCE, HILLY, GABE, AND the Cererians stood atop a large hill whose summit was capped with three piles of boulders. Just a few days past the new moon and the inky sky appeared as a black canvas splattered with brilliant white and yellow stars. The landscape spilled away from them in a shadowy darkness toward the distant horizon.

"We're standing on Foel Drygarn, which means 'the hill of three cairns,'" Gabe explained. "If I recall my history properly, this is a hill fort from the Iron Age and these three mounds of rocks are burial cairns."

Hilly glanced skyward. "This is beautiful. The darkness is magnificent. I feel I could stretch up on my tip toes and pluck a star out of the sky." She reached upward with both hands.

"Reminds me of my excursion to move mountains," Chance said. "Wild, open space that rambles on forever."

"We weren't far away," Alden said. "About a hundred and fifty miles to the east from here."

"The area is secure. I've confirmed the Yfel are not present," Benedict announced. "Is this rocky crag the location of your crystal, Chance?"

"No," Chance responded. He walked to a six-foot pillar lying sideways on the ground and glanced westward. He closed his eyes and raised his hands. After many moments, he turned to the others. "I sense the gem lies southwest of here." He pointed into the darkness.

"Aye, you're pointing between Carn Goedog and Carn Breseb," Gabe confirmed. He grabbed Chance's hand and moved it slightly to the left. "Now, you're pointing at Carn Menyn."

"You've been to these places?" Alden asked.

"I've not been to Goedog," Gabe replied. "But I am familiar with Breseb and Menyn. You'll find piles of bluestone boulders on both hills, which are surrounded by patches of marshy ground. With the damp weather we've had this month we should tread lightly."

"How far is Goedog?" Chance asked.

"About twenty-four hundred meters," Gabe replied.

"In miles?"

Gabe rubbed his chin and stared at the ground. "I figger it must be about one and a half miles away."

A shooting star streaked across the sky from west to east. Everyone followed the celestial body's fiery trail until it disappeared into the black void. "It's a different world out here, indeed," Hilly commented. "There's a sense of being completely isolated yet totally surrounded at the same time." She closed her eyes and breathed deeply. "I smell rain."

As if on command, a drizzle swept the hilltop. "Follow me," Gabe said as he trotted for a cluster of vertical boulders. "These chambers have pockets within them that will offer us shelter." One by one they squeezed between the stones and huddled together under a rocky overhang. Benedict's gangly frame bent at odd angles within the cramped space.

As fast as it had arrived, the rogue cloud sped away pushed by stiff winds.

"That was interesting," Hilly observed.

"Welcome to the Preseli," Gabe commented. "Expect the unexpected."

"Speaking of the unexpected," Alden interjected. "We need to locate the crystal. Chance, which way should we head?"

"We go to Goedog," he replied with confidence. "I'm sure it's over there."

"I have informed Darrius and the others of our plan," Benedict mentioned as he nodded to Alden.

Chance climbed around the boulder at the edge of the summit. "Stop, Chance," Gabe cried out. "There's a pathway over here that we can take down to the valley. Remember these are ancient sites, and we should treat them like treasures."

"Excuse me," Chance teased as he rolled his eyes. "Where's the trail? It's hard to see anything in this darkness."

"It's over here. It's steep, so walk carefully so you don't slip on the pebbles." Gabe led the way down the winding dirt trail to the moor below. Once everyone reached the bottom, he oriented on Carn Goedog and began to walk west. "It'll take about twenty-five minutes hiking cross country. Be careful not to step into a bog," he cautioned.

"Hold up, Gabe," Chance said as he gripped his cousin's arm. "Here's an idea. Why don't you and I race to Goedog? Hilly, Alden, and Benedict can flit there in an instant. We'll all meet on the top."

"That's a fab idea," Gabe agreed. "Is that okay with everyone?"

"We can't allow that," Benedict bluntly remarked. "That means we'll be separated."

"Only for a matter of seconds," Chance countered. "How could that cause problems?"

"The Yfel only need seconds to steal a magician's soul and magic," Alden affirmed.

"We're cloaked, and Benedict didn't detect any of the Brethren in the area. My cousin and I don't get to use our supernatural speed very often. This would be a perfect opportunity to release some of our pent-up energy."

"No, my friend." Alden gripped Chance's shoulder and smiled gently. "While I appreciate your enthusiasm in embracing your powers, this is not the time. Benedict is correct. We can't allow you to be away from us even for seconds."

Alden continued to grasp Chance's shoulder as he turned to Hilly. "Would you please open a portal that will deposit all of us on the top of that cairn in the distance?"

"Absolutely," Hilly replied.

"This isn't fair, Alden," Chance complained. He pushed forward, but Alden's grip pulled him back.

"I won't sacrifice your life to satisfy your ego," Alden calmly explained. "Run another day when the conditions are not so dangerous."

"Humph," Chance uttered in disgruntled resignation.

Hilly mouthed an incantation as she waved her hands from the sky to the ground. The gaping maw of the entryway loomed dark before them. "Stay together," she warned.

When the portal opened on Carn Goedog, Alden released his grip on Chance who scowled at him.

"Interesting," Alden commented as he walked toward the edge of the hill. "The energy on this cairn is heightened."

"Yes," Benedict agreed. "The atmosphere is electrified as though we are near a vortex or some other energized anomaly."

"Could it be the remnants of the portal?" Hilly asked.

"No," Benedict responded. "There is a powerful energy source nearby." He turned to Alden. "Yfel?"

"No. This is different. There's a primal pulse to the energetic flow as if it emanates from deep beneath us."

A deep grunt followed by several high-pitched whistles pierced the night air.

"What the fuck was that?" Chance asked as he whirled with his hands raised, ready to fight.

"Back to back!" Alden ordered. At his command everyone assembled into a circle with their backs toward each other. Hilly withdrew her sword, Raven. Chance held his blade at the ready, and Gabe unsheathed his triskelion weapon. Eyes darted back and forth searching for danger as the group slowly turned in a circle.

An ear-splitting squeal shattered the stillness.

"Argh!" Chance cried out as he fell to his knees on the ground. He grabbed his right arm and moaned.

"Chance!" Hilly yelled. "What happened?"

"I don't know. There's a burning pain on my arm."

"Let me see," Alden said. Chance rolled up his sleeve. A barely perceptible symbol was burned onto his bicep. Alden ran his finger over the mark and sniffed it. "Blood."

"A triskelion," Gabe gasped. "He's been marked!" Gabe whirled and anxiously searched the hilltop.

"What does the symbol mean?" Alden asked.

"It means we're not alone," Gabe replied. "Chance has been marked by an earth spirit."

Another grunt followed by a series of thundering stomps crashed from above. Pebbles and small rocks rained down on them. The group gazed upward. Twenty feet above, on top of the largest boulder at the apex of the outcropping stood an immense creature.

"'Tis bigger than a house!" Gabe yelled.

It moved quickly between the shadows of the night. A ghastly wail screeched from above, sending shivers down Gabe's spine. "It screams like a banshee!" he cried. "'Tis an entity of the Preseli come to claim a soul I wager."

"I sense no malice in this creature," Benedict calmly observed.

"Agreed," Alden said.

Chance slowly rose. His sleeve was still rolled up and exposed dark trickles running freely down his arm. He raised his arms and closed his eyes. "Are you here for me?" he yelled at the beast above him.

The creature bugled and thumped the earth causing more rocks to fall upon their heads. Chance stepped back as a boulder thudded the dirt where he had been standing.

"Looks like he...or she...is trying to kill you," Hilly noted.

"I don't think so. I don't feel those kinds of emotions from it. I sense a familiarity, like it's family but that doesn't make sense, does it? I'll ask a different way." Chance raised his hands and spoke again. "I'm Chance Easton Drury, son of Chauncey and Jane, son of the earth family and one of the four fated to restore peace to the world. Were you sent to guide me on my journey?"

As if a light switch had been flicked on, a luminescent glow radiated from the creature that stood above them. Green in color, the light shimmered and swirled around a massive white stag. The huge deer snorted and shook its massive head.

"Look at the size of that buck," Gabe marveled. "'Tis a ghostly spirit."

The white stag vanished.

"What does that mean?" Hilly asked.

"Shit. I think I pissed it off," Chance replied.

Several deep grunts erupted from within the cairn in front of Chance. Startled by the sound, he staggered back several steps, his blade at the ready. Hilly and Gabe stood on either side of him, holding their weapons at attention.

As if moved by unseen hands, boulders lifted away from the front of the cairn and were carefully stacked in two piles on either side of the outcropping. After several moments, a luminescent light shone through a crevice between two boulders.

"The monster is coming," Gabe whispered in a trembling voice.

Chance placed a hand on his cousin's shoulder. "Steady, Gabe. I think we'll soon be in the presence of something amazing."

The last two rocky pillars lifted away, leaving behind a widened entranceway. Chance gawked at the cavity, and the white creature emerged and slowly approached him. Six-foot tall at the shoulder and carrying a sixteen-point rack on its head, the large buck bent down until his eye was even with Chance's face.

"It has bright blue eyes," Gabe whispered in awe.

The animal blinked several times before it sniffed Chance's hair and then the triskelion mark on his arm. It opened its mouth and Chance tensed but did not pull away. A long black tongue lolled out of the deer's jaws and the stag gently licked the marking until it faded away.

Fear me not, son of the earth.

"What?" Chance asked shocked by the thought that drifted through his brain. The stag backed up and tilted its head quizzically at Chance.

I've been sent by Lord Yr Wyddfa to welcome his son.

Unaccustomed to mind speaks, Chance struggled to respond using his mind. "I've never spoken via telepathy."

"The stag is communicating with you?" Hilly asked.

"Yeah, in my mind. I don't know how to answer."

"Focus, Chance. Stay calm and try." Hilly patted his hand reassuringly.

The stag stomped its foot. *The earth spirit of Mount Snowdon, Lord Yr Wyddfa, wishes to welcome you to his realm. I am your spirit guide.*

Chance squeezed his eyes to remove all visual distractions. He grimaced as he focused on his response. *My spirit guide?*

Well done, magician. Yes, I am your spirit guide. You seek your crystal, do you not?

Chance nodded.

I will assist you on your journey.

Chance rubbed his arm. *Why did you burn the triskelion into my arm?*

I did not mark you. 'Twas the only way the Lord could identify his son to me. It was his action carried through my voice that left the symbol upon your body.

Chance nodded.

"What do you think they're discussing?" Gabe whispered as he leaned toward Hilly.

"Shh!" she responded.

The white stag disappeared.

Chance opened his eyes and smiled. "Well, that was interesting. I've never chatted with a spirit guide with my mind before."

"Can you tell us what he said?" Hilly asked.

"I can tell you that his name is Hildred, and he will lead us to the crystal."

"So, the crystal is not located on this cairn?" Alden asked.

Chance shook his head. "No, Gabe was right. It's on Carn Menyn. The reason I was driven to come to this hill was so Hildred and I could meet. Carn Goedog possessed the gateway for Hildred to enter into this world." He grinned at Hilly. "It was an arranged date set up by Lord Yr Wyddfa, my earth father."

"The lord of Mount Snowdon is your earth father?" Gabe asked excitedly.

"Apparently. He seared the brand onto my arm so Hildred could identify me."

"We have company," Benedict warned as he pointed into the darkness toward Foel Drygarn. "They just arrived. I noticed the pulse from their teleportation."

Alden and Benedict closed their eyes. After several moments they turned toward the others. "There are three, all Cererian," Alden advised.

"Jake's father is not with them?" Hilly asked.

"Unless he has transformed into a Cererian, Ryan Pierson is not among the group in the distance," Benedict explained.

"Jake's in trouble," Hilly blurted. "I'll alert him."

"I've already advised Darrius of the situation," Benedict stated.

"I'm sure you have, Benedict, but I want to ensure Jake gets that information from me." Hilly stared into the darkness and opened her mind.

Jake, be on alert for your father. The Brethren arrived, and Ryan's not with them. I'm sure he plans to intercept you and the others. Please respond.

Hilly anxiously awaited Jake's reply. After several moments, she turned to the others. "He hasn't responded."

"I reached out to Darrius," Alden said. "Jake is battling his father."

Chapter 19

A Dimensional Battle

JAKE HAD SENSED HIS father lurking on Cadair Idris long before everyone gathered at the glacial lake Llyn Cau. His father's taunts mentally prodded him as he flew toward Wales with Kai. Closing his mind to Ryan's insults only produced a brain splitting migraine as his father's mental tirade slammed against his head like giant fists pounding on his skull.

Talk to me, Jake, his father insisted.

Jake refused, but his father's powers were noticeably stronger. *How much has he changed since he joined the Yfel Brethren?*

Encountering his father had been inevitable. Ryan was intent on stealing the crystal of air to halt the predictions of The Cererian Prophecy and stop the worldwide peace the Yfel yearned to prevent. Killing Kai and Fen would only be a bonus.

Jake reached out to the Sentinel boulder for answers. *Sacred spirit, please guide me as I face this inevitable battle with a man whose powers are unknown.*

My son, what you seek is within you. The earth spirit, bound by the restrictive nature of The Cererian Prophecy, could share only that which was allowed.

Jake was not surprised by the Sentinel's answer. Intuition and instinct were his greatest allies, and the Sentinel alluded to their value in his reply.

Of course, Jake's battle daggers, Cathal and Cadmar, were worthy companions as well.

As he joined Fen, Kai, and Darrius at the lake, Jake decided not to tell anyone about his father—not yet. Not until he confirmed Ryan was on the mountain. Why burden Fen and Kai with the added stress of being stalked by a killer.

Jake remained vigilant as he led the others up the slope. The misty rain and fog complicated matters and made the landscape more treacherous. Jake wondered if Ryan conjured the weather to delay their arrival at the Guardian boulder.

With each step, he grew more bitter toward the man.

Hilly had once described her relationship with the evil Stygian as one mind sharing two bodies. She felt he was always close, probing for information he could use against her and slipping inside her brain and befuddling her thoughts. Banishing him into an interdimensional cell had removed him from her life, but the connection remained because they were bound by blood.

Jake felt the same way about his father, a man he hadn't seen since he was five. Ryan was a magician who betrayed his friends and family in exchange for power and the lust for magic. He had become a monster—neither man nor Cererian—but he was still Jake's father.

Several months earlier, while attending the ritual for the crystal of fire in the Alaskan Mat-Su Valley, Jake had learned of his father's existence from the Sentinel boulder. The news shattered Jake's world, but despite his anguish, he knew the earth spirit had shared the information because he and his father would meet soon.

That day had come.

As Fen rested in the grassy area, Jake had seen a dimensional glimmer, a quick opening of someone flipping between dimensions. Ryan had been snooping on them by jumping between realms. Time was of the essence. "We need to move," Jake ordered as he trudged up the trail.

Once he reached the junction of the paths, the hairs on his neck stood up. Ryan was nearby, having tracked the group like a starving predator. When Jake left to investigate, he found his father perched on the summit.

As Jake approached him, Ryan telepathically reached out, *I will soon kill both of the shamans and steal the crystal of air. I will be well rewarded by the Yfel.* Then he vanished into another dimension.

Seconds later, Jake returned to the group and informed Darrius of the encounter. "I will engage my father once Fen and Kai have safely reached the Guardian," he whispered into the Cererian's ear.

Darrius nodded.

"Over there in the clearing," Jake said as he directed Fen and Kai to the Guardian. As the siblings opened their minds and communicated with the earth spirit, Jake turned to leave.

"Be well," Darrius said. It was an acknowledgement typically reserved for Cererians going to war, and Jake felt humbled by Darrius' simple words.

Jake glanced one more time at Fen and Kai before vanishing in search of his father.

Led by the heat markers left behind by Ryan, Jake moved in and out of dimensions, which spanned space and time. Each world appeared the same with distinct differences. He materialized on the summit, but the boulders glowed technicolor, illuminating various hues from deep within their rocky surfaces. Flipping into another dimension on the summit, the landscape appeared crystalized like sugar granules.

Here I am, boy! Ryan screamed into Jake's brain.

Jake knew his father couldn't be trusted, and even as he stood at the summit, he knew in his gut, his father had betrayed him yet again. He psychically scoured the dimensions sensing for Ryan's whereabouts. The information he received made no sense. Ryan appeared to be everywhere and yet nowhere.

"Doppelgangers," Jake hissed.

Fen and Kai are in danger! Jake tensed at Darrius' urgent message.

Body doubles had led Jake on a wild-goose chase while Ryan stalked the siblings. Jake had left his friends only seconds earlier, but in dimensional travel where time stood still, Ryan could kill them and flee in the blink of an eye.

Jake flipped to the original dimension where he had left the Kemps and stood on a cliff above the Guardian boulder. He detected Fen's fear and Kai's fury. *Stay still!* he messaged to them. *I won't let him hurt you!*

When Jake dropped between his father and Kai, Ryan hesitated. Before Ryan could react, Jake tackled him and pulled him into a parallel universe far away from the Guardian boulder.

They tumbled out onto the icy peak of Penygader, the prominent summit of Cadair Idris. Gales howled as snow and ice swirled around them.

"My sweet boy," Ryan cooed as he regained his footing. "Surely, you're aware I've alerted the others."

Jake circled his father with Cathal and Cadmar gripped in his hands. He sneered and lunged forward to measure his father's reaction.

"You've grown into a fine magician," Ryan placated as he calmly walked out of striking range while holding his sword pointed toward the ground. "I understand from my Brethren friends that you've been marked by the Cererian Prophecy, and you carry the sacred text on your body."

A breath caught in Jake's throat.

Ryan smiled and continued, "Imagine my surprise and delight, that my very own son had been selected to carry the Word." Ryan licked his lips. "Imagine how sweet and satisfying your magic must taste."

Ryan bolted into the air.

Jake launched after him.

The two men raced toward space, fifty miles above Earth. As they flew, Ryan flipped in and out of dimensions. Jake followed, switching between realms on the heels of his father.

They soared through galaxies millions of light years away, then zipped toward the Aurora Borealis as it shimmered above the North Pole. The men flipped into a cubist dimension where the planets appeared as boxes with square moons in orbit before they switched into a realm of complete darkness, then finally returned to their original dimension.

Jake soared close to his father's boots and thrust Cathal forward.

But Ryan halted, turned, and struck Jake in the ribs as he flew by.

Jake inspected his side. A twelve-inch gash sliced along the left side of his ribcage. Blood soaked his shirt. He growled and soared after his father.

Ryan plummeted back to Earth. "You're too slow, my boy!" he yelled as he hurtled toward the summit.

Jake found his father waiting for him atop a steep cliff. "You run away from me like a coward," Jake ridiculed. "Stand and fight. Or are you waiting for the Yfel to handle your battles?"

Ryan's eyes turned onyx. He sneered and his lips pulled away into a ghoulish smile. "I'll teach you respect," he hissed. "You don't talk to your father that way."

Ryan thrust his sword forward so swiftly the movement was blurred.

Jake reacted as quickly, and the two men bounded along the cliffs locked in battle.

From below, Darrius followed the combatants with his mind. He stood on the pathway in deep meditation, fingertips pressed together.

He sensed the siblings approach and opened his eyes.

"Has Jake returned," Fen asked.

"No," Darrius replied.

The battle raged on.

Darrius couldn't interfere. As Observer, he could only watch as the battle unfolded. He closed his eyes and opened his mind. Images flashed in his brain: blood trails spattered each dimension that Jake and Ryan visited as they chased each other, wounded and weakened.

"Where is he?" Fen asked as she gently touched Darrius' hand and immediately pulled away. "Jake needs our help!"

"There is nothing we can do," Darrius replied.

"Where is he, Darrius?" Kai asked. "I may be weak, but I can help."

Darrius placed a hand on Kai's arm. "The Cererian Prophecy has already dictated the outcome. Nothing we do can change it."

"Fuck the Prophecy!" Kai yelled.

"Kai!" Fen intervened. "Darrius is our friend."

"So is Jake. Without him, we won't be able to find the other Guardian boulders." Kai turned to Darrius. "Please tell me where he is so I can help fight."

A flash of lightning illuminated the black sky, followed by a clap of thunder that shook the ground around them.

Darrius bowed his head. "The battle is over."

"How do you know?" Fen asked.

Before Darrius could answer, a blue light flickered high above them, and Jake's body dropped from the sky.

He slammed into the ground face first and didn't move. Cathal and Cadmar stabbed deep into the dirt several feet away.

"Jake!" the siblings cried out together.

Jake lay on his stomach with his head turned to one side. One arm twisted unnaturally over his back while the other remained pinned under his body.

Fen and Kai knelt beside him and gently rolled him over. "Oh, the smell," Fen gasped as she held her nose. "Like roasted meat." Smoke smoldered from what was left of his clothes, which were charred and tattered.

Fen placed two fingers on his throat. "There's a pulse. It's weak, but he's still with us." She hovered her hands over his body and scanned for injuries. "Almost every bone is broken, and he's lost a lot of blood. Kai...Darrius, help me heal Jake."

Fen pulled charred clothing away from Jake's skin and threw them to the ground. Once she removed the remains of his shirt, the full extent of his wounds became apparent. A long, gash trailed down his ribcage, exposing bone and sinew where stab marks peppered his torso.

Blood covered everything.

"Kai, check for injuries on his arms and legs," she requested. "Remove any scraps of clothing you find."

"Darrius, please help me," Fen implored. "My healing energy hasn't returned since working on Kai and the Guardian boulder."

The Cererian didn't move. He remained in meditation with his hands pressed together and his eyes focused on Jake's body as he mouthed a soundless prayer.

"Darrius?" Kai asked. "Please help us. We need to save Jake."

Jake jerked and moaned.

"Jake?" Fen swiped the blood from his eyes. "Can you hear me?"

He jerked again, this time so violently his arms and legs jumped from the ground.

A soft blue light pulsed on his chest, quickly followed by a blue strobe on his stomach, and another one along his ribs.

"What the...?" Kai said. "What's with the lights?"

"The Word is trying to heal itself," Darrius stated as he knelt beside Fen. He ran his hand over Jake's skin, removing the gore and revealing the black tattoos covering his body from his neck to his upper thighs. "Jake carries the written text of the Prophecy on his body," he said pointing to the black markings.

Cleansed of the blood smears, the markings flashed blue one at a time and in no particular pattern. Slow at first, the pulsing quickened until the tattoos flared rhythmically to Jake's heartbeat. "Ryan's attack has disrupted the holy Word," Darrius said. "If we're not able to save Jake, the world will be plunged into chaos."

"Are you saying Jake is the Prophecy?" Fen asked.

"No. Jake is the Chronicle, the vessel for the Prophecy."

Jake began violently shaking.

"Remove the remainder of his clothing...quickly!" Darrius ordered.

The trio removed the remains of his jeans, some portions of which had fused to his skin. Kai and Darrius tugged off his leather boots that had melted around his ankles. Once all clothing had been removed, Jake's skin glistened raw and angry.

"Kai, invoke a gentle rain, one that carries healing droplets from the goddess Airmed," Darrius instructed.

"Airmed?" Kai asked.

"Just do it!" Darrius barked. "We're running out of time!"

Kai raised his hands toward the night sky, closed his eyes, and mouthed inaudible words, an invocation to the deity known as Airmed. Soon, a fine drizzle drenched them all as they huddled around Jake.

Darrius hovered his hands over the body. "This healing ceremony is sacred, and you must *never* talk about this to anyone, not even Hilly or Chance," Darrius said sternly. "Don't even discuss it between yourselves. Is that understood?"

The siblings glanced to one another. Concern etched their faces.

"I promise," Fen said.

"I promise too," Kai added.

"And forget what I told you about Jake and the Prophecy," Darrius added. "Loose words could be his death sentence."

Fen and Kai exchanged worried looks. "We understand," Fen whispered.

"Very well. Let's proceed. Fen, stay at Jake's head and calm his mind as I assist the Word in healing itself. Do not remove your hands until I tell you. Is that clear?"

"Yes, Darrius." Fen sat on the ground, placed her fingers across Jake's forehead and mouthed healing words.

"Kai, join your sister in steadying your friend. Once the healing begins, Jake might become incoherent and combative."

Kai sat at Jake's side and placed a hand on Fen's arm. Energy vibrations rippled between them. Kai bowed his head and focused on calming thoughts for his friend.

Darrius pressed his hands together and bowed over the body acknowledging the sacred text that softly glowed in response. The supernatural rain had washed blood residue from the skin. While simple scratches had healed under the beneficial droplets of Airmed, the deep lacerations revealed black-red clots the size of a fist.

Placing a hand each on Jake's chest and torso, Darrius chanted Cererian healing words and tapped his fingers lightly on the tattoos.

Despite their combined work, the tattoos flashed weakly and erratically, and no longer pulsed to Jake's heartbeat.

"Jake is dying," Darrius warned. "And so is the Prophecy."

Chapter 20

The Betrayal

THE THREE YFEL BRETHREN materialized atop the ancient hill fort, Foel Drygarn.

"This desolate space reminds me of when I first set foot on this planet a millennium ago," Aaron Aningan remarked gesturing toward the massive boulders jumbled around them. "This fort was being used by the local people when I passed through here on a reconnaissance mission."

Aaron strolled among the pillars and touched the rocks, letting his fingers trail along their surface as he walked to the edge of the summit. He paused and stared up into the night sky. "It seems like only yesterday..."

He sighed and turned back to his men. "Balor, were we detected upon landing?"

"Yes. As you commanded, lord," the young man replied. "I allowed our teleportation signature to be noticed for a fraction of a second."

"Excellent. I'm anxious to see their next move."

Aaron pressed his fingertips together and scanned the moor with his mind. Gradually, a thin smile spread across his face. "The sensor on our agent is doing an excellent job. I'm able to look through his eyes and hear with his ears without anyone noticing. Our prey is on Carn Goedog. Besides the magicians, Chance and Hilly, and that meddlesome Benedict, another Cererian by the name of Alden is with them. I'm not familiar with him, but he won't stand in our way since he is bound, as is Benedict, by The Cererian Prophecy and cannot interfere.

"Can we trust the defector?" Cary asked. He stood at attention beside his brother Balor. Both muscular and stocky, the twins dressed in matching dark gray suits in the same manner as their leader. Long white hair cascaded down their shoulders.

Aaron faced the soldier. "He will do my bidding. I have something he wants very much."

"When shall we attack, lord?" Balor asked. His fingers flexed and contracted at his side.

"Patience, my young soldier," Aaron whispered. "You'll have your chance soon." Aaron resumed gazing over the valley toward Carn Goedog. "If all goes according to plan, we will feast on magicians very soon."

Aaron abruptly looked north and closed his eyes.

He chuckled and nodded. "Our comrade, Ryan, has just confirmed the shaman, Jake, is on Cadair Idris with the magicians Kai and Fen, and Darrius."

He had last seen Darrius in Aningan, Alaska when Darrius arranged to have him arrested and taken back to Ceres for exploiting and killing the inhabitants of the town. Aaron had been imprisoned for only a few months before he brokered a deal with the two young Cererians, Cary and Balor who yearned to be Yfel Brethren and with the rogue magician, Ryan who had mysteriously visited him in his cell unbeknownst to the guards.

The two Cererians had been easily influenced but Ryan was unpredictable. He possessed powers Aaron didn't quite understand. Regardless, the four men shared a common goal: to find and kill the four chosen magicians along with the shaman, Jake.

Aaron absently licked his lips and mused. *How savory that magic will taste. Stygian would be proud. And if my plan unfolds the way I've designed it, Stygian will soon be free and will reward me greatly.*

Aaron gazed across the moor again and reached out to the defector. *Distract them. I will be paying Hilly a visit very soon.*

A vibration raced across the moor and throughout the numerous cairns that peppered the landscape. Only the magical populations and nature's spirits could sense the gentle shockwave that passed over them like a soft whisper.

The energy wave carried the Guardian boulder's message that the Crystal of Air had been successfully placed upon its seat of power.

"Kai and Fen were successful!" Hilly shouted. She clamped her hand over her mouth and glanced toward Foel Drygarn. "Sorry," she whispered.

"Yes," Alden nodded. "The second crystal has been restored."

The white stag snorted and pawed the ground with his hoof.

"Hildred is anxious to show me the location of the crystal," Chance said as he stroked the buck's muscular neck. "Now that Kai has united his crystal, the pressure is on for me to find mine."

Benedict gazed at the nearby hill fort. "Despite our cloaking, any movement on our part will be detected by Aaron and his men," he warned.

"We can't stay here," Chance said. "I need to get over to Carn Menyn as soon as possible."

"I could cause a diversion," Hilly blurted.

"No, you must stay with us," Alden emphasized. "Aaron would love to get his hands on you."

"How about me?" Gabe asked. "I'm no value to the Yfel, but if they chase me, that might give you enough time to find the crystal."

Benedict and Alden faced each other and discussed the option telepathically. Finally, they parted and faced the others. Gabe searched their faces.

"Benedict and I have discussed the matter," Alden began. "There are merits to your proposal, Gabe. It's urgent that Chance finds his crystal and that we're able to depart before Aaron and his team can interfere—"

"I have an idea," Chance interrupted. "Since Carn Menyn is far away and Carn Breseb is close by, why don't I switch the cairns? I'll use my superpower and move the mountains." Alden gazed across the valley and studied the two hilltops and then looked back to Chance.

"That might work," Alden said. "Benedict, what do you think?"

The Cererian looked toward Foel Drygarn. "How fast is the process?" he asked.

"Seconds," Alden replied.

"The movement will be detected by the Yfel. But if Gabe can also create a diversion while Chance is switching the cairns, it might work."

Gabe grinned and rubbed his hands together. "I'll be happy to help."

"All activity must be synchronized," Benedict continued. "Gabe, what diversion will you perform?"

"I'll run swiftly across the moor to Carn Menyn. That will draw their attention," he answered.

"If I was Aaron, I'd only send one soldier after you since they will quickly detect you are not Chance," Alden interjected.

"Then that leaves you with only two Brethren to deal with," Gabe replied. "With Hilly and the two of you, you can easily handle the other two. Once the Cererian reaches me, I'll flick back to the cottage."

As the group discussed the details of their plan three black shadows silently glided across the darkened sky. Alden and Benedict glanced upward.

"Did you see something?" Hilly asked.

"Something flew overhead," Alden replied.

"It was only for a second," Benedict added. The Cererian squinted at Foel Drygarn. "Very odd. The Yfel are no longer cloaking their whereabouts. It's as though they want us to know they are nearby."

"I'm suspicious by that action," Alden warned.

"There are still three individuals on that hilltop," Benedict observed. "And they appear to be observing us."

Gabe studied Alden and Benedict as they chatted about the Yfel Brethren. He, too, had seen the shadows sweep by overhead but said nothing...he wouldn't dare. A slight movement by the entrance to the cairn snatched his attention. Out of the corner of his eye, he saw Hilly sneaking quietly around the massive boulders while turning her head back and forth as if listening for something.

Gabe opened his mouth to say something and then bit his bottom lip and stared at the ground. He clenched his fists at his side and turned to face the moor. A single tear trailed down his cheek.

Hilly was ten feet from the others but was completely hidden by towering bluestone pillars that framed the entrance to the cairn. Something had captured her attention, and she was intent on finding it. It wasn't so much an audible sound, but a soothing vibration within her brain that compelled her forward.

Hilly.

The call was familiar. One she had heard on Mount Denali's slopes. Her heart quickened anticipating an encounter with her earth mother, Denali. She arrived at a crevice running the length of a thirty-foot rock, just wide enough for her to shimmy through.

She squeezed through the opening. Her jacket snagged on the rough edges, and she abandoned it so she could reach the other side. Once she emerged, she stood on the edge of a cliff sixty feet from the heather below.

Hilly.

Her intuition pulled at her. Doubt filled her mind. "Mother?" she whispered softly as she peered into the inky void that stretched before her.

No reply.

The hair on the back of her neck stood up, and she tensed. *That never happened in the presence of Denali*, she thought as she backed up toward the crack in the boulder.

CAW!

Hilly stopped and scanned the rocks above her. It was a raven.

A shadow crossed in front of her, its movement detected only because the stars blinked, their light momentarily blotted out as the shape passed by.

Gravel cascaded down the rock face.

Hilly shuddered and looked up.

A giant raven perched on a boulder above and peered at her with glinting eyes.

CAW!

Hilly smiled, recognizing the bird as her spirit animal bestowed upon her by Denali. She yearned to be with the corvid, but her instincts held her back.

CAW!

It ruffled its feathers and stretched its neck toward her. Hilly extended her hand upward toward the black bird as she mentally messaged, *Did the mother send you to me?*

Her fingers lightly trailed along the curve of its beak but as she reached the ebony feathers framing its face the bird snapped its bill around her arm and launched into the air at such a speed Hilly's senses dulled.

Fighting unconsciousness, she beat at the raven's legs and wings with her free hand to no avail. The stars blurred as the bird sped northward at a blinding speed.

Darkness descended upon Hilly's mind, and she knew she was passing out. With one final burst of energy, she screamed telepathically, *Help me!*

An evil thought drifted through her foggy brain. *No one will hear you, Hilly. I've cloaked us. Your cries will fall on deaf ears.*

Hilly shivered. She knew that voice.

It belonged to Aaron Aningan.

"Hilly!" Jake screamed as he bolted into a sitting position.

"Easy, Jake," Darrius soothed as he helped guide the shaman back to the ground.

Fen cradled Jake's head and stroked her fingers across his brow as she spoke magical healing words.

"What do you think that was about?" Kai asked.

Darrius fluttered his hands across Jake's naked body, which began to show some signs of healing along his arms and legs where white scars snaked like zippers.

"Darrius?" Kai pressed. "Was that a feverish outburst or could Hilly be in trouble?"

The Cererian kept his head low and chanted while dispelling healing magic upon the shaman.

"Darrius?" Kai asked again.

Darrius stopped and glared at Kai. After several tense moments, Darrius spoke. "Continue your work, shaman. Healing Jake is your priority. Nothing else."

Darrius bowed his head and continued with his conjuring words.

Kai and Fen exchanged anxious looks before Fen jutted her chin, encouraging Kai to continue healing their friend. She mouthed encouragement. *All will be okay.*

Kai bowed his head and mouthed inaudible words. Fen didn't join him right away. She watched Darrius and her brother as they worked on Jake who twitched and mumbled. She knew Hilly was in danger and there was nothing she could do, except ensure Jake survived.

"Hey, where's Hilly?" Chance asked.

Alden and Benedict whirled.

"Hilly's missing?" Benedict asked, a hint of uneasiness in his tone.

Alden dashed to the tumble of nearby boulders.

Gabe didn't move. He faced Foel Drygarn with his shoulders hunched and his hands in his pockets.

"Who saw her last?" Benedict asked.

"I remember her asking about what you saw in the sky," Chance replied. "But then Hildred became antsy, and I had to calm him down."

"Gabe, did you see Hilly?" Benedict asked.

"Aye," he answered without turning around.

"Where?" Benedict pressed.

"She whar over by them rocks," Gabe replied as he pointed at the cairn entrance. He swiped at his eyes and stared at the ground.

Alden returned holding something in his hands.

"What's that?" Chance asked.

"Hilly's jacket." Alden held it up. "Found it by a crevice between two pillars at the cairn entrance."

"Gabe said he saw Hilly over there," Benedict reported.

"Oh?" Alden faced Gabe who stared at the ground. "What was she doing?"

Gabe shifted his feet and dug his hands deeper into his pockets.

"Gabe?" Alden grabbed the young man's chin and forcibly lifted it until he could peer into his eyes. The two men stared at each other while Alden's eyes pulsed and flashed. After several moments, he withdrew his hand. Gabe bowed his head while Alden strode to the edge of the hill. "Benedict, a word, please."

The Cererians stood shoulder to shoulder as they conversed telepathically.

Hilly has been taken by the Yfel, Alden explained. *I probed Gabe's mind and found that he is being manipulated by Aaron.* Alden pointed toward Foel Drygarn. *Those are their doppelgangers staring at us. Perfect duplicates of the three Cererians who shapeshifted into ravens and flew right over our head.*

How did we miss that? Benedict replied.

I can't explain it, Alden responded. *We have failed at protecting Hilly.*

I will alert Darrius, Benedict stated as he bowed his head and pressed his fingertips together.

Benedict sighed as he faced Alden. *The Yfel have been busy. Jake lies near death after battling his father, Ryan. Apparently, the shaman heard Hilly's cry for help and sat up during the healing ritual.*

Why did we not hear her? Alden asked.

Perhaps Aaron's magic has evolved. Jake may have heard her since he hovers near the veil of death. Darrius, Fen, and Kai are focused on healing the shaman and can't assist in locating Hilly. It falls on our shoulders. And we must ensure Chance finds his crystal.

We must divide our resources, Alden assessed. *I'll remain with Chance as he searches for the gem and then guide him safely back to the sanctuary of the cottage. You search for Hilly, and I will join you as quickly as possible.*

What about Gabe? Benedict asked as he peered over his shoulder at the young man. *He is not to be trusted. Everyone's life is in jeopardy as long as he lives. Aaron will use him like a puppet.*

Agreed. Alden turned around. "Gabe, look at me." The man trembled as he gazed up at Alden.

"What's going on?" Chance asked as he stepped beside his cousin.

"This does not concern you, Chance," Alden replied, shoving Chance aside.

"Hey!" Chance rushed Alden, but the Cererian raised a hand and Chance lifted into the air held aloft by invisible forces. He struggled against the unseen hands as he dangled six feet above the ground.

"Do not interfere, Chance. Do you understand?"

Chance wrestled harder and kicked but couldn't break free of Alden's invisible grip. Alden swept his hand to the side and Chance flew several feet away and landed against some boulders. He fought to stand but was pinned to the ground.

Satisfied that Chance was secure, Alden returned to Gabe. "Gabe, we know Aaron is using you to spy on us."

"What?" Chance sputtered as he rolled on the ground trying to break free.

Gabe gazed at his cousin with tears in his eyes. He shivered and chewed his bottom lip.

"You can no longer be trusted. Our lives and mission are in jeopardy because of your deception. We cannot allow you to be in our midst, nor can we allow you to go back to the cottage."

"What are you saying, Alden?" Chance yelled. "You can't kill him! He's family." Chance struggled harder.

"I had me reasons," Gabe whispered. He looked at Chance. "I meant ye no harm, cousin. They only wanted Hilly."

"It's true?" Chance asked. "You betrayed us?"

"Aye." Gabe hung his head. "I only wanted me mum back."

"You said she was dead."

"Aye. That I did. But the Yfel have her."

"Where are they holding your mother?" Alden asked.

Gabe silently shook his head and sniffed back tears. "I don't know."

"Alden, is there another way to handle this?" Chance asked.

"Your sister's life is at stake because of this traitor," Benedict answered sharply. "You waste time discussing this matter. Gabe must be dispatched, immediately." He turned to Alden. "Do your duty, brother."

Alden nodded and raised his hand toward Gabe. "This will not be painful."

"Wait, you can't do this!" Chance yelled out. "He's kin!"

Alden's hand fell on Gabe's head and the man disappeared.

"You reduced him to dust, you bastard!" Chance yelled.

Alden casually brushed debris from his suit. "I did no such thing. Your cousin is suspended in a different dimension. He still lives."

"You should have killed him," Benedict rebuked.

"Perhaps, but at least the situation has been handled for now." Alden turned to Chance. "You and I will search for your crystal while Benedict searches for Hilly. Time is truly of the essence." He turned to Benedict. "Be well, brother. I will inform you when I can join you."

"Be well, Alden." Benedict abruptly disappeared.

"Chance, we should get started," Alden instructed as he strode to the edge of the hill and gazed across the moor. He waved his hand, releasing the force field holding Chance to the ground.

"Thanks for not killing Gabe," Chance said as he joined the Cererian.

"Death is still a possibility. But banishing him was the easiest decision considering our urgent timeline. Now, let's find your crystal."

Chapter 21

Hilly's Torment

THE THREE RAVENS FLEW north toward Yr Wyddfa.

We have shaken the world by stealing the Firewalker witch, Aaron telepathically boasted to his soldiers. *Soon Lord Stygian will be released.*

Hilly dangled from Aaron's beak as he rocketed toward the summit of the mountain also known as Mount Snowdon. Having blacked out, her eyes had rolled back into her head and a blue tint spread across her skin.

Minutes after taking Hilly, Aaron and his henchmen landed near the peak. When their feet touched the ground, they shapeshifted back into their Cererian form. Aaron kicked Hilly, and she rolled like a rag doll along the ground.

"Balor, bring the witch into that cave," Aaron barked. "Cary, seal the area with cloaking magic. Be quick about it!"

Balor lifted Hilly into his arms and carried her inside as Aaron followed behind. "Over there," Aaron ordered as he pointed toward a large rock. "Bind her to that boulder."

Balor held Hilly's body against the rock as he mouthed binding magic. Instantly her body spread eagle against the boulder, her hands and feet held by an invisible force.

"Step aside, Balor," Aaron directed. He faced Hilly and lightly stroked her lips with his index finger until her mouth grew faint and disappeared."

"The cloaking magic is dispensed, Lord," Cary advised as he joined the others in the cave.

"Good," Aaron replied. "Now, no one will find her, and no one will hear her." He stepped back and scrutinized his captive. "To think that such a pitiful creature could ensnare Stygian. I'll soon remedy that!"

"Lord, did you hear the Guardian boulder's message?" Cary asked.

"Idiot!" Aaron screamed, slapping the soldier across his face. The Cererian careened into a nearby wall. Cary regained his footing and held his cheek, stained with a crimson imprint of Aaron's hand.

"Of course I heard it," Aaron raged. He clenched his fists and menaced the soldier. "It means Ryan has failed, and the second crystal has been restored."

Aaron eyed Hilly. "That means we will need to expedite our plan for the witch."

Jake gasped and sputtered. His eyes bulged, and he clawed at the sky.

"Roll him over, quickly," Darrius ordered.

Fen and Kai pushed Jake onto his side right as he vomited black bile. He retched several times while Fen rubbed his lower back. Her fingers inadvertently brushed one of the tattoos

She snatched her hand away.

"Ow!" she cried out.

"What happened?" Kai asked.

"One of those symbols bit me."

"His body is healing," Darrius observed. "The Prophecy is protective of the Word, and you must have come in contact with an important passage." He studied the shaman as he lay panting on his side. "You and Kai have witnessed an event no one is allowed to see. The Prophecy and Jake share a body. The tattoos are alive as much as your friend or you and me. To look upon the sacred symbols is blasphemous."

"We were healing Jake, not being disrespectful," Kai argued.

Darrius held up a hand. "I did not accuse you of sacrilege. I am informing you of the Word's importance. Now, I have a dilemma." Darrius touched Jake's temple, causing the shaman to shudder and mutter.

"What's your dilemma?" Fen asked.

"You and Kai can't tell anyone about what you witnessed today—not even Hilly or Chance. The only way I can ensure that will never happen is to erase your memories."

"No way, Darrius!" Kai stood and glared at the Cererian. "Fen and I can keep Jake's secret."

"Under pain of torture?" Darrius probed.

"What do you mean?" Fen asked.

"If the Yfel capture you, they have methods for extracting information, and if that occurred, Jake's life and the existence of the Prophecy will be compromised."

"They...won't...tell," Jake sputtered in a hoarse whisper as he lay on his side.

Darrius looked down at the shaman. "You can't take that chance, Jake."

"We won't tell," Fen asserted. "Kai and I would never betray our friend." She gently stroked Jake's forehead, and he sighed.

"Have faith in us, Darrius," Kai added. "Fenny and I can be discreet when we need to be."

"They'll be fine," Jake croaked as he struggled to sit up. "I know they won't talk about what happened today."

"What happened?" Kai asked winking at his friend.

"Very well," Darrius said. "I will not erase your memories, but I will be watching."

"Hilly's...in...trouble," Jake said haltingly. He spit phlegm onto the ground.

"She's been taken by the Yfel," Darrius revealed as he wrapped a cloth around Jake's shoulders. "You need more time. The Word is still healing."

"There's no time," Jake replied in a husky voice. "She needs my—our help." Jake sat hunched with his chin on his chest. He wheezed slightly.

"I heard her cry out," Fen blurted. Kai and Darrius stared at her. "When Jake sat up and screamed her name. I, too, heard her cry for help."

"Interesting," Darrius replied. "You and Jake were the only ones who heard her. Not even Benedict or Alden knew she was in trouble."

"How?" Kai asked.

"Jake was on the threshold of death," Darrius replied. "And Fen...you're a healer who hovers between the veils of the dying and the living. In the realm Aaron has taken Hilly, only those who walk in the shadows can hear her."

"I need to go to Hilly." Jake struggled to stand, then fell back to the ground. He stretched his hand toward Darrius. "Help me up, Darrius. Get me to my feet."

The Cererian grabbed Jake around the chest and lifted him effortlessly.

"Where are my clothes?" Jake asked. "I can't leave like this." He dropped the cloth and exposed his naked body. Ashen scars snaked everywhere. Most of the tattoos were black and no longer flashing, but a few of the symbols near his chest pulsed a somber gray, indicating their healing was ongoing.

Darrius snapped his fingers and a pair of jeans, a button-down shirt, and a pair of boots appeared on the ground.

"Those look like the clothes Jake was wearing earlier," Kai noted. "Perhaps when this adventure is over, you can whip up some new clothes for me, Darrius." Kai wiggled his eyebrows at the Cererian who stared back unamused.

"They are exact duplicates," Darrius replied as he handed them to Jake and steadied him as he got dressed. Jake's fingers cramped while buttoning his shirt, so Fen took over. While fastening the buttons, she gazed into his bloodshot eyes, the sclera completely red. "Jake, is your father dead?"

The muscles in Jake's jaw bunched. Finally, he released a long sigh. "I don't know, Fen. I honestly don't know how I even got back to this dimension. All I know is I don't sense him around here."

"What happened?" Kai asked.

"Ryan and I battled each other through different dimensions...so many parallel worlds that I lost count. Time was measured in nanoseconds. But we can talk about that later. Right now, I need to find Hilly."

Jake stretched his head to the right and then to the left. He lifted his arms up and down. "I'm a bit stiff, but I think the kinks will work out once I get going."

"You're not ready," Darrius cautioned. "The Word is not fully healed."

"I need to leave whether it is ready or not. I can't let anything happen to Hilly." He frantically searched the ground. "Where's Cathal and Cadmar? Did they come back with me?"

"Easy, Jake," Kai said as he stepped forward with the battle swords. "They dropped out of the sky like you did." Jake looked at Kai with a puzzled look. "Long story, Jake, we'll discuss it over a drink once this is said and done."

"Where do we go?" Fen asked.

Jake smiled gently and placed a hand on Fen's shoulder. "*You* are going nowhere. The healer needs to remain out of harm's way."

"Fen, you'll remain with me," Darrius instructed.

"You've changed your tune about me leaving?" Jake asked the Cererian.

"I don't think you should go in your state, but I can't stop you," Darrius replied. "I'll send Kai with you."

"You will?" Kai asked, his eyebrows arched.

"Yes," Darrius responded. "You and Kai will travel to where you think Hilly is located. Fen will stay with me in case Hilly calls out again. That way I'll know where to go. Where will you start?"

Jake closed his eyes and drew in a long breath. He recalled Hilly's cry for help. He analyzed the pitch, the distance, the emotions. When he opened his eyes, he firmly announced, "I'm going to the summit of Yr Wyddfa. Aaron is holding her there."

"Very well," Darrius commented. "Be well, Jake. Be well, Kai."

Jake clamped his hand on Darrius' shoulder. "Be well, Darrius." He turned to Kai. "Come on, brother. Be prepared to fly fast."

The two men launched into the night sky and disappeared.

Hilly awoke to a distorted world. She struggled to see, but her eyes wouldn't focus. With her strength sapped, her head lolled side to side. When she tried to speak, her mouth wouldn't function.

She grunted in frustration.

"Ah, the witch is awake," Aaron purred as he slid a finger down the side of her face. She pulled her head away, and he chuckled. "No sense in trying to scream, you need a mouth to make noises." He jabbed a finger into her face.

Clarity filled her mind, and her eyes widened in fear and anger. She thrashed against the invisible restraints pinning her to the boulder.

"There, there, magician, it will soon be over," Aaron cooed as he leaned closer and stroked her hair.

She recoiled. The heat and stench of his breath sickened her.

What do you want! she screamed telepathically.

A twisted grin spread on Aaron's face as he pressed his forehead against hers. "I want Stygian," he hissed. "And you will deliver him to me."

Aaron pulled away and brushed her cheek. His finger trailed down the curve of her jaw and then down her neck. He toyed with the fringe of the scarf she wore around her neck before he yanked it off revealing the blue opal.

The nugget nestled securely in the notch in Hilly's neck. "What do we have here? A gift from Denali? Is this the stone that quiets the voices?" Aaron circled the base of the gem with his finger.

Hilly shivered at his touch and goose bumps rose all over her body.

Aaron placed his hand on her forehead and shoved her head back. With his other hand, he gripped the blue gemstone. "What do you think would happen if I removed this beauty?" he teased.

Hilly's eyes widened. She twisted under his hold.

Aaron dug his fingers into the skin around the gemstone, his fingernails penetrating a quarter inch into her neck, and he ripped out the blue opal.

Aaron held the jewel in front of Hilly's face. "Behold the beginning of your end."

Once the nugget was removed, voices of all the murdered souls Hilly had inhaled during her battle with Everild raced forward screaming for help. The blue opal had quieted the restless souls but now their pleas reached a piercing pitch. Blood trickled from her ears as the mournful howls echoed in her head.

She swung her head side to side. In desperation, she thumped her head on the boulder. Anything to quiet the screams.

"There, there, my little Firewalker," Aaron soothed as he gripped her head in both hands. "I will replace the opal once you have released Lord Stygian. The voices will be quiet once again if you'll only give me what I want." He leaned forward and kissed her forehead before he turned around and walked away.

"Just scream when you're ready to release Stygian," he called out.

Chapter 22

Crystal of Earth

ALDEN STOOD ON THE edge of the cairn and faced the moors, head bowed.

Chance observed the Cererian. Alden's signature bowler hat had vanished in the rush to find Hilly and streaks of gray matter—the result of the wind and rain—coated his black suit. A slight smile softened Alden's face.

The Cererian hummed a melody and rocked gently.

A cockeyed grin popped up on Chance's face. Minutes earlier Alden had shoved him to the ground and exiled Gabe to another dimension. Now, he appeared peaceful and harmless.

"This is what Cererians do to center ourselves," Alden whispered.

"Sorry. I didn't mean to disturb you."

"No need to apologize." Alden glanced at Chance and then resumed his reverie. "I enjoy your company."

They stood in silence.

Alden's eyes flashed open. "Darrius is on his way. He's bringing Fen with him."

"Does that mean Jake is healed? Or does that mean he died?"

"The shaman lives. He and Kai are flying to Yr Wyddfa to find Hilly."

Gravel crunched behind them, and the men whirled.

"Chance!" Fen cried as she ran to her brother.

Chance threw his arms around her and lifted her into the air before carefully setting her back down. "Hilly's been taken by the Yfel," he said solemnly.

"I know," Fen replied. "I heard her cry for help."

"What?" Alden exclaimed.

"Yes," Darrius affirmed. "Both Jake and Fen heard Hilly's cry. Nobody else did. I can only ascertain that it's because Jake and Fen are both closer to the veil of death. The realm Aaron has imprisoned Hilly must be in the land of the shadows."

"At least you and Kai were successful with the crystal," Chance added.

"We would have never found the Guardian boulder without Jake's help," Fen replied.

"How is Jake?"

"The shaman has left with your brother against my wishes," Darrius interjected. He turned to Alden and whispered, "The Word is not completely healed."

"What Word? What are you talking about?" Chance asked.

Darrius glanced at Fen who looked away. "It is our word for something sacred," Darrius explained.

"Oh, I see," Chance replied. "It's Cererian jargon."

"Something like that. And it does increase the urgency for what we need to do. Where do you stand on searching for your crystal?"

"Chance will switch Carn Menyn with Carn Breseb to expedite his search," Alden explained. "But we must deal with the doppelgangers on Foel Drygarn." He pointed toward the hill fort in the distance.

"Will they attack?" Fen asked as she stared at the three figures who gazed back at her.

"Most definitely," Darrius replied. "The imposters will act in the exact manner of their host forms—Aaron and his soldiers. Any departure on our part will compel them into action."

"The Prophecy prevents us from killing the doppelgangers, but we can distract them," Alden added. "While Chance and Hildred search for the crystal, we will need to create a ruse."

"Who's Hildred?" Fen asked.

Chance took Fen's hand and led her to the cairn's entrance where the immense white stag rested. As Chance approached, the buck snorted awake and stamped his hoof.

"Oh, my goodness!" Fen exclaimed. "He's so beautiful!"

Chance stroked the buck's muscular neck and invited Fen to join him. "Come meet Hildred," he urged.

Fen reached up to Hildred's muzzle and gently rubbed the sensitive skin around his nose and lips. The animal didn't pull away. Instead, he lowered his head and allowed Fen to slide her hands up to his ears and tickle the base of his antlers. She massaged his forehead and hummed.

"You're putting him to sleep," Chance observed.

"He's such a lovely stag. Where did he come from?"

"Lord Yr Wyddfa sent him to me. He's my spirit animal, and he'll help me find the family crystal."

"What a clever buck you are," Fen said as she stroked both sides of its face. Satisfied grunts filled the air as the creature's eyes slowly opened and closed.

"Lord Yr Wyddfa sent this stag?" Darrius asked.

"Yes," Chance replied.

"He is your earth father as Denali is Hilly's earth mother," Darrius stated. "He is aware of the Prophecy and has chosen to aid on your behalf. This is very fortunate. It means you'll find the family crystal much faster."

Darrius pressed his fingertips together in front of his chest.

Several moments passed.

"Benedict has located Jake and Kai," he announced. "They are searching the summit for Hilly." He turned to Chance. "It's time for you to put your plan into action."

"I'm ready. But what about our unwanted guests?" Chance jutted his chin at the doppelgangers.

"I have an idea." Fen strode to the edge of the summit. "I have a special power I recently discovered on my trip to Denali. Chance, you probably have it too, but I know Hilly, Kai, and I possess the ability to intensify our magic, especially when we're all together."

"How will that help?" Darrius asked.

"If the doppelgangers move, I will combine my energy with Chance's and stop them before they can reach Chance."

"What do you mean, 'combine my energy with Chance's'?" Chance demanded. "I'll be a little busy searching for the crystal."

Fen chuckled. "Chance, you're projecting energy even as you stand there not doing a thing. I'll take what I can and combine it with my power." She glanced at the Cererians. "Believe me, I can really do this."

"Why don't I know about this special ability?" Darrius asked.

"You don't know everything about us, Darrius," she replied. "As you've stated, the Prophecy doesn't divulge all the details." She grinned wide. "Don't worry, it will work. I promise. And, unlike you and Alden, I can kill the imposters if needed."

"Brother, I say we give it a chance," Alden added. "If it doesn't work as Fen wants, you and I will dissuade them as much as possible."

"Very well," Darrius responded. "But don't kill the imposters, Fen. If you dispatch them, Aaron will sense they've vanished and may send his soldiers to investigate."

"Move your mountains, Chance," Alden directed as he nodded toward Carn Menyn.

Chance led Hildred to the edge of the hilltop. "Once I've moved the cairns, Hildred and I will disappear."

Remembering what he'd been taught, Chance drew in several deep breaths to steady his mind and then raised a hand toward Carn Menyn and another hand toward Carn Breseb. He closed his eyes and probed the depth and breadth of both mounds with his mind. He envisioned the vastness of the living communities on each cairn, from the microorganisms to the mammals. Taking care to maintain the integrity of their existence, he rotated his left hand in the air. Carn Menyn slowly rose into the dark sky. Simultaneously, he turned his right hand and raised Carn Breseb from the moor. The hills passed each other quickly and settled on the ground in their new locations.

The process took less than three seconds.

Chance scrambled onto Hildred's back. "Wish me luck!" he called out as he and the stag vanished.

"Where did they go?" Fen asked.

"Hildred has taken him to Carn Menyn to search for the crystal," Alden replied. "Don't worry, he'll be fine."

"Look!" Darrius called out. "The doppelgangers have mobilized. They are flying to intercept Chance on Carn Menyn."

"We'll see about that!" Fen declared as she faced the imposters. She held her hands toward the three approaching forms. "Come on, Chance, give me some of your energy," she uttered as she clenched her jaws and grimaced.

A pulse of white energy radiated from her outstretched fingers, spreading up her hands and arms until her entire body was illuminated with a lustrous glow. As the doppelgangers drew near, Fen threw her hands outward, deploying a bright white bubble that rocketed toward them. The dome of light encased the men who ceased moving the moment the energy touched them. With the three imposters safely ensnared, Fen maneuvered them back to Carn Goedog and settled them onto the summit.

"It will be less taxing on my power if I keep them on the ground near me instead of in the air at a distance," said. "Now, if Chance can find his crystal before I tire maintaining this energetic web around my hostages..."

The white stag materialized beside a large boulder jutting from the summit on Carn Menyn. Chance jumped to the ground and tripped over a large rock. When he righted himself, he realized the entire hilltop was littered with bluestone fragments of varying sizes. He collected several smaller specimens and stuffed them into his pockets.

The stag trotted toward the center of the cairn. He pawed the ground and stared back at Chance.

"Is that where I'll find the crystal?" Chance asked.

The beast shook his massive antlers and responded telepathically. *The precious one slumbers in the carn's bosom.*

Those are the words Sybil shared with me, Chance responded. *She highlighted that passage in the Family Records.* He glanced around. *I don't see anything.*

Hildred reared up and stomped the ground with such force the cairn shook violently. *That which you seek lies in the bosom...it slumbers underground.*

Chance stared at the ground where the animal impatiently paced. *Oh, I get it. I suppose I need to dig for it, or will you help me?*

Hildred snorted. Strands of thick mucus shot from his snout and splattered Chance's chest. The beast grunted and shook his head.

I'll take that as a no, Chance said as he removed his shirt, which was now slick with snot.

He knelt in the dirt. Raising one arm, he jerked his elbow skyward with the fingers and hand pointing downward like an arrow. With a strong thrust, he knifed his fingers into the dirt like the point of a blade. His fingers crumpled against a slab of rock two feet below the surface.

"Ow!" he howled. He shoved his wounded hand into his armpit and cursed under his breath. When the throbbing subsided, he held up his hand and wiggled the fingers. "Bruised and bloodied but not broken."

Hildred paced nervously and bugled.

Chance glanced toward Carn Goedog. Fen had her captives pinned to the ground. Only minutes had passed, but he knew he had to work fast.

Okay, Hildred, let me try another way. Chance stood and planted his feet on the ground while hovering over the small hole he had created. Cupping his hands like miniature shovels, he dug into the ground at a furious pace like a dog determined to find a buried bone.

His supernatural strength and speed made it so Chance was able to dig rapidly, creating a mound of dirt ten feet behind him within seconds. Any boulders he encountered were stacked neatly on the surface. Once the hole was large enough for him to stand in, he jumped down and dug again, flinging arcs of soil between his legs.

A pile of debris rose into the night sky.

Twenty feet below the surface, he encountered a four-foot-thick bluestone pillar. A circular niche had been carved out of its middle. The boulder sat vertically in the hole with ten feet of it exposed. *I reckon there's at least that much still underground,* Chance commented to Hildred.

The buck snorted and stomped the ground.

With no moonlight to illuminate the darkness, Chance used his fingers to feel along the stone and explore the spherical nook. He deftly brushed off debris as he probed the smooth edges of the hole.

The entrance is too tiny for my thick fingers, he told Hildred.

The stag nodded and stamped the earth. *You must try. The precious one lies within the bluestone. Hurry!*

Relying on his instinct, Chance plunged his hand into the hole and wedged a finger into the recess. As he wiggled it around, he felt a sharp point. He withdrew his hand. *I felt something pointy.*

Chance repositioned himself in the shaft to allow more room to maneuver his hand back into the pillar. Twisting his arm and rotating his hand he enlarged the nook's opening to three inches, allowing two fingers to enter. They instantly contacted a faceted nugget.

Chance stopped and panted. *I found it, Hildred!*

Steadying the object with the two fingers, he twisted his thumb into the recess until it touched the gem's hard surface.

He pinched the small object and extracted it from its sacred sanctuary. Once his hand emerged from the nook, he closed his fist over the nugget. He squeezed hard for fear the tiny jewel would tumble out and be lost in the darkness.

But he was curious.

He opened his hand and gently explored the stone with the fingers of his other hand. There were four smooth, primary sides and a crown peppered with miniature facets.

I have it, Hildred. I'm coming back out!

He clenched the jewel, then squatted, and propelled upward using his powerful legs. He shot several feet above the shaft opening and landed softly on the cairn surface.

Chance extended his hand toward Hildred, his fingers unfurling like flower petals as he held the stone under the stag's nose.

Is this the Crystal of Earth? Chance asked.

Yes, the beast replied.

Chance deposited the gem into a small, leather pouch slung around his neck.

Now I need to replace the rocks and dirt.

Mindful that the cairn needed to be reconstructed in the precise manner it originally existed, Chance worked swiftly until the hole was replaced with the dirt and boulders as it was before.

He was filthy.

A fine layer of dirt covered his naked upper body. Brown furrows creased his forehead and muddy lines trailed away from his eyes. He brushed off what dirt he could before replacing his shirt and carefully tucking the pouch inside.

Now would be a great time for a shower, Chance joked as he searched the dark sky for rain clouds.

Hildred bobbed his head. *I will take you back to Carn Goedog but then I must leave you. The Lord beckons me.* The stag nudged Chance to climb onto its back.

Once Chance mounted, they vanished and reappeared atop Carn Goedog. Chance jumped off, and the massive buck instantly disappeared.

"I was successful!" Chance yelled as he approached the others. "Now I need to move the cairns back to their original locations."

"About time," Fen snarled through clenched teeth. Sweat poured down her reddened face. "I don't think I can hold this energy field much longer."

"Can you redirect them back to Foel Drygarn?" Darrius inquired. "If you can do that while Chance moves the cairns, there might be a chance the imposters won't be aware we moved anything at all."

"It's worth a try," Fen responded.

Chance held his hands toward the two hilltops and nodded at Fen. "Let's get this done, Fenny." While Chance moved the two mounds back to their original locations, Fen redirected the gelatinous energy ball encasing the three doppelgangers across the moor and back to the hill fort. She settled them onto the ground and then removed the energy.

Fen crumpled to the ground and panted.

"Are you okay?" Chance cried out as he knelt by her side.

"Just extremely worn out," she replied flashing a quick smile.

Alden studied the three forms on Foel Drygarn. "The doppelgangers are staggering around the summit like drunkards. Fen's power may have drained them."

Chance held Fen and lifted her to her feet.

"I could have used a little more of your power, Chance, but I didn't want to weaken you too much," Fen said as she gently kissed his cheek.

"Good thing you didn't take too much," he responded. "Because I needed to dig twenty feet through bedrock to find my crystal." He withdrew the leather pouch and removed the tiny gemstone. "It's much smaller than the others," he said as he presented the stone.

"But it's just as important," Darrius added. "I suggest you put it away to keep it safe."

"The imposters are staring in our direction but are not moving," Alden reported.

"Excellent," Darrius stated. "I think the plan has worked."

"What will happen if we leave?" Fen asked.

"We will need to fashion body doubles for ourselves before we leave," Alden suggested. "If you agree, I'll create them as we teleport."

"Agreed," Darrius said. "It's critical that we get Chance and Fen to the safety of the cottage as soon as possible—"

"Wait, Darrius," Chance interrupted. "We need to save Hilly."

"The only thing *you* need to do is protect the crystal. And Fen needs to be out of harm's way."

"But—"

Darrius held up a hand. "No further discussion. Both of you will stay with Alden in the cottage.

"Alden, please accompany Fen back to Amesbury, and I'll transport Chance."

"I can flick back to the house on my own, thank you," Chance insisted. He crossed his arms and scowled.

"I'm aware of that, but I also know you're stubborn and may flick to a location elsewhere so you can run to Mount Snowdon and help free Hilly." Darrius placed a hand on Chance's shoulder. "You will come with me. I insist."

He tightened his grip, and Chance bent under the pain. "Ow! Okay. I'll go with you."

"I appreciate your understanding," Darrius responded. "Once we're back in Amesbury, I'll share more about the situation with the Yfel."

"I'm ready to deploy our doppelgangers, Darrius," Alden advised.

"Very well. Let's reconvene at the cottage." Still gripping Chance's shoulder, Darrius disappeared with the magician.

Alden wrapped his arm around Fen, and they vanished as well.

Chapter 23

Denali's Plea

HILLY'S TELEPATHIC SCREAM HURTLED around the globe, racing along the invisible magnetic ley lines and rushing through the ether—the magical realm of existence.

My daughter! Denali called out, knowing her message would never be delivered. The Yfel Brethren had used high magic to prevent communication of any sort and to cloak Hilly's location.

But Denali knew.

The Prophecy had revealed where Hilly would be held captive, but Denali could do nothing to save her earth daughter.

Still, a natural connection existed between them. Despite the cloaking magic, Denali could hear, see, and feel everything Hilly experienced. And when the blue opal was ripped from her throat, Denali screamed in her ice castle just as Hilly's agonizing cry ripped through her brain.

Denali pounded the icy walls of her sanctuary. Waves of avalanches cascaded down her slopes, causing glaciers to crack and buckle. An enormous blizzard swirled clockwise around her summit and unleashed torrents of snow and ice crystals.

The pain did not subside. Her anguish only grew.

My child, I will set things right. I will restore the blue opal and silence the voices again.

She received silence in response.

Denali wept.

Icy tears slid down her frosted crystal dress and shattered on the frozen floor.

Disturbing images of tortured souls flashed in Denali's mind. They demanded that Hilly die so they could escape their wretched existence locked inside her body.

Denali sensed Hilly neared the brink of madness as she struggled between delirium, sanity, and rage. Hilly would go mad. Denali was sure of this. If she didn't intervene, her daughter would not survive.

Denali needed assistance. She would reach out to Lord Yr Wyddfa, the earth spirit who ruled the dominion of Mount Snowdon.

But it would not be easy.

She had insulted Yr Wyddfa fifty-six million years earlier when she rose from the tectonic plates and grew into the tallest mountain in North America. Like an unruly child, the young earth spirit had announced her arrival to the rest of the world by abusing her powers and causing chaos and destruction around the globe.

She offended the ancient spirit with her headstrong ways.

Denali had created a schism between them, and Lord Yr Wyddfa severed all communication.

Now, Denali needed him. After millions of years, would he even listen?

She would need to be contrite. A sincere apology, one with her ego in check, might open the door that she slammed shut so long ago. Denali sat on an icy bench in her sanctuary and prepared.

Calm and composed, she reached out.

Lord Yr Wyddfa, I beseech you. Denali paused.

Silence.

Lord Yr Wyddfa, I'm in need of your help.

No reply.

I treated you unfairly so long ago. Regrettably, I acted like a spoiled child, an ignorant brat who thought she knew more about the world than anyone else. I am ashamed of my behavior. I would not tolerate those insults from another, and I don't blame you for rebuffing me. I apologize, and I'm in great need of your assistance. My earth child, Hilly, has been taken prisoner in your realm. Please, Yr Wyddfa, help me.

The Firewalker is bound by the Prophecy, as we are, he responded apathetically.

Denali gasped. His unexpected response gave her hope.

Yes, but I know you intervened on behalf of your earth child, Chance, to improve his chances of finding the crystal. How is that not interfering with the design of the Prophecy? How would it appear if Hilly perishes on your slopes and the hope of peace for this world is forever gone?

She must endure what she must endure, he tersely remarked.

Are you saying you will not aid my child? Denali asked, her words biting and direct.

You try my patience, Denali. I did not claim I would not help your child. I merely stated that the Firewalker witch is destined to endure pain at the hands of the Yfel. I cannot interfere. To your point, Hildred aided in speeding up the process of Chance locating the crystal, but Chance would have found it eventually. There is a difference.

Denali's anger exploded. Shockwaves propelled ice daggers upward through the mountain and into the atmosphere. *How dare you preach to me! I was the one who witnessed their battle on my slopes. I was the one forced to stand by while the tortured souls of thousands transferred into my daughter's body. I did not intervene in any of those instances because of the Prophecy. If you do not stop the course of destruction unfolding on your slopes, this world will be plunged into darkness.*

Denali sighed. Her unchecked fury would surely end the conversation with Yr Wyddfa. She followed with a softer voice. *We are so close. Hilly and Kai have restored their crystals to their seats of power. Chance has located his crystal and Fen will soon begin her quest for the fourth gemstone. But if Hilly should perish, we will no longer have the four who will restore peace. That responsibility lies firmly on your shoulders.*

Denali stopped talking. She wondered if her last comment was too demanding. Would Lord Yr Wyddfa be insulted and not respond?

Several quiet minutes passed.

I am not without a soul, Denali, Yr Wyddfa responded. *I am not without feelings. We have lived on this planet since its inception. We have seen destruction, and we have enjoyed moments of peace. We endure.*

The shaman has appeared on my slopes along with the magician, Kai, and a Cererian named Benedict. It won't be long before the shaman sets the wheels of the Prophecy in motion once again. He will try to free the Firewalker witch.

And he will fail. Yr Wyddfa sighed.

I know, Denali replied. *I am desperate regarding this outcome. What is it that we can do that will not interfere with the Prophecy?*

The earth spirits remained quiet and pensive for some time.

Denali, I may be able to offer some assistance, Yr Wyddfa offered.

Will you be able to save Hilly?

Of that I am not sure. Humans are fragile beings. Humans with magical abilities even more so. I will talk with the giants of Snowdon. They have protected my slopes for centuries. The giants may be able to help. But I make no promises.

I understand, Denali responded. *I will accept any help you are willing to provide. I will await word on what transpires. I trust you'll tell me before I sense it.* Denali delivered her last sentence tinged with spitefulness.

I will turn a deaf ear to your contempt, Denali, Yr Wyddfa growled. *You err because of your daughter. Never forget this is my kingdom, not yours. Now go.*

Very well. Denali paused before continuing. *I am grateful, Lord Yr Wyddfa for anything you do. She is my only earth child and to lose her would be too painful to bear.*

Denali, Yr Wyddfa said with tenderness and respect, *whenever we lose our children, the pain of their passing is forever carved on our soul. But your daughter, and my son, are destined to restore our world to the peaceful existence we knew at the beginning of our times. There are two others who will join them and together they will clear the way for the Chronicle to ascend to the throne and cleanse our world of these murderous Yfel.*

Lord Yr Wyddfa sighed. *I understand your plight. You are at a distance unable to assist the Firewalker witch. So, I say to you, have faith. We will gain nothing if Hilly perishes. But the Prophecy is unyielding, and the outcome has already been determined.*

Denali whispered, *The fate of my child lies in your hands. I will have faith.*

Chapter 24

The Rescue

MINUTES AFTER LEAVING THE Preseli Hills, Jake and Kai landed near the summit of Mount Snowdon. When his boots hit the snow-packed ground, Jake collapsed to his knees, then rolled onto his side and hugged his ribcage.

"You okay?" Kai asked as he knelt beside his friend.

The shaman grimaced. "Fine." He touched his right side and inspected his hand. Blood.

"You're not fully healed," Kai cautioned. "You should wait until we have backup."

"Backup?" Jake growled as he struggled to sit up. "Darrius? Benedict? Alden? The Cererians can do nothing but observe. "It's just you and me, Kai."

"Not exactly," a male voice said. Benedict walked out of the shadows and approached them. "I may not be able to kill a Brethren, but I can detain them."

"All...due...respect..." Jake gasped. "But you...can do...nothing." The corner of his mouth jerked up into a sneer and then disappeared as he groaned and doubled over.

"The Word is trying to heal," Benedict observed. "You should be resting."

"There's...no...time," Jake panted. "Get...me...up."

Kai hooked Jake under the armpits and pulled him to a wobbly standing position.

"Humans are exhausting," Benedict chastised. "Especially magicians. So, tell me, shaman, what is your plan for finding and freeing your friend when you can't even stand on your own?"

Jake stumbled to a nearby boulder and glared at the Cererian. "Benedict, sometimes you...can be a prick."

Kai looked between Benedict and Jake. "Something tells me you two don't get along."

"We tolerate each other," Benedict replied as he stepped toward Kai. "Managing Aningan with your friend is a challenge, at best. Let's just say we have a difference of opinion."

Jake retched and spat a gob of phlegm at Benedict's feet.

Kai patted Jake's shoulder. "I'm just a casual observer, but this attitude is not going to find Hilly. We need to work together."

Jake narrowed his eyes and then dropped his gaze. "You're right, Kai." His shoulders slumped forward.

"ARGH!" Jake cried out and fell to his knees. Kai knelt and pried Jake's hand away from his right side. The blood had spread.

"I'm going to take a peek." Kai unbuttoned Jake's shirt and carefully looked at his ribcage. Three tattoos pulsed electric blue erratically. Each time a marking flashed, Jake bit his lip and grunted as though he had been punched in the gut.

"The Word is trying to heal, shaman," Benedict said as he inspected the wound. "You should wait."

"Instead of lecturing me..." Jake paused to catch his breath. "Why don't you heal it!" Jake clutched his side and moaned.

Benedict stood. "I cannot. Darrius, Kai, and Fen have given you all the healing energy they can. Only the Word can heal itself at this point."

"Benedict is right," Kai observed. "If you find Hilly, you're in no shape to fight the Brethren. There's three of them and one and a half of us—and you're the half."

Jake fell to the ground and nudged his back against the boulder. He panted and looked up at Kai with bloodshot eyes. "I may be only a half, as you put it, but I'm the toughest half."

Benedict interjected. "I've just heard from Darrius. Chance has found his crystal."

"Great, then he can help us," Kai reasoned.

"No. Chance won't be joining you," Benedict stated. "He must protect the crystal at all costs. He is with Fen and Alden at the cottage in Amesbury."

"Great..." Jake seethed.

"But Darrius will join us shortly," Benedict added.

"And that still leaves us with one and half people to fight the Yfel." Jake closed his eyes. *Where are you Hilly?*

Help me! Hilly's voice drifted through Jake's brain like a zephyr.

Hilly! I'm on Yr Wyddfa. I have Kai with me. Where are you?

NOOO!

Hilly's scream pierced Jake's brain. He grabbed his head with both hands.

"Are you okay?" Kai asked.

"Hilly's nearby," Jake whispered. "She reached out to me."

Help me! Stop the voices! Hilly's cries pummeled Jake's brain telepathically.

"Interesting," Benedict noted. "Darrius mentioned you might be able to hear her because she's in the land of the shadows. "What did she say?"

Jake massaged his temples. "She screamed for help."

"What are they doing to her?" Kai demanded as he strode across the snowy summit. "Come out, you bastards!" Kai craned his neck and looked up the sheer cliff. He clenched his fists and yelled at the top of his lungs, "Hilly!!"

"Please be quiet, Kai."

Kai whirled to find Darrius walking toward him.

"Darrius, where'd you come from?"

"I've left your brother and sister with Alden in Amesbury." He glanced at Jake on the ground. "How goes the healing, Jake?"

"Fine," Jake spit the word through clenched teeth.

Darrius turned to Benedict. "Any sign of the Yfel?"

"I've scanned the entire summit and cannot detect any evidence that they are on the mountain," Benedict reported.

"They're here," Jake said. "I heard Hilly."

"Interesting," Darrius commented. Aaron has deployed powerful cloaking magic that prevents us from seeing or sensing their exact location. Darrius walked to Jake and stared down at him. "Jake, are you well enough to fight?"

Gasping, Jake looked up at Darrius. "Any...time." The Cererian grabbed Jake's right arm and pulled him to his feet. Jake wobbled but stayed erect.

"Show me," Darrius demanded.

Jake licked his cracked lips and narrowed his eyes at Darrius. In a split second, he snatched both Cathal and Cadmar from the sheaths on his back and held them inches from Darrius' throat.

The Cererian did not flinch.

"You were slow," Darrius uttered as he turned his back on Jake and joined Benedict. The two Cererians conversed telepathically as Jake seethed.

"Slow?!" Jake yelled. "You sanctimonious shit!" Holding his battle daggers toward Darrius, he took one step forward before crumpling to the ground.

Darrius knelt beside him and gently rolled him over. The blood had spread across the entire front of his shirt. Darrius undid the buttons and inspected his torso. Two markings pulsed violently between purple and midnight blue. "Two symbols are still injured."

"Please heal them, Darrius," Jake begged as he lay on his back with his eyes closed.

"I've done all I can for you. The Word needs time."

Kai sidled up to the pair. "There were three angry markings ten minutes ago. Since one healed in that amount of time, Jake might be back on his feet in less than thirty minutes."

"Or not," Jake replied through gritted teeth. "In the meantime, Hilly is suffering."

"Why don't I lead the charge?" Kai asked.

Jake looked at his friend and chuckled, which soon turned into a strangled cough. Darrius rolled him onto his side. When he recovered, Jake whispered, "Nobody leads me into battle. But I appreciate the offer, Kai."

"I fear that if we do not act soon, we may lose Hilly," Benedict stated as he joined the group. "We know the Brethren came to this mountain, but they have made it impossible to find them."

"I know where they are," Jake said as he lay on his side. He gazed under Darrius' knee to a collection of rocks stacked in a pyramid shape against the side of a cliff. "They've used a clever cloaking magic. Very different. I've not seen anything like it before." He pointed toward the cluster of rocks.

Everyone looked where Jake was pointing. "I don't see anything," Benedict said. "I don't feel anything, either."

"Is he delirious?" Kai added.

"He sees the gateway to the land of the shadows," Darrius observed. "His closeness to the veil of death allows him to see beyond our capability."

"Tell me what you see," Darrius requested.

Jake licked his lips and continued. "The cloaking veil looks...it looks like a shimmering waterfall of many colors—a kaleidoscope somewhat. Constantly changing, constantly moving. Beyond the veil is a cave entrance." He gazed upward and around. "The cloaking field goes about thirty feet high and extends to either side the same distance." Jake swallowed hard before continuing. "It appears to penetrate the rocky ground." He rolled onto his back and sighed. "It's a big ass magical force field."

Darrius glanced at the area Jake described. "This rock face does appear to be odd for a mountain. Look, Benedict. There are no natural formations nor imperfections along this cliff. It's as though it is a smooth wall...a manufactured barrier."

Benedict scanned the area. "I agree. I've penetrated this rock as far as I can but detect nothing but quartz and dirt. There are no Yfel."

"They're there." Jake pulled himself up and kept one hand touching the rock to steady himself. "I can clearly see the cave entrance." He paused and glanced around. "So far, I don't see Yfel."

"What is your plan, Jake?" Darrius asked.

Jake held his ribs and listed to one side. "First, I need to confirm where Hilly is located." Jake glanced toward the cave. "Then I go in and get her."

"Simple enough," Darrius commented.

"Darrius?" Benedict said quizzically.

Darrius held up a hand toward Benedict before addressing Jake again. "So, you run in, brandishing your weapons, and kill the three Cererians. Is that correct?"

Jake stared at the Cererian. "Stop, Darrius. I know I'm outnumbered, but I need to do something and that's the only plan I have. Hell, I'm the only one who can see the cave entrance."

"I'll follow you," Kai blurted. "You lead the way, and I'll be right behind you." He withdrew his blade and waved it in the air.

"I appreciate all the help I can get, Kai." Jake smiled weakly at his friend. *STOP!*

Hilly's voice stabbed Jake's brain. He winced and staggered backward.

"Jake?" Darrius asked. "What's wrong?"

"Hilly." Jake gripped the boulder and gazed wearily at the ground. *Aaron! No! HELP!*

Jake's eyes widened. "She's in trouble. I've got to help her!" Snatching Cathal and Cadmar, he sprinted toward the cavern.

"Wait!" Kai cried out as he chased after him.

The wall of rock loomed ten feet in front of them, and Jake rushed through it and disappeared. Kai slammed headfirst into the rocky barrier and crumpled to the ground.

Kai lay unconscious in the snow. Blood oozed from a jagged gash across his forehead.

Darrius placed his hand across the wound and mouthed a healing incantation while Benedict scanned his body for additional injuries.

"It appears his head took the brunt of the collision," Benedict assessed.

Kai's eyes fluttered open. "What happened?"

"You ran into the side of the mountain," Darrius replied.

Kai rubbed his head. "Jake was right in front of me."

"Jake disappeared into the land of the shadows," Benedict reported.

Kai stared at the Cererians. "You mean he got through the force field, but I didn't?"

"Yes," Darrius responded.

"I tried to communicate with the shaman but have received no answer," Benedict said.

Darrius gazed into the cliff's shiny surface and ran his hand along its smoothness. "Hilly's salvation rests in Jake's hands. There is nothing we can do to help him."

"He was almost healed," Kai added. "Maybe he'll gain his strength before he encounters the Yfel Brethren."

"Hopefully," Darrius solemnly responded. "If not, I fear we will lose both Jake *and* Hilly."

Chapter 25

Madness Descends

"MAKE YOURSELVES COMFORTABLE WHILE I make tea." Alden left Fen and Chance in the lounge and entered the kitchen. He stared out the window as he filled the kettle. It had been a clear night in the Preseli Hills, but a vicious winter storm pelted the backyard of the Amesbury cottage.

Darrius had departed for Mount Snowdon minutes earlier.

The clock in the hallway chimed.

Five in the morning.

Alden leaned against the range and ran his fingers through his hair. He missed his bowler hat, which had been lost somewhere on Carn Goedog. *I feel undressed,* he thought as he brushed dirt off his rumpled black suit and gazed at his ruined leather shoes.

The tea kettle whistled, and he snatched it from the burner.

"Tea is served," Alden announced as he entered the lounge holding a tray. "I found some biscuits as well."

Fen nestled against Chance on the sofa. His arm curled around her shoulder and his head leaned against hers. With their eyes closed, they appeared as though they were napping.

Alden placed the tray on the table in front of them.

The siblings didn't stir.

"I brought the sugar cubes you like." Alden poured three cups of English breakfast tea.

They didn't reply.

He extended a cup toward Fen. "Tea, Fen?"

Silence.

"Chance? Tea?"

Again, silence.

Alden returned the cup to the tray and studied the siblings. The movement of their eyelids indicated they were either in a deep sleep or a meditative trance. Their breaths came extremely slow and synchronized.

Fen's lips moved slightly.

Alden leaned closer and strained to hear what she was saying. *She's casting a spell,* he thought. Chance's lips also faintly moved. *They're combining their magic.*

He immediately contacted Darrius telepathically. *Fen and Chance are conjuring.*

To what end?

I don't know. I found them in a deep trance. Their actions are synchronized, so I assume they are combining their power to aid Hilly in some manner.

Darrius sighed. Jake had just plunged through the shadowy veil to search for the Yfel, Kai lay on the ground recovering from his head injury, and now the siblings were attempting to interfere. *Wake them!* he ordered.

Alden hesitated. *What if they can make a difference?*

Disobedience, Alden? That's unlike you.

We witnessed Fen's power against the doppelgangers. What if she and Chance can direct their magic? Since Fen can hear Hilly's thoughts, perhaps she can also communicate with Jake.

It is frustrating not to be able to use my powers, Darrius responded. *I have never felt so impotent. I'm not accustomed to depending on humans.*

Ego, Alden replied. *You...me, we don't like to lose control.*

Indeed. Perhaps you are correct. Fen and Chance may be able to penetrate the veil with their magic. Keep me apprised of their progress.

I will. Were you aware of this development in their powers?

Darrius paused before responding. *I have learned over the millennium that the Prophecy is the only entity in control. While I always believed the Word shared all its secrets with me, recent events have demonstrated that that is not the case. The Kemps are changing at an incredible rate, transforming into the warriors they were destined to be. Although I have knowledge of the ultimate outcome, their actions...their abilities...continue to surprise.*

Darrius! Alden interrupted. *Their eyes—*

What's going on?

Fen and Chance are staring at me with opaque eyes. Alden waved his hand in front of their faces. They didn't flinch or react. *They appear like alabaster statues.*

They've entered the realm of the shadows, Darrius concluded.

With Cathal and Cadmar leading the charge, Jake plunged through the veil that cloaked the cave entrance. Once he passed through the multi-colored waterfall, he stopped and glanced back.

Kai lay unconscious on the ground bleeding from a head wound.

Benedict was administering aid to Kai, and Darrius stared into the rock face, seemingly peering directly into Jake's eyes.

Can Darrius see me? He messaged Darrius. *I made it through. What happened to Kai?*

Silence.

Darrius turned away and helped Benedict with Kai.

"I guess I'm on my own," Jake mused as he absently stroked his ribcage. Although his side ached, the pain was tolerable.

He glanced around. Blackness filled this side of the veil. The inky void swirled with no beginning and no end, disorienting the shaman.

Engaging his intuition, he turned away from the entrance and peered into the darkness, trying to detect the presence of the Yfel or Hilly. Stretching his hands out to either side, he shuffled one foot forward, probing for rocks or holes that might trip him up and then stepped through with the other foot. He repeated the slow gait, waving his hands back and forth at eye level.

When his left hand scraped the rocky side of the cave, he moved closer to the wall and used it as a guide while his eyes strained to see anything in the darkness. He continued along trusting his hands, feet, and intuition.

Then his boot bumped into something solid. He leaned forward until his right hand connected with a smooth, cold surface and ran his hand up and down and side to side. The path was blocked by a massive boulder.

He followed the curve of the rock until he entered a shaft on the other side. He paused. Shadows flickered across the wall in front of him.

Torches, he thought. *The Brethren must be nearby.*

The flame silhouettes danced on the rocks compelling him to push forward.

Help me, please! Hilly's mental scream ripped into his brain. Jake grabbed his head and groaned.

I'm here, Hilly. Where are you? he messaged back.

No response. Uncontrollable sobbing filled his head. The choked crying tore at his heart. He sensed Hilly's sanity slipping away.

He drew in a sharp breath and crept further into the bowels of the mountain. The shaft enlarged and the light grew brighter as a fine scent of sandalwood wafted.

Cererians, Jake thought.

He stopped behind a cluster of large rocks at the entrance to an immense cavern. He hugged the boulders and peered into the chamber.

The ceiling soared upward and disappeared into a black void. Flickering torches lined the curved wall of the circular room and illuminated an enormous boulder in the middle of the space.

Two figures appeared in front of it.

Jake's breath caught in his throat.

One figure was Hilly. She leaned against the rock, arms and legs spread eagle, suspended by invisible restraints. She rolled her head from side to side while Aaron Aningan tormented her.

A chill raced up Jake's spine. The Cererian licked Hilly, his black tongue flicking across her eyelids, her nose, and down her cheek. The shiver was not from fear but from explosive rage.

Hilly shook her head violently. Aaron slowly drew his finger along her forehead and then down her neck. Her head lolled toward Jake, and his anger escalated.

That bastard removed her mouth. He tightened his hands around Cathal and Cadmar.

His fury boiled.

Steady, Jake, he calmed himself. *Don't go running headlong into trouble—not yet.*

He glared at the back of Aaron's head as he abused Hilly. "There, there, Hilly. Just give me what I want, and I'll silence the voices. Is my old friend Everild still demanding that you kill yourself?"

Go away! Leave me alone! Help!

"No one can hear you, dear," Aaron placated. "I've seen to that. Our cloaking magic prevents anyone, including your Cererian friends, from hearing you or finding you. So, you might as well give me what I want before you go insane."

His low chuckle echoed off the chamber walls as Aaron ran the back of his finger along Hilly's face.

A single tear trailed down her cheek.

Jake. The unified voices entered Jake's mind.

He flattened against the wall and searched for the source. *Jake, it's Fen and Chance.*

Fen and Chance? he responded with skepticism. *How?*

We combined our magic. We fused our consciousness to amplify our nat-ural powers. The sibling's reply was a single voice that carried the quality of a finely blended androgenous duet.

Jake was not quick to believe. *I don't trust you are who you say you are. Tell me what symbol is tattooed on Chance's foot.*

Triskelion, the reply came quickly.

Jake grinned. *Correct. I need your help, Aaron is torturing Hilly.*

How can we assist you?

Are you able to talk with her?

We are only able to hear Hilly. Our sister has not returned our psychic messages.

I need to free her, Jake replied. *How can you help?*

We can combine our power with your magic.

How?

Do you recall the incident in Alaska when Kai and Fen drained Hilly's magic and prevented her from leaving the car until she acquiesced to our demands?

I do, Jake responded. *It scared the hell out of me.*

That's the power we wield. We will enhance any conjuring you do against the Yfel. But we need to prepare...

Hilly thrashed against the rock as strangled giggles filled his mind. Jake jolted and his attention went to the center of the chamber. Her chatter ranged from maniacal laughter to uncontrollable sobs.

We need to hurry, he warned Fen and Chance. *She's babbling in various voices.*

We will combine our energy with yours now, Jake.

A soothing sensation like a gentle wave seeped into the soles of the his feet and crept up his legs. The warming vibration rushed through his torso and chest before spreading into his arms and extending up his neck. As the tingling filled his head, beads of sweat sprouted on his forehead.

Jake gasped.

His heart raced, and he panted as though he was running a marathon. The pain at his side abruptly disappeared. He lifted the edge of his shirt. The tattoos had returned to normal.

The Word is healed! he relayed to Fen and Chance.

You're welcome.

How? Darrius said only the Word could heal itself at this point.

Darrius doesn't yet understand our united power. But we are glad that you benefited from the joining of our energies.

HELP ME!!! Hilly's telepathic scream pierced Jake's brain and simultaneously stabbed into her siblings' minds.

I...we...need to help her, Jake announced as he advanced into the middle of the room with Cathal and Cadmar stretched in front of him.

Wait, Jake! We still need more time for our powers to balance.

He ignored them as he crept closer.

Balor and Cary, stood on either side of the boulder facing Hilly as Aaron raised his arms toward his captive. "Hilly, this is your final chance to release Lord Stygian and save yourself."

She twisted away from his reach, but he grabbed her head with both hands and squeezed. Peering into her eyes he demanded, "Release. Stygian. Now!"

Jake launched into the air and twirled the battle daggers in his hands, the points jutting downward. He arced toward Aaron's back, and thrusted both blades at the Cererian.

Hilly's eyes widened at his approach.

Aaron turned and halted the shaman midair. Sweeping his hand to the side, Aaron shoved Jake upward with such force that the shaman slammed into the chamber ceiling twenty feet above them. A jagged stalactite punctured his thigh.

Jake yelled.

Back in Amesbury, Fen and Chance winced. *Sorry, Jake. We were not prepared for Aaron's conjuring. The magical souls he has consumed has greatly heightened his magic. We need more time.*

Jake dangled from the ceiling by his impaled leg. *You need to speed it up. Aaron is demanding that Hilly release Stygian now.*

Aaron sneered at the shaman and turned back to Hilly. "Your beautiful eyes betrayed your friend's position, my dear." Once again, he thrust his hand toward Jake. The stalactite vibrated and agonizing pain burned through Jake's body. He clenched his jaw and moaned.

Stop hurting him! Hilly wailed telepathically.

Aaron smirked. "You're fond of the shaman, aren't you?" He glanced between Jake and Hilly. "How sweet. You've been resistant to save yourself, but will you be so bold if Jake faces the same fate? Release Stygian or watch as I behead the shaman and consume his magic."

Hilly pounded her head on the rock. Aaron gripped her head and squeezed. "Now, Hilly. Release Stygian now."

If you return my mouth, I will do as you demand. Hilly squeezed her eyes shut and brokered the deal. *And I will release Stygian once you remove Jake from his restraints.*

A twisted smile spread across Aaron's face. *Finally, Stygian will return from his prison, and when he does, he'll have only me to thank.*

"Cary...Balor...remove the shaman from the ceiling and stand him over there!" Aaron demanded, pointing to an area near the wall. The soldiers floated up to where Jake dangled, grabbed him on either side of his body, and yanked him off the stalactite. Gliding back to the ground, they dragged him along the ground and forced him to stand on his injured leg between them.

Jake looked at Hilly with melancholy eyes. *Why, Hilly?* he messaged. *They'll kill us anyway.*

Aaron sneered as the shaman passed. He then faced Hilly and lightly brushed his finger across her face and restored her mouth. The instant her lips appeared, she screamed an incantation.

Aaron held up a hand. Hilly choked on her words, and Jake was whisked away from the twins and sent crashing into the ceiling. This time the stalactite punctured his back and exited out his stomach.

Black blood jetted from Jake's mouth.

Hilly gagged.

"Don't try your tricks, witch," Aaron threatened. "I want Stygian." He looked at Jake and pointed. "His pain is *your* fault."

Hilly gazed pitifully at Jake who hung limply with his eyes closed. Intermittent groans were the only indication he was still alive.

Aaron cupped Hilly's face and pulled her forward until their noses touched. He opened his mouth. Stale, fetid air wafted. "Produce Stygian...NOW!"

Jake, the dual voices of Fen and Chance spoke into his brain. *Don't react to our words. We are still with you and will prevent Stygian from harming you or Hilly. Trust us.*

Too bad you couldn't have stopped Aaron, he replied.

Aaron needs to believe he is winning.

Even I believe he's winning. Jake coughed and spat bloody phlegm to the ground.

Angry tears streamed down Hilly's face. Her mouth twisted as she snarled, "If you want Stygian, you can have him! By the powers of the north, the east, the south, and the west, return to me, my lord. Stand with me as it was in the beginning and as it will be in the end. Return to me n ow!"

Hilly's head shot back against the rock as if it had been yanked backward. She wheezed, each ragged breath slower than the previous one.

The chamber's atmosphere thickened, and the torches sputtered.

"Where is he?" Aaron yelled as he frantically searched the room looking for Stygian.

Electrical charges snapped and popped. Hairs stood in response to the static electricity.

Hilly's head rocketed forward, and her eyes widened. Her brilliant green eyes were solid black. "Stygian comes!" she croaked.

A clap of thunder rumbled through the cavern shaking the walls, floor, and the stalactite in Jake's body. He groaned.

A black line, about five inches wide, zippered from the ceiling to the floor. The twins backed away, but Aaron stepped toward it confidently. He approached the pulsing line with his head bowed. "Lord Stygian. I await you!" he cried out.

The black bar stretched and widened until it morphed into the shape of a translucent doorway. The pressure rose in the chamber as frenetic energy bounced off the rocky walls. A high-pitched whine pierced the room. The door violently bent and buckled.

Aaron stared at the spectacle unfolding before him.

The entryway convulsed, contracting and expanding with tortured breaths. The movements quickened and intensified until the anomaly vibrated and blurred.

BOOM!

The entryway exploded outward pelting the chamber with sharp shards. The blast snuffed out the torches.

Silence. Darkness.

Abruptly, the flames reappeared and illuminated the chamber.

Stygian appeared in the middle of the room.

Standing well over six-feet-tall, the flaxen-haired young man with intense green eyes and pale skin glared around the space.

Aaron dropped to his knees, hands raised upward. "My Lord!"

Mimicking their commander, Balor and Cary also fell to their knees.

Stygian sneered.

Then he locked eyes with Hilly bound helplessly to the boulder.

Stygian marched to Aaron. "How dare you torture my child!"

"But...but..." Aaron stuttered.

"Silence!" Stygian roared. The cavern quaked. Loose rocks fell to the floor.

Aaron averted his eyes and held his hands upward, his fingers trembling. "I am yours to command, Lord Stygian."

Stygian stared at Aaron's bowed head and grimaced.

He snatched Aaron from the floor, ripped off his head, and consumed the magical souls that snaked from his body as they sought to reach the ether.

Then he flung the carcass against a wall and smacked his lips. "It's been a while since I've eaten. That was quite satisfying."

The twins fell to the floor and pressed their foreheads to the ground.

"Fear not, soldiers," Stygian said as he approached. "I will not harm you. Rise and face me. I want to see the eyes of those who will go to battle with me."

Balor and Cary jumped to their feet. "Yes, my Lord!" they shouted in unison.

Jake messaged Fen and Chance. *Stygian has been released and he has killed Aaron.*

It is time for us to put our plan into action, the siblings announced. *Extend your hands toward Stygian.*

I can barely lift my head, Jake responded.

A wave of energy filled the shaman's body as the siblings' full power pulsed through Jake's veins. *Try now.*

Slowly, Jake lifted his arms and pushed his hands toward Stygian.

Time for the magic, Fen and Chance chorused.

Summoning their combined magic, the siblings directed their energy through Jake until a luminescent glow manifested around his fingers and hands. The soft light crept up his arms, spread throughout his torso, and eventually radiated from his entire body.

And so it begins, Fen and Chance said calmly.

A fine beam of intense light discharged from each of Jake's fingers. Concentrated toward the Cererians, the energy filled the space between them, and expanded outward until the men were swaddled in a dazzling radiance.

Then the conjuring exploded.

The concussive pressure wave detonated outward filling the cavern. It burst through the shafts and blew out the cave entrance.

Then the shockwave quickly reversed sucking the energy back into the mountain and rushing back to the heart of the chamber. Tornadic winds pummeled the interior as spontaneous lightning stabbed the floor and walls.

BOOM!

The torches extinguished.

After several seconds. The torches reignited one by one.

Two figures remained.

Jake lay face down on the chamber floor. Beside him, Hilly curled against his side, her arm reaching across his body.

Chapter 26

The Giants of Snowdon

Fᴇɴ ᴀɴᴅ Cʜᴀɴᴄᴇ ᴄᴏʟʟᴀᴘsᴇᴅ against one another.

Alden quickly scanned their bodies with his mind. There were no injuries, but he noted their bodies were completely depleted of energy. Their hearts had slowed to fifteen beats per minute.

Fen and Chance have blacked out, he messaged to Darrius. *They are uninjured but their bodies have slowed as though they have entered hibernation.*

There has been an enormous explosion inside the mountain, Darrius responded. *The cloaking magic has been removed. We're going in.*

Be well, Darrius!

"I'm going with you," Kai declared.

"I suggest you wait here while Benedict and I investigate what has happened within the cave," Darrius responded.

"I won't stand by while Hilly's and Jake's lives are in danger." Kai grabbed his blade and marched to the cave entrance.

"Very well," Darrius acquiesced. "But don't get in our way." Darrius and Benedict rushed by Kai and plunged into the dark tunnel. Their keen Cererian eyes allowed them to see clearly in the pitch blackness, avoiding rocks jutting from the ground. Kai followed close behind but tripped over obstacles he couldn't detect with his weaker human eyes.

As the men rounded the large boulder blocking the pathway, lights flickered along the wall ahead. Darrius raised his hand, and the group stopped. He telepathically reached out to Benedict and Kai. *I sense only two individuals and neither is Cererian.*

It must be Jake and Hilly, Kai replied as he pushed past.

Kai entered the bright chamber and skidded to a stop. "Uh-oh," he whispered.

Darrius and Benedict pulled alongside him.

Three giants towered over Jake and Hilly and glared at the intruders.

I don't sense them at all, Darrius noted. *It's as though they don't exist.*

The gigantic trio ranged in height from eight to ten feet. Shaggy, black hair spiraled out in all directions around their heads and cascaded to their shoulders where the wild strands merged with unruly thatches of thick beards that drooped mid chest. Each wore a leather apron on top of overalls constructed of brown human hair and animal fur.

Hypnotic icy-blue eyes stared at Benedict, Darrius, and Kai.

"Ya trespass in the realm of the laird," the tallest one roared as he stepped over Jake and Hilly. The giant cracked his hairy knuckles as he stomped forward. Vibrations rolled through the ground with each step.

Kai backed up, but Darrius and Benedict didn't move.

The giant stopped six feet from the Cererians and sneered.

"We're here for our friends," Darrius explained.

"Go," the giant ordered as he pointed down the tunnel. "Leave this place."

"Stand down, Bran," a male voice said softly.

The giant growled and turned.

An ethereal being floated forward. As the entity, not quite a man, drifted closer, his aura undulated between flashes of purple, blue, and green. His electric-blue eyes darted from an angular face sculpted from gray granite.

His body, arms, and legs were also chiseled from stone, the edges sharp and gleaming. A modesty patch of moss covered his lower body while curls of fungus draped about his head.

The giant lowered his head as the entity neared.

"I am Lord Yr Wyddfa," the spirit announced. "This is my kingdom. These are my giants." He swept his hand toward the three colossal beings.

"I'm—" Darrius began

The entity held up a hand. "I know who you are, Darrius. Behind you, the magician, Kai, trembles in my presence while your associate, Benedict, attempts to probe my mind." The being floated to the bodies of Jake and Hilly. "And these two are the great shaman, Jake, and the Firewalker witch, Hilly."

He faced the Cererians. "Bran is correct. You are trespassing."

"We want our friends," Darrius said sternly.

A kaleidoscope of colors danced across the chamber walls as Yr Wyddfa's aura brightened and flashed. "You will demand nothing of me, Cererian. Proceed with caution, or I will banish you from my slopes like Shasta was forced to do after your indiscretions."

Darrius and the ethereal being stared at each other.

"You care for the humans," Yr Wyddfa observed. "That is evident."

"We want to heal them," Darrius said quietly.

"You can do nothing for the Firewalker. Only my giants can soothe the torment she endures." He motioned to Hilly. "Ellis, turn the witch over and show our visitors."

The smallest giant knelt and carefully rolled Hilly away from Jake until she slumped onto his chest. Then he gently cupped her chin and pulled her head up, revealing the ragged hole in her neck where the blue opal had once been fastened. Her carotid artery pulsed deep within the black cavity encrusted with scabs and gore.

"Behold," Yr Wyddfa said. "The gem that silenced the voices within the witch has been removed. The restless souls scream relentlessly to be released. Insanity is the witch's constant companion. Only my giants can cure her. Denali has personally requested we save her earth child."

Kai gawked at the gaping hole in Hilly's neck. He stepped in front of Darrius and bowed his head toward the entity. "Lord Yr Wyddfa. Hilly is my sister. I request your permission to visit with her."

"Magician, your sister is not conscious," Yr Wyddfa explained. "Her soul does not exist in this world. Your siblings, Fen and Chance, projected their combined powers within this sacred space and banished the Yfel to other lands while preserving the bodies of the shaman and Firewalker. To achieve this, the souls had to be safeguarded in another dimension. Your siblings are very clever magicians. They eradicated evil while maintaining the lives of their comrades."

"If we can't take Hilly with us, may we leave with Jake?" Darrius asked with his head slightly dipped toward the entity.

"There is hope for you yet, Darrius." The ethereal being smiled and floated forward until he was directly in front of Darrius. "You may remove the shaman. My commitment to Denali is only for the Firewalker. But, be forewarned, uniting his soul and body may be difficult. The magicians who cast the original spell will need to reverse the conjuring."

"You don't need Fen and Chance to save Hilly?" Benedict asked.

A low chuckle echoed around the cavern. "No, Cererian. I am an earth spirit. I possess the original magic of the universe. I was born with the ability to create or erase any life." Yr Wyddfa narrowed his gaze at Darrius. "I was present at the creation of the Prophecy, as were you, Darrius. You know the strength of my power."

"Hilly is in capable hands," Darrius said. He turned his head and gave Benedict a serious look, and the Cererian nodded his understanding.

The entity gestured toward the bodies on the ground. "You have my permission to take Jake with you but leave my realm...now."

Kai ambled to Jake's body. Ellis held Hilly in his arms and gazed up with expressive eyes full of kindness and compassion. Kai knelt. "I'll see you soon, Hilly. I promise." He kissed his fingertips and brushed them lightly against her cheek. Then he reached under Jake and scooped up his body. Kai gazed at Hilly one more time before turning his back and carrying Jake away.

"How long will you keep Hilly?" Darrius asked.

"As long as it takes to restore Denali's earth child to full health," Yr Wyddfa replied. "Bran, take the Firewalker. Ellis, collect the blue opal. It's time for us to go."

"How will we know when Hilly is healed," Darrius pressed.

"The Firewalker will contact you when she is well." The spirit turned abruptly and drifted away. He paused by a stone wall, and Bran folded Hilly into his arms, then Ellis located the blue opal against a far wall. The gigantic men walked through the rocky barrier as though it didn't exist. Yr Wyddfa exited last.

"They vanished into solid rock," Kai observed.

"Come, let's return to the Amesbury cottage," Darrius ordered. "If Fen and Chance hold the key to uniting Jake's body with his soul, we should meet with them right away. Benedict, teleport with Kai. I will teleport with Jake."

"Interesting," Benedict said. "I couldn't probe their minds nor sense the existence of the giants and Lord Yr Wyddfa. It was as though they were projections and did not exist on this physical plane."

"Yes, I experienced the same phenomenon," Darrius concurred.

"So, were they actually here?" Kai asked as he turned to leave.

"Nature's spirits are truly a mystery," Darrius replied.

Chapter 27

Anguish of the Unknown

JAKE AND HILLY'S SOULS drifted along a bright yellow current of energy.

Unaware of each other, the luminous spirits meandered, floating through space and time like lustrous bubbles carried on currents of psychic wind.

Temporarily separated from their bodies by Fen and Chance's explosive banishment spell, the spirits explored their surroundings. Not a small room nor a vast landscape, the space they occupied continually contracted and stretched, forever shifting between dark and light, and solid and liquid.

Though Jake and Hilly were not conscious of each other's existence, when their soul orbs bumped against each other, they would linger for a second, a flurry of warm colors racing across their skins, before they would part and journey onward in the realm of the undead.

"I left them as they were," Alden said as he led Darrius and Benedict to the lounge where Fen and Chance leaned against one another on the sofa. "It's been an hour."

Kai remained upstairs with Jake.

After teleporting back to the Amesbury cottage, Darrius immersed Jake in warm bath water infused with healing oils and potions that once belonged to his friend, Prasad. Then he and Benedict dispensed healing magic, paying special attention to the nasty puncture wound caused by the stalactite.

The shaman's body was horribly battered and bruised.

But he was alive.

Afterward, Darrius carried Jake to bed for a recuperative sleep. Kai volunteered to remain with him while the Cererians departed to the lounge, anxious to talk to the siblings about their unusual conjuring.

Fen and Chance hadn't stirred.

Darrius mentally scanned their bodies and frowned. "I don't know what to make of this. There is nothing physically wrong with them, yet their minds have retreated."

"They dispensed powerful magic, the likes we've never seen," Benedict added. "Perhaps this is their manner for recharging."

"I was not made aware they planned to combine their powers," Alden reiterated.

"Fen is the key," Darrius noted. "She has been the instigator during each occurrence: in the Aningan hotel room, disarming Hilly's magic in the car, and her control over the doppelgangers. Like her siblings, Fen is evolving at a rapid pace."

"We need them to heal the shaman," Benedict stated bluntly. "Can we force their wakefulness?" Benedict stepped forward and stretched a hand toward the siblings.

"No!" Alden shouted and hurried in front of Benedict, his arms spread wide protectively. "You talk about them like they're foreign entities, not our friends. Leave them alone. They will return to us when they're ready."

"I meant no disrespect, brother," Benedict stated. "But time is of the essence. We don't know the full results of their magic. Where are the Brethren? Jake and Hilly are alive, but their souls are adrift in the land of the undead. What else did their spell impact?"

"Alden is right," Darrius noted. "Despite our needs, despite Jake's needs, we should honor what Chance and Fen require. They are unable to talk with us, so we wait until they can."

"What's going on?" Kai asked as he strode into the lounge. "We can hear you upstairs."

"We?" Darrius asked.

Kai grinned. "Jake's awake, but—"

"I need to talk with him," Darrius interrupted. He rushed out of the room.

"Darrius!" Kai shouted. Darrius stopped at the bottom of the stairs. "Jake's awake. But he's not all back."

Everyone went upstairs and found Jake sitting up in bed. His skin glistened with a purplish sheen, a result of the healing oils in the bath water. Jake stared with vacant eyes.

"Jake?" Darrius said as he sat on the edge of the bed.

The shaman didn't acknowledge him.

Darrius touched his arm. "Do you know where you are?

Unblinking, Jake stared ahead.

"It is as Yr Wyddfa claimed," Benedict observed. "This is the shaman's body, but his soul has not yet returned." He turned and glared at Alden. "To return his spirit, we need Fen and Chance."

"Benedict, please," Darrius admonished as rubbed his forehead and walked toward the window. The morning sun draped the trees in a golden glow. Pale pink clouds billowed on the horizon. He pressed his fingertips together in front of his chest and closed his eyes in meditation.

When he turned, determination filled his face.

Great Denali, your child is in great hands, Yr Wyddfa reaffirmed.

Her soul is missing. Where is her soul? Denali pounded her fists on the ice bench in her sanctuary. Icy shards scattered onto the floor.

The magicians, Fen and Chance, cast her soul to the realm of the undead. They sought to protect their sister from their psychic blast that banished the Yfel.

When will she return to me? When can I hold her again?

My giants must first reset the blue opal and heal her before they can invite the soul to reoccupy her body.

Invite her soul?

Yes. Her soul may decide to remain in the land of the undead. I, nor my giants, can force her to return.

Unacceptable, Yr Wyddfa! Denali stomped around her ice palace. Each step convulsed the snowpack on her slopes.

The decision is beyond your control, and there is nothing I can do to intervene. If the Firewalker witch decides not to return, then the world will never know peace.

But the Word was clear, Denali insisted.

And it has altered its course over the millennium.

Denali ceased her rant. She swiped at the ice water tears that trickled down her face. *I...I await your word on my child.*

I will keep you apprised of everything we do.

"Laird?" Bran asked softly. Yr Wyddfa hovered in the middle of his chamber with his eyes closed.

"You may approach," Yr Wyddfa said as he faced the giant. "Denali is anxious for her earth child to return."

Bran bowed his head and stepped into the chamber. "We are about to begin the restorative process. Will you be present?"

The glinting skin of the spirit flashed a myriad of colors before resuming a steady blue gray. "No, Bran, I shall remain here." The earth spirit floated to the giant and placed a stony hand upon his shoulder. "I have faith in your abilities."

"Thank you, laird," With his head lowered, Bran backed out of the room.

Fen and Chance hadn't moved for almost two hours. Darrius stood at the back door gazing into the garden, his hands clasped behind him. Benedict sat across from the siblings and fixed his gaze on them, his eyes continually watching. Alden sat by the fireplace and straightened the crease of his pants. He had recently changed into a new suit and shoes.

Kai sat on the loveseat beside his friend, Jake, who he dressed in jeans and a blue, long-sleeved shirt. The shaman stared straight ahead at the wall across the room.

"Shouldn't Jake blink every now and then?" Kai's question shattered the tension. Benedict and Alden looked at him.

When no one answered, Kai stood and gestured toward Jake. "Look at him. He hasn't blinked since he woke up. That's fucked up in my book. His eyes are going to dry out or something."

Still staring into the backyard, Darrius responded softly. "He'll be fine."

"Fine?" Kai pressed. "How do you know?"

Darrius whirled and glared at Kai. Then he bolted across the room, his image blurring. In seconds, he stood face to face with the magician. "Because I know," Darrius seethed through gritted teeth.

Kai's eyes widened and his fingers trembled. "Okay, Darrius. I believe you." He sat back on the loveseat and peered up at the Cererian. "I didn't mean to upset you."

"Who's upset?" a weak female voice whispered.

All heads turned toward Fen and Chance. The siblings yawned and stretched as though they had emerged from a long nap. "Someone's upset," Fen reiterated. "Who?"

Kai dashed to her side. "Fenny!" He threw his arms around her neck and hugged hard.

"What about me?" Chance whined.

"Sure!" Kai replied as he leaned toward his brother.

Chance grabbed him and pulled him across his lap and planted a kiss on his cheek. "I've missed you, Kai," Chance said chuckling.

"Yuck!" Kai complained playfully as he tumbled onto the floor.

Darrius, Benedict, and Alden stood in front of the siblings.

Fen exchanged puzzled looks with Chance. "Is something wrong?"

"Where is the—" Benedict started.

"Benedict!" Darrius shouted as he gripped the Cererian's shoulder and forced him back into his chair. Benedict glared at Darrius. For several moments, the two Cererians stared at each other.

Darrius turned to Fen and Chance. "Welcome back. We've missed you." He spread his arms wide and leaned down to hug each one.

Fen shot a side glance toward Chance and shrugged. "Um, we missed you, too, Darrius?"

"What's going on?" Chance demanded. "Why all the drama?"

"You've been asleep for two hours," Alden added. "Almost three hours, if you count the time you spent conjuring."

Fen stared at her hands, which fidgeted in her lap. "Oh, that." She gnawed on her bottom lip. "I'm sorry for not telling you, Alden." She glanced at Chance. "But we wanted to do something to save our sister."

"Yeah," Chance added. "We were forced to stay in this cottage while everyone else rushed to the rescue. We had to do something."

"You could have warned me," Alden said as he knelt in front of Fen. "I was concerned. We were completely in the dark. And that wasn't considerate."

"Fair enough," Chance said. "Perhaps we should have told you, but time was of the essence."

"As it is now!" Benedict exclaimed.

"Benedict," Darrius warned. "Protocol."

"While you slept," Benedict pressed. "Jake's soul has been wandering. And we have no idea where the Yfel are."

"The Yfel?" Fen asked

Darrius stepped forward. "Fen, what did you and Chance do with the Brethren that were in the cave?"

"Perhaps we should start from the beginning," Fen said softly.

"Finally!" Benedict exclaimed.

Fen frowned but continued, "When Alden left the room, I conferred with Chance on combining our abilities to help Hilly." Fen smiled and patted Chance's hand.

"I thought it was a great idea," Chance added. "I felt castrated sitting in this house doing nothing. Plus, I was anxious to see if I could meld my power with Fen's like Kai and Hilly."

"The ability comes easier and quicker each time I perform it," Fen explained. "Chance and I combined our powers in seconds. Unfortunately, we were not able to communicate with Hilly, as we had hoped. Apparently, Aaron conjured magic to block outsiders from reaching her. But we could communicate with Jake."

"We didn't anticipate the strength of Aaron's power," Chance added. "Jake sustained injuries when he was thrown against the ceiling the first time."

"The first time?" Kai said.

"We regret that that occurred," Fen said, shaking her head. "But we underestimated Aaron's power fueled by all the magicians' souls he has feasted on. When Jake informed us that Hilly had released Stygian—"

"Stygian is free?!" a collection of voices chorused.

"Oops, I hate being the bearer of bad news," Fen apologized. "Hilly agreed to release Stygian after Aaron slammed Jake against the ceiling the second time and the stalactite punctured his stomach."

"That explains the condition of his body," Kai uttered.

"Is Jake here?" Fen asked. "Is he okay?"

"We'll talk about him later," Darrius interjected. "Please tell us the rest of the story."

"Well, Chance and I needed to reassess our abilities and find a way to increase our power," Fen continued. She gazed sheepishly at Kai. "We may have borrowed some of your power, Kai."

"I wondered why I felt so weak," he complained.

"You hit your head on a rock," Benedict said dryly.

"Yeah, but my body felt kinda puny too," Kai added.

"Once we felt our magic had fully charged," Chance chimed in, "We reached out to Jake and told him we would protect him and Hilly against Stygian."

"That's when we exploded the psychic bomb," Fen summarized.

"Fascinating," Alden said, nodding his head. "And what was the purpose of this bomb?"

"To propel the Yfel into space," Fen replied. "*And* to direct Jake and Hilly's souls into the realm of the undead."

"To be clear," Darrius began. "Where exactly did you send the Brethren?"

"To Ceres," Chance replied.

"I'll contact Ceres immediately." Darrius rushed out of the room.

Benedict watched him exit and then turned to Fen. "And what about the souls? Where are the souls?"

"The land of the undead," Fen replied. "We can restore their souls once their bodies are healed."

Benedict leaned closer. "Jake is healed. When can you start?"

"What about Hilly?" Chance asked.

"Lord Yr Wyddfa wouldn't allow her to come back with us," Kai explained.

"Lord Yr Wyddfa?" the siblings chorused.

"The earth spirit who rules over Mount Snowdon," Darrius said as he returned to the room. "The blue opal had been ripped out of Hilly's throat. Yr Wyddfa said only his giants knew how to reset the gem, heal her body, and restore her soul."

He turned to Alden and Benedict. "Ceres has confirmed they have Stygian as well as Balor and Cary in containment, but they noted that Aaron did not return with them."

"So, what happed to Aaron?" Fen asked as she gazed at Chance. "Did we miss somebody?"

"Darrius," Benedict interjected. "If we restore the shaman's soul, we'll have his account of what happened in the cavern. Perhaps he knows what happened to Aaron."

"Agreed," Darrius said. "Fen, are you and Chance rested enough to perform the ritual to restore Jake's soul?"

"I am," she replied. "Chance?"

"I'm willing, but I have no idea what I'm doing."

"Don't worry, we'll work together like we did in the cavern." Fen patted Chance's hand and smiled up at Darrius. "We're ready when you are, Darrius."

"Good, let's return Jake to the land of the living."

Chapter 28

Return of the Souls

ELLIS CIRCLED THE BLUESTONE slab. He gently tucked Hilly's arms along her sides, straightened her legs, and smoothed her clothes. He pulled hair strands away from her neck and eased them behind her ears. Lifting her chin, he swabbed the ragged hole in her neck with a black, viscous ointment that turned violet the moment it contacted her skin.

He folded his hands and stood back to inspect his work. His eyes widened. Flecks of dirt dotted her cheek. He rushed to her side and softly brushed the debris away.

"Done?" Bran barked as he entered the room.

Ellis jerked. "J-just—finishing—u-up," he stammered.

"Stop yer fawning over the Firewalker witch, Ellis," Bran said as he joined his brother. "Ya not her type." Bran cackled.

Ellis stared at the floor. The apples of his cheeks glowed red above his bushy auburn beard.

"So, this is the magician who will restore peace," Bran commented as he stared into Hilly's face, her emerald eyes wide open and staring into space.

"One of four magicians," Ellis whispered.

"She's puny for a warrior. Hard to imagine her overpowering Stygian."

"She carries his blood," Ellis added softly.

Bran glared at his brother. "Aye, ya know everything, dun ya? Where's Dylan? We need to get started."

"He's collecting the herbs," Ellis replied.

Moments later, Dylan entered the chamber. "What a trip!" he exclaimed. "Couldn't find most of my herbs in Wales—had to venture into England to snatch a few. Thank the gods for interdimensional travel." He positioned an ebony tray on a nearby table. Holding a burlap sack, he extracted foxglove, yarrow, pimpernel, and mistletoe and positioned the stems on the tray.

Bran reviewed the plants and pointed to the pimpernel. "That's a tricky one to work with. Ya can kill the witch."

Dylan moved Bran aside. "That's why I'm the one in charge of working with the herbs, dear brother." Dylan carried the tray to the bluestone slab and gazed down at Hilly. "'Tis disturbing to see the Firewalker witch staring at me with those big green eyes."

"The laird said her soul journeys in the land of the undead," Ellis added.

"Speaking of the laird," Dylan said as he glanced around the room. "Where is he?"

"He has faith in my abilities," Bran emphasized.

Ellis and Dylan exchanged glances.

"You mean *our* abilities," Dylan added.

Bran glared.

Dylan took his position on Hilly's left side, near her heart. "Very well. We should proceed while the herbs are still flush with medicinal magic."

"I'm in control of the ritual, Dylan," Bran growled. "Take your place, Ellis."

Ellis positioned himself at the foot of the slab near Hilly's feet while Bran stood at her head.

"First, we heal her body and reset the blue opal," Bran instructed. "Dylan, begin your healing ritual. Ellis, have the blue opal at the ready."

Ellis pushed his hand into his apron pocket and withdrew the gleaming jewel. Taking precautions not to dispel its sacred magic, he had already cleaned it of dirt and gore.

Dylan looked to Bran and then to Ellis. He raised both hands into the air. "I invoke the power of our ancestors, the ancient healers that roamed this land since the beginning of time. Join us within this sacred circle and guide our hands as we heal the Firewalker witch."

A misty ribbon descended from the rocky ceiling above them and unfurled blue tentacles to the four corners of the room. Miniature flashes sparkled within the vaporous sash.

"The ancestors' life force is present. We are ready to begin," Dylan said nodding to Bran.

A tremor rippled throughout the land of the undead. Jake and Hilly's soul orbs jostled against one another. Burgundy colors skittered across their skins. They lingered, touching for a second before the lustrous bubbles ricocheted in different directions as if yanked by unseen hands. Jake's soul entered a bright white room while Hilly's soul ventured toward a dark, narrow passageway.

Jake was prone on the kitchen table, eyes staring vacantly into the overhead light. Fen stood at his head while Chance stood at his feet. Kai and the Cererians assumed positions on either side of the table.

"Once we start, please don't interfere," Fen warned.

"What should we expect?" Darrius asked.

"Honestly, Darrius, I'm not sure," Fen replied. "This is the first time I've reversed the spell."

"Fen, that doesn't give me a warm, fuzzy feeling," Chance quipped.

She smiled gently at her brother. "You'll be fine."

When she nodded, Chance cupped Jake's heels in his palms, and Fen cradled the back of the shaman's head.

"We begin," she announced solemnly.

The siblings closed their eyes. Within seconds their eyelids moved furiously, and their lips quivered but made no sound.

"They're casting their spell," Darrius observed.

The kitchen air thickened. "It's hard to breathe," Kai gasped. "I feel like I'm underwater." Darrius touched Kai's side along his ribs. "Ah, much better. Thank you, Darrius."

"High magic has an extraordinary impact on others," Darrius explained.

Fen and Chance continued their conjuring. Soundlessly, their lips moved faster and faster.

Soon, a light glowed like an aura around their hands. The brightness stretched onto Jake's body and engulfed the shaman in a healing white light. The brilliance ebbed and flowed, pulsing through various pastel colors before quickening its cadence and strobing rapidly.

Kai shielded his eyes, but the Cererians were transfixed by what they were witnessing and maintained their focus on the spectacle before them.

The luminescence enlarged, spreading outward until it filled the room with a dazzling bright light.

Suddenly, the kitchen reverberated with a muffled explosion. A shockwave raced away from Jake's body and penetrated the bodies of all in attendance.

Kai grabbed his chest, but the Cererians didn't move.

Seconds later, an implosion sucked the explosive force back toward the shaman. Once it reached Jake's body, the energetic bomb detonated within him.

The concussion shoved Kai and the Cererians backward.

Fen and Chance opened their eyes.

Kai and the Cererians scrambled off the floor and stared at Jake.

The shaman's eyes were closed.

He breathed slow and controlled.

Chance and Fen removed their hands.

"It is complete," Fen announced. She lightly stroked Jake's forehead. "Wake up, Jake."

"Hilly!" The shaman yelled as he bolted up. Eyes wide, he grappled at the air.

Darrius grabbed Jake's arms. "Easy, Jake," he soothed. The two men stared at each other. Wild-eyed, Jake looked around the kitchen and then back to Darrius with a puzzled look.

"Where am I?" he demanded. "Where's Hilly?"

"You're in Amesbury," Darrius replied.

"Hilly was here," Jake said, pointing to a wall. "She was going down a dark corridor."

Fen wrapped her hand around Jake's. "Hun, we just brought your soul back from the land of the undead."

"Was Hilly there too?" he asked.

Fen glanced at Darrius before responding. "Yes. She was there. Chance and I sent you there when we psychically blasted the Cererians out of the cave."

"The cave," Jake whispered. "I remember…" Jake rubbed his forehead. "Stygian!" he yelled. "Hilly released him!"

"I know, hon," Fen soothed.

"Stygian killed Aaron!" he shouted before collapsing against Fen. His face was coated with sweat.

"Darrius, please help me," she requested.

Darrius eased Jake from the dining table and guided him to a nearby chair. "You saw Stygian kill Aaron?" he asked.

Jake nodded.

The Cererians exchanged glances.

Fen brought Jake a glass of water, which he chugged. He grabbed her hand. "So, if you brought me back, then where's Hilly?"

Fen gazed at Darrius for help.

"Lord Yr Wyddfa and his giants are healing Hilly," Darrius responded.

"What the fuck?" Jake replied.

"Yr Wyddfa is the king of Mount Snowdon, where you and Hilly were held captive. He would only allow us to take you from the cave."

"Then, he has Hilly?" Jake asked.

"Yes."

Jake tried to rise from the chair, but his legs gave out. "We need to get Hilly," Jake said as he struggled to stand.

"You're going nowhere, shaman," Darrius ordered.

Chapter 29

Restoring Hilly's Soul

HILLY LAY ON A bluestone slab. After invoking his ancestors, Dylan walked clockwise around the slab three times before he returned to her left side.

"Grant me your power, oh wise ancestors, so I can heal this Firewalker witch," Dylan requested. The ethereal sash of the ancients undulated and drifted across the herbs on the ebony tray by Dylan. A low thrumming filled the room as though a million honeybees had entered.

As the misty ribbon brushed over each herb, Dylan selected the plant, carefully picked off the leaves and dropped them into his mortar. Once he had added all the plants, he used his pestle to grind them together. "With the essence of the foxglove and yarrow, I enrich your heart. With the assistance of mistletoe, I boost your immune system. With the pimpernel I heal your wounds."

Using the paste from the plant juice, he dabbed it upon the ragged hole in Hilly's neck, taking care to push it gently into the cavity until the wound was completely full. He set the mortar and pestle aside. He placed his hand gently on her neck and mouthed a healing incantation as he closed his eyes and envisioned the gaping injury repairing itself.

Without opening his eyes, Dylan spoke to Ellis. "Give me the blue opal, brother." Ellis reached forward with the gleaming jewel and deposited it in Dylan's outstretched hand.

"Here it is," Ellis announced.

Dylan invoked the ancients once again. "Bless this jewel, the gemstone gift from the great earth spirit, Denali, who sacrificed her sight so the voices in her daughter's body would be quieted." The ancestral mist swirled around the blue opal as Dylan maneuvered it toward the wound in Hilly's throat.

"Tilt her chin up, Bran," Dylan instructed. Bran curled his fingers along Hilly's jaw and gently pulled upward.

"Through the power of the ancients, we unite this sacred stone with the Firewalker witch," Dylan proclaimed as he firmly pushed the gem into the juggler's notch. The herb paste oozed out and hardened around the base of the blue opal as the misty ribbon churned along Hilly's neck, stroking her skin with smoky fingers.

The giants patiently waited as the supernatural ribbon swirled up and down coating Hilly's neck in a thick blue haze. The friction discharged miniature bolts of electricity that danced across her throat.

Vivid blue strobed the room.

Whiffs of ozone filled the air.

Slowly the tendril of mist retreated to the ceiling.

Dylan gazed at Hilly and smiled. "The blue nugget has been successfully affixed.

"But her eyes still stare at me," Bran said, panic edging into his voice.

"Calm yerself, brother," Dylan soothed. "We've only healed the body. Her eyes will close once we restore the soul."

Bran coughed into his fist. "I knew that," he lied under his breath.

"Assume your positions," Bran barked. Ellis cupped Hilly's heels, Bran cradled her head, and Dylan pushed his right hand under her back until his palm rested parallel to her heart.

"Do not break your contact with the Firewalker witch," he ordered. Ellis and Dylan nodded.

"So it begins," he uttered. The three giants closed their eyes. Within seconds their lips soundlessly moved as they recited the conjuring.

Hilly's soul rushed down a long, dark corridor. Snakelike, the wormhole undulated and twisted as Hilly's energy raced along the dark passageway. Her pace slowed when she arrived in a small blue chamber.

She hovered, unsure of where she was.

Flashes of electric blue snapped and popped around her.

We invite you to return to your body, a male voice called out. The request vibrated within Hilly's essence like a cool breeze.

The words were calm, but she was afraid. Her last physical memory was of the blue opal being ripped from her throat, allowing thousands of magicians to torment her with their screams.

She didn't know where she was, but at least the blue chamber was quiet.

She had no desire to return to chaos and the relentless voices.

She floated toward the opening that would lead her back through the wormhole.

Return, Hilly, the male voice invited. *Return to your body.*

Hilly didn't know the voice drifting through her soul. That concerned her. What if it was a trick?

Her soul moved out of the blue chamber and entered the passageway.

Yr Wyddfa tensed.

Monitoring the healing ritual from the confines of his rocky lair, he grimaced at Hilly's reluctance to return to her body. *Bran is losing his opportunity*, he thought. *If he doesn't act, we'll lose the witch.*

Yr Wyddfa drifted into the healing chamber and approached the blue-stone slab. He gazed down at Hilly who stared unblinking back at him. The three giants were deep in a trance, their lips moving furiously as they recited the magic that would restore her soul.

Yr Wyddfa telepathically inserted himself into their conjuring. *The witch resists returning to her body.*

I will convince her to return, Bran replied.

You had your chance, Yr Wyddfa said. *The witch is moving further away. I will handle this.*

Yr Wyddfa propelled his soul into the realm of the undead.

Hilly had entered the passageway, but she stopped near the entrance and listened to their conversation

Yr Wyddfa's soul orb drew alongside Hilly. *I bring you greetings from the great Denali.*

A flash of purple burst along Hilly's skin.

Yr Wyddfa reached out again. *She longs to hold her earth child once more. If you do not return to your body, you will make her unhappy.*

Who are you?

I am Lord Yr Wyddfa. Mount Snowdon is my kingdom.

Is that where we are?

No, you are in the realm of the undead. Your sister and brother sent you here to protect you when they exploded their psychic blast and banished the Yfel.

Stygian!

Yes. Stygian and the twins.

Is Jake here?

The shaman's soul has been restored. He is recovering and awaiting your return.

I'm not sure. The screams...the voices...

I assure you that Denali's blue opal has been restored to your body. The voices have been quieted once again.

Yr Wyddfa moved away from the passageway and toward the center of the blue chamber. *Please join me. I will not harm you.*

Hilly hesitated, but something about the spirit who pulsed pleasing purples and blues convinced her to follow him.

You are safe with me, Yr Wyddfa reassured. *I have given my word to Denali that you would be returned to her.*

Denali, Hilly repeated. Her soul drew beside Yr Wyddfa in the middle of the chamber.

Your body awaits you within the protective cliffs of Mount Snowdon. My giants are conjuring high magic to illuminate the pathway so your soul can reunite with it.

You promise that the voices are quiet?

I promise. My giants have healed your body. It now awaits your soul.

Then I will follow you.

Yr Wyddfa pulsed a flurry of blues and purples. *Very well. I invite you, Hilly Kemp, to return to your body.*

Continuing their healing magic, the giants worked furiously. The ancestral sash swirled around the chamber as though directed by tornadic winds, twirling wildly until the air flowed with a fine mist.

The explosion and implosion occurred almost simultaneously. The giants arched their backs with the initial psychic detonation as the blast pushed through their bodies and raced toward the walls of the room. Then the brothers were violently forced over the slab as the energy rushed back into Hilly's body.

Vibrations rolled through the walls and along Mount Snowdon's slopes. Then absolute silence.

Bran opened his eyes and sighed with relief. Hilly's eyes were closed. "It is done," he announced.

Dylan and Ellis stepped away and joined their brother. "Her heart and breathing are strong," Dylan confirmed as he quickly scanned her vitals.

"The Firewalker witch didn't want to return," Yr Wyddfa stated as he drifted nearby.

"I can explain—" Bran started.

Yr Wyddfa held up his hand. "I need no explanations." He peered at all of them. "This witch is very different than the other magicians. You should have been better prepared for her mental strength."

"Yes, laird," they chorused as they dipped their heads.

"Wake her, Bran," Yr Wyddfa commanded.

Bran stroked her forehead with a calloused finger. "Wake up, Firewalk-er," he ordered.

Hilly murmured but didn't open her eyes. Bran peered at the laird.

"Again," Yr Wyddfa ordered.

"Let me," Ellis interjected. Bran grimaced at his brother's impudence.

"Granted," Yr Wyddfa replied.

"What?" Bran demanded

"Bran, let your brother wake the witch," Yr Wyddfa ordered.

Bran shuffled aside as Ellis approached Hilly's head. He lightly touched her forehead with his finger and leaned close to her ear. "Wake up, Hilly," he whispered.

Her eyes fluttered open and then widened when she saw Bran grimacing at her. She bolted into a sitting position and raised her hands in defense. "Where am I?"

"Still yourself, Firewalker," Yr Wyddfa said calmly. "You have returned to your body within Mount Snowdon." The earth spirit drifted near Hilly and flashed purples and blue hues across his rocky skin.

"You are familiar," she said, squinting at Yr Wyddfa. "Have we met before?"

A rich chuckle echoed off the stony walls. "Indeed, we have," he replied. "We met in the realm of the undead."

"What?" she asked as she ran her hand across her forehead. "The land of the undead?"

"It matters not," Yr Wydffa continued. "You are with us now. Your soul and body reunited."

"Who are they?" Hilly asked as she glanced around the room.

"My giants," the laird replied. "Bran, Dylan, and Ellis." The three brothers bowed.

Hilly smiled weakly and nodded back at them.

"The blue opal!" she shouted as her hand clutched at her throat. She sighed when her fingers touched the nugget. Her fingertips lingered on the facets and traced the seal that held the jewel to her skin.

"I did promise that the voices had been quieted," Yr Wyddfa reassured. "I do not break my promises."

Hilly smiled at the earth spirit. "Thank you."

"Bran, assist the witch up from the slab," the laird commanded.

The giant extended his hand, which was ten times larger than Hilly's. She stared at his thick, calloused fingers for a second before she placed her hand in the middle of his palm and slid off the bluestone.

"Is Jake here as well?" she asked.

"The shaman is recuperating in Amesbury," Yr Wyddfa explained.

"Then I will join him," she responded.

"No, you won't," the earth spirit replied.

Hilly's cheeks flushed red. "You don't tell me what I can or cannot do." She lifted her hands, but no portal appeared. "What did you do?" she demanded as she faced Yr Wyddfa

"Your magic will not work here, Firewalker," Yr Wyddfa said as he drifted out of the chamber. "You will be my guest a little while longer."

"Bran, show the witch to her room," the laird ordered.

Chapter 30

Fen's Disappearance

A CONSTANT DRIZZLE FELL on the Amesbury Cottage. Jake stared out the lounge window, his palm pressed flat on the glass.

The golden morning sky retreated as the gray winter storm approached from the west.

Darrius sidled up beside him.

"It's as if Hilly doesn't exist," Jake whispered. "I can't detect any trace of her anywhere."

"Yr Wyddfa has taken her beyond the veil on Mount Snowdon," Darrius said softly. "No one can see beyond the veil except earth spirits."

Jake curled his fingers, and the window squeaked as he made a fist against it. "I need to find her."

"And you will, but not now." Darrius placed a hand on Jake's shoulder. The shaman tensed and then relaxed.

Fen gazed at Jake as she sat with Chance and Benedict near the fire.

"Your healing spell was most impressive to watch," Benedict noted. "Your powers amaze me."

"I'm always surprised by what I can do, too," Fen admitted. "Not long ago, I mourned the loss of my husband and retreated into myself. Then Darrius' letter arrived announcing the death of my parents." She glanced toward Darrius. "I hated him when I received that letter. I hated him and didn't even know him. It's not that way anymore. Darrius is a true friend."

"I felt the same way, Fen," Chance chimed in. "The last thing I wanted was to return to The Nine Muses and see all of you."

"Hard to imagine that was only six months ago," she said. "Now look at us. Powerful magicians on a quest to reunite four crystals and restore peace."

Chance and Fen shared a glance before they broke into laughter.

"Yeah, it sounds like something you'd read in a comic book," Chance chuckled.

Benedict stared at the siblings, confused. "You don't believe in your abilities?" he asked.

"Yes and no," Chance replied. "It's hard for me to wrap my mind around being a magician. I recently found out three of my kids can also perform magic, but my wife and my oldest sons have no supernatural powers."

"Folk," Benedict noted.

"Yeah, they're Folk," Chance said as he gazed into the fire.

"I think I've always known," Fen said.

"Known what?" Chance asked.

"That I was different. I could predict events way before they happened. My husband called it a sixth sense. Even before I opened Darrius' letter, I knew what was inside."

Chance wrapped his arm around his sister and kissed the side of her head. "You've always been special to me, Fenny."

"Dinner's served," Kai called as he poked his head through the doorway. "Alden and I whipped up some delectable delights."

"You mean Alden did," Chance joked as he helped Fen to her feet.

"No food for the mean man," Kai said, pointing to his brother. "But the rest of you are welcome to the feast." He held the door and gestured toward the kitchen.

Fen kissed Kai's cheek as she passed, followed by Chance who playfully sneered.

"Jake? Darrius?" Kai asked. "Care to get a little something in your belly?"

"Come on, Jake," Darrius urged. "You need to eat after what you've been through."

Darrius pulled Jake away from the window and toward the kitchen. "Thank you, Kai," Darrius said as they passed. "I look forward to your feast."

"Welcome!" Alden greeted as Jake and Darrius entered the kitchen. "What would you like to drink? I have coffee, juice, and water." Alden pointed to three decanters sitting in the middle of the table.

Jake glanced around the table and sighed.

"We'll start with coffee, Alden," Darrius replied as he led Jake to an available seat.

Kai added a platter of grilled sausages, onions, and a bowl of broiled potatoes with fresh peas.

"Anyone want fried bread?" Alden asked.

Three hands shot up.

"Coming up," Alden responded cheerfully.

The kitchen quieted as everyone ate and drank. Murmurs of delight mingled with Chance's occasional belches.

"Eat slower," Fen requested as she patted Chance's hand.

"Do you even know me?" he replied.

Jake leaned his chair back until it teetered on the back legs. He slowly chewed a sausage link stuck on the end of his fork and stared into space.

"Alden, I've been meaning to ask you a question," Fen said.

"Yes?" Alden replied.

"Where is Gabe?" Chance squeezed her knee under the table, and she yelped.

Fen glared at him.

Alden coughed into his napkin.

"I thought he was with you and Chance on Carn Goedog," she pressed.

Chance squeezed her knee again, and she smacked his arm. "Cut it out," she snapped.

"Gabe is being punished," Alden replied between sips of coffee.

"For what?"

"He betrayed us and allowed Aaron to kidnap Hilly."

"Is this true, Chance?" she asked, searching her brother's eyes.

"Yeah...but he did it out of desperation," Chance responded.

"How so?"

"Gabe said Aaron was holding his mom captive and would let her go if he did a little spying for the Yfel." Chance heaped potatoes onto his plate and avoided Alden's stare.

"Still, he betrayed us," Alden remarked.

"Is he dead?" Fen asked.

"Gabe has been banished to another dimension until I determine his fate," Alden replied.

"Darrius, can't you do something?" Fen implored. "Gabe is family."

"This is Alden's choice," Darrius replied.

Fen crossed her arms and huffed. "Well, I think this is unfair. You should at least allow him to plead his case."

Benedict changed the subject. "Fen, I noticed you have something around your neck that I've not seen before.

Fen gently touched the silver chain around her throat. She hadn't wanted to talk about the Guardian Boulder's gift but now all eyes stared at her. "Um..." she stammered.

"Yeah, Fen," Chance stated. "I noticed a white feather poking out of your shirt earlier but forgot to ask you about it."

"Well," she continued. "It's a—"

"It's a gift!" Kai blurted

"Kai!" Fen shouted.

"Just tell them, Fen."

Fen glared at everyone. "It's hard to keep things private around here. Okay! It's a gift."

"From whom?" Chance asked.

"From the Guardian boulder as a way of saying thank you for my healing power."

"May I see it?" Alden urged.

Fen withdrew the small pendant from inside her blouse.

"A dream catcher?" Chance's eyebrows arched in surprise.

"Yes. It's been fashioned from white feathers and bluestone chips." Fen held the three-inch pendant between her thumb and index finger and showed everyone at the table.

"Very pretty," Benedict acknowledged.

"Incredibly potent," Darrius noted. "What did the Guardian boulder tell you when he bestowed it?"

"He said it would keep me safe in the future," she replied.

"Interesting," Alden said. "It's not often that nature's spirits interact with humans on this level. You should feel honored."

"I do," Fen responded. She gazed lovingly at the necklace before tucking it back inside her blouse.

The room quieted as everyone finished their meal.

Chance patted his stomach and croaked small belches into his fist. Fen frowned at him, which caused him to chuckle. "Well, I've had my fill of this fine feast," he announced. "How about a little after-dinner drink in the lounge?" He rose, grabbed the Woodford Reserve bottle, and marched out of the kitchen.

Alden tied an apron around his waist and collected the dinner plates from the table. "Kai, would you help me clean up?" he asked as Kai was halfway out the kitchen door.

Kai's shoulders hunched, and he turned around. "Sure, Alden."

Everyone else settled in the lounge.

Jake resumed his position at the window. The rain was heavier. Gusts splattered droplets against the windowpane

Chance threw more logs onto the fire and watched the wood snap and pop in the blue-yellow flames.

"Anyone fancy a drink?" Chance held the bottle of whiskey in the air. No replies.

He poured a glass for himself and plopped into the chair by the fire.

Alden and Kai strolled into the room. "My poor dishpan hands!" Kai claimed dramatically.

Alden sat beside Darrius and Benedict while Kai joined Fen on the loveseat. Chance watched Kai pass by.

"Drink, Kai?" he asked, wiggling his glass.

Kai grinned. "Absolutely. After everything that happened today, I damn well deserve a drink." Chance carried a drink to his brother and they clinked glasses before they took a long sip. "Ah, that's what I needed. Let's see...my crystal was restored to its seat of power and Chance located his jewel. Care to show her off, big brother?"

Chance's eyes twinkled. "She's a little different than what you and Hilly had."

"Well, I hope she's a lot different than the one that fused with my chest," Kai said as he absently rubbed his chest.

"Very true." Chance withdrew the leather pouch hanging around his neck and pulled the opening apart. Turning the bag upside down above his palm, he gave it a slight shake. A tiny object fell onto his skin.

Kai and Fen leaned forward and squinted.

"I saw something," Fen said. "But it was tiny."

Chance pushed his hand toward his siblings. Their eyes widened as the faceted one-inch jewel flashed a mossy green.

"Looks like an emerald," Kai noted.

"Or jade," Fen observed.

"It's a perfectly cut bluestone," Alden stated as he joined the siblings.

"That's impossible," Kai replied. "You can't facet a bluestone."

"You can with magic," the Cererian replied. "That's a very rare specimen, Chance. Keep it safe."

Kai sipped his whiskey. "All we need to do is find Fen's crystal and then restore Chance's and Fen's gems with their respective Guardian boulders. That'll be easy...right?"

"They're coming," Jake said under his breath.

"What did you say?" Darrius asked.

Silence.

Darrius touched Jake's shoulder. "Jake, what did you say?"

Jake turned and looked at the Cererian. "They're coming."

"Who?" Darrius peered into the backyard, but the sheeting rain distorted everything.

Chance, Kai, and Alden stood behind Darrius. "Did he say someone was coming?" Chance asked.

Darrius nodded as he gazed out the window.

"This cottage is impenetrable," Alden explained. "Nobody could break through the magic used to enforce this home and the surrounding grounds."

A flash of light flickered outside.

BOOM!

Thunder crashed and the house went dark.

"They're here," Jake whispered.

Seconds later the lights flickered back on. "Well, that was interesting," Kai observed. "Reminds me of the storm at The Nine Muses."

"Yeah, it kinda does," Chance agreed. "Fen, what do you think?"

Silence.

Chance whirled.

Fen was gone.

"Fen!" he cried out. He rushed to the couch where she had been sitting. A small white feather lay on the cushion. He picked it up and looked back at the others with concern.

"Search the house," Darrius ordered.

"No need," Jake said softly

"What do you mean?" Darrius demanded.

Jake peered into the storm and didn't answer.

Darrius grabbed him by the shoulders and turned him around. "Jake, what do you mean there's no need? What do you know? Tell me!"

"There's nothing we can do. Fen was taken by her ancestral tribe."

"How?"

"They entered on the threads of a another dimension, snatched Fen, and fled the same way. Fen lies sleeping within the medicine wheel."

Thank You

Thank you for taking the time to read **Bluestone Shadows** , book 4 of Chronicle of Ceres.
Please take a moment to write a review.

It's so important for a book to have social proof, and I'd love your help sharing this series with others who embrace their magic.

Leave a review or star rating at your favorite book retailer

For new releases, giveaways, and fun info, subscribe to my newsletter by visiting www.cllavigne.com

Acknowledgements

My readers and my fans who challenge me in my writing and keep the spirits of the Kemps and Cererians alive.

My husband, Chris, who weathers my emotional storms, calms me, and urges me to finish my fantastical tales.

John, Judy and Steve—how could the Kemps come alive without having you in my life?

Super Jimmy who lives on in my fictional Flanagan's Irish Pub.

Brittany and your amazing editing. Imagine my stories without your intervention.

About Author

Born in Alaska and raised in England, CL is an Elemental Specialist who writes magical realism novels that have witch fantasy overtones. Her stories feature real people and natural magic, all controlled by the Spirits of Nature and otherworldly beings.

Residing in the Sunshine State with her husband, three cats and six goldfish, CL incorporates elements of magic, mysticism and mythology into her writings. It's not unusual to encounter dragons, elemental spirits, Leotes (glowing orbs) and even big foot as you follow her characters on their adventures.

Her current fantasy series is Chronicle of Ceres, which will feature 5 books. The final installment will be released summer of 2025.

CL has published a collection of short horror stories under the title of "Tales From the Crows." A second volume is expected in 2025.

Embrace your magic!

Find the magic and stay informed about special deals, giveaways, new releases and other great updates by subscribing to her **NEWSLETTER**.

Discover CL's magic:

www.cllavigne.com

www.facebook.com/CLLaVigneAuthor

www.instagram.com/cllavigneauthor/

Also By

Chronicle of Ceres Magical Realism Series

Beginning of Tomorrows, book 1

Denali Rising, book 2

Shasta Beckons, book 3

Tales From the Crows

Horror short story collection

www.ingramcontent.com/pod-product-compliance
Lightning Source LLC
Chambersburg PA
CBHW070923260626
47162CB00007B/2774